"What do you want, Eva?"

He asked her in a tight voice.

She met his green eyes and saw unmistakable arousal flashing back at her. The smart thing to do would be to walk away, but her feet refused to comply.

Tate waited a few seconds, then sighed when she still didn't answer. "Fine. We'll deal with this later. I'm getting dressed."

She blocked his path, swallowing hard. Her gaze dropped to his towel, then moved back to his face. A wry note entered her voice. "Don't bother."

His eyes narrowed. "Don't bother what?"

"Getting dressed." She brought her hand to his chest and stroked the spot between his pecs. "We both know any clothes you put on will come right off, anyway."

Tate inhaled sharply, and she felt his pectoral muscles quiver beneath her fingers. "You're playing with fire, sweetheart."

Dear Reader,

I'm thrilled to be launching a new three-book miniseries with Harlequin Romantic Suspense—The Hunted! I think the series title says it all: we're going to be following the stories of three military heroes who are being hunted. By whom and why? Well, that's what these determined alpha males are trying to figure out!

First up is Captain Robert Tate, gruff, ruthless and undeniably sexy. Tate has one problem, though: he doesn't trust anyone. Especially the gorgeous, raven-haired woman who tracks him down and asks him to undertake a very dangerous task for her. Eva Dolce also has reasons not to trust—her last relationship turned her into a prisoner, after all. Needless to say, these characters' journeys were incredibly fun to write—jungle treks, mountain caves, endless bickering, steamy sexual tension. But more than that, their journey is about opening yourself up and learning to trust again.

I really hope you enjoy Tate and Eva's story. Next month you'll get the chance to read Sebastian Stone's book, as the journeys of these special forces soldiers continue....

Happy reading!

Elle

ELLE KENNEDY

Soldier Under Siege

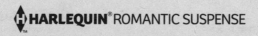

Recycling programs
for this product may
not exist in your area.

ISBN-13: 978-0-373-27811-4

SOLDIER UNDER SIEGE

Copyright © 2013 by Leeanne Kenedy

Printed in U.S.A.

ELLE KENNEDY

A RITA® Award-nominated author, Elle Kennedy grew up in the suburbs of Toronto, Ontario, and holds a B.A. in English from York University. From an early age she knew she wanted to be a writer, and actively began pursuing that dream when she was a teenager. She loves strong heroines and sexy alpha heroes, and just enough heat and danger to keep things interesting.

Elle loves to hear from her readers. Visit her website, www.ellekennedy.com, for the latest news or to send her a note.

To Danielle, Alex and the twins for their invaluable plotting help. Some of your ideas were…*interesting,* but the ones that made it into the book? Pure gold.

Also, special thanks to Keyren Gerlach and Patience Bloom for being so enthusiastic about this new miniseries!

Prologue

Eight Months Ago
Corazón, San Marquez

The gunfire finally came to a deafening halt.

Silence.

Captain Robert Tate ignored the ringing in his ears and swept his gaze across the village. It was like looking through a gray haze. The smoke filled his nostrils and stung his eyes, the odor of burned flesh making his stomach roil. Orange flames continued to devour what used to be the church, the only structure left intact. Everything else had been reduced to ash—the ramshackle homes, the schoolhouse, the dusty village square…nothing but ashes.

He covered his mouth and nose with his sleeve and looked around, doing a quick head count. Sergeant Stone was bending over the bullet-ridden body of a rebel. Second Lieutenant Prescott was wiping sweat and soot from his brows. Lafayette, Rhodes, Diaz and Berkowski. Where was Timmins? There, maneuvering his way through heaps of charred flesh and mangled bodies.

Tate released a ragged breath. Miraculously, all of his men were accounted for. Despite the thick smoke choking the air, despite the stifling heat from the flames, despite the shootout with the rebels, they'd managed to— *Wait.* Where the hell was Will?

His shoulders stiffened. "Stone," he shouted. "Where's Will?"

Through the smoke, he made out the younger man's bewildered expression. "Haven't seen him, Captain. I think he—"

Tate held up a hand to quiet his men. Then he listened. The trees rustled and swayed. Flames crackled. Birds squawked. The wind hissed.

Footsteps. There. Through the brush.

Raising his assault rifle, he broke out in a run, nearly tripping over the body of a raven-haired woman burned beyond recognition. One of the villagers.

Later. Think about the villagers later.

As his heart drummed in his chest, he slowed his pace and moved stealthily through the canopy of smoke toward the tree line. His ears perked. Footsteps. He glimpsed a dark blond head, a flash of olive-green. The silver glint of a blade.

"Don't move," Tate ordered.

His prey froze.

With his finger hovering over the trigger, Tate took a few steps forward, just as the rebel holding the knife turned.

Tate's heart dropped to the pit of his stomach.

"Drop your weapon, amigo." Hector Cruz's voice was soft, soothing almost.

An uncharacteristic vise of terror clamped around his

throat. He couldn't tear his gaze from the knife. From the resigned expression in Will's green eyes.

The rebel tightened his grip on Will, digging the blade deeper into his prisoner's neck. "Drop the weapon," Cruz said again. "Drop it, and I'll let him go."

"Don't do it," Will burst out. "Don't do it, Captain."

"Shut up," Cruz barked at his hostage.

Tate swallowed. He stared into the black eyes of the rebel, seeing nothing but dead calm reflected back at him. The knife sliced deeper into Will's throat.

Fingers trembling, he lowered his rifle a fraction of an inch.

"That's it," Cruz said in encouragement.

"No!" Will shouted. "He'll kill me regardless."

The rifle dipped lower.

"For the love of God, shoot the bastard." Agony rang from Will's voice. "Forget about me, Robbie. Forget—"

Tate tossed the gun onto the warm brown earth.

Triumph streaked across Cruz's harsh features. Followed by a grin that lifted his lips. "Bad call," he said lightly.

And then the rebel slit Will's throat.

Chapter 1

Paraíso, Mexico

This is a mistake.

Eva took one look around the dark, smoky bar and nearly sprinted right out the door. It took her a second to gather her composure, to force her feet to stay rooted to the dirty floor. She couldn't chicken out. She'd already come this far, traveled over seven thousand miles and crossed two continents to come here.

There was no turning back now.

Squaring her shoulders, she drew air into her lungs, only to inhale a cloud of cigar smoke that made her eyes water. She blinked rapidly, trying hard not to focus on the dozen pairs of eyes glued to her. Some were appreciative. Most were suspicious. It didn't surprise her—this place didn't seem as though it catered to many law-abiding citizens. She'd figured that out when she'd first spotted the dilapidated adobe exterior with its crooked wooden sign, the word *Cantina* chicken-scratched onto it.

The interior only confirmed her original assessment. The bar was small and cramped, boasting a wood counter that would probably give her splinters if she touched it, and a handful of little tables, most of them askew. Across the room was a narrow doorway shielded only by a curtain of red and yellow beads that clinked together. All the patrons were men; a few wore sombreros, several didn't have any shoes on, and all were looking at Eva as if she'd just gotten off a spaceship.

Ignoring the burning stares, she made her way to the counter, her sandals clicking against the floor. Her yellow sundress clung to her body like wet plastic wrap. It was nearly seven o'clock, and the humidity refused to cease, rolling in through the open front door like fake fog from a horror movie.

The bartender, a large man with a thick black beard, narrowed his eyes at her approach. "What can I do for you, señorita?" he asked.

He'd spoken in Spanish, and she answered in the same tongue. "I'm looking for someone."

He winked. "I see."

"I was told he's a regular here," she hurried on before the bartender misinterpreted her intentions. "I have business to discuss with him."

Gone was the playful twinkle in the man's eyes. He looked suspicious again, which made her wonder just how many times he'd heard this same old line before. Hundreds, probably. Paraíso wasn't the kind of town you visited on business, at least not the legitimate kind.

In her research, Eva had discovered that this little mountain town was a frequent stop for drug runners, arms dealers and men involved in all other sorts of nefarious activities. It was also the perfect place to hide. According to her sources, Mexican law enforcement turned the other cheek to what went on here, and with its mountainous landscape and neighboring rain forest, it was easy to disappear in a place like Paraíso. Its name translated to *paradise.* Irony at work.

"I'm afraid you'll need to be more specific," the bartender said curtly. He swept an arm out. "As you can see, there are many men here, almost all of them regulars."

She swallowed. "The one I want goes by the name Tate."

Silence descended over the room. The laughter of the patrons died. Even the music blaring out of the cheap stereo over the bar seemed to get quieter. From the corner of her eye, Eva noticed that the gray-haired man at the other end of the counter had blanched, his tanned leathery skin turning a shade paler.

So she'd come to the right place. These men knew Tate. And they feared him—she could feel that fear palpitating in the stuffy air.

"I take it you know him," she said to the bartender.

His dark eyes grew shuttered. "Actually, I can't say I've ever heard that name before."

She suppressed a sigh and reached into the green canvas purse slung over her bare shoulder. She fumbled around until her hand connected with the roll of American bills she'd secured with an elastic band. She peeled off four one-hundred-dollar bills and set them on the counter.

The man's jaw twitched at the sight of the cash—about five thousand pesos after the conversion.

"What about now?" she asked softly. "Have you heard of him now?"

Greed etched into his harsh features. "No, still doesn't ring a bell."

She added two more hundreds to the pile.

Smirking, the bartender pocketed the cash and hooked a thumb at the doorway in the back. "I believe you'll find Mr. Tate at his usual table, stealing money from poor, hard-working souls."

With a quiet thank-you, Eva headed for the doorway and slid through the string of beads.

The corridor was narrow, illuminated by an exposed lightbulb that dangled from the ceiling on a long piece of brown twine. Only one other door in the hall, all the way at the end, and she heard muffled male voices coming from behind it. A burst of laughter, a few Spanish curses and then…English. Someone was speaking English. She immediately picked up on a faint Boston inflection. Having spent her entire childhood and adolescence in New York, she knew an East Coast accent when she heard one.

Tate was definitely in Paraíso.

Eva's legs felt unusually weak as she made her way down the corridor. She instinctively reached into her purse, tempted to grab her cell phone and call the babysitter just to make sure Rafe was all right, but she resisted the impulse. The quicker she did this, the faster she could get back to her son.

Still, she hated leaving Rafe alone for even a few minutes, let alone the two hours she'd already been gone. She worried that if she let him out of her sight, she'd never see him again.

Lord knew her son's father was doing his damnedest to make that happen.

Her stomach clenched. God, what a fool she'd been. And as humiliating as it was to admit, she had nobody to blame but herself. *She* was the one who'd left New York to volunteer with the relief foundation in San Marquez. *She* was the young and idealistic fool who'd actually believed in Hector's cause. *She* was the idiot who'd fallen in love with an outlaw rebel.

But now she had the chance to be free of Hector Cruz. After three years of running, after five close calls and half a dozen fresh starts, she finally had the opportunity to vanquish her personal demon once and for all.

Assuming Tate agreed to help her, of course.

Tucking an errant strand of hair behind her ear, she approached the door and knocked, then opened it without waiting for invitation.

"Who the hell are you?" a rough male voice demanded in Spanish.

Eva did her best not to gape. Her gaze collided with four men sitting at a round table littered with colorful poker chips and a pile of crumpled cash. A lone cigar sat in a cracked plastic ashtray, sending a cloud of smoke curling in the direction of the door. Two of the men were dark-skinned, with matching shaved heads and menacing expressions. The third looked like a fat little character from a Mexican cartoon, boasting bulging black eyes and a generous paunch.

But it was the fourth man who caught and held her attention. He was sitting down, but she could tell he was tall, judging by the long legs encased in olive-colored camo pants. A white T-shirt clung to a broad chest and washboard stomach, the sleeves rolled up to reveal a pair of perfectly sculpted biceps. His chocolate-brown hair was in a buzz cut, and his face was ruggedly handsome, its most striking feature being eyes the color of dark moss.

This had to be Tate. The man had military written all over that chiseled face and massive body.

"Tell Juan thanks, but we have no need for a whore," he said gruffly.

"I'm not a whore," she blurted out.

She'd spoken in English, and she noticed his eyes widen slightly, then narrow as he studied her. His gaze swept over her sweat-soaked sundress, resting on her bare legs and strappy brown sandals, then gliding up to her cleavage, which he assessed for an exasperatingly long time. She supposed she couldn't fault him for thinking she was a prostitute. In this heat, skimpy clothing was really one's only option.

"Who are you, then?" he demanded, switching to English. "And what do you want?"

She took a steadying breath. "Are you Tate?"

The room went silent, same way it had out in the bar. The two men with shaved heads exchanged a wary look, while the chubby one began to fidget with his hands. All three avoided glancing in the dark-haired man's direction.

"Who wants to know?" he finally asked.

"Me," she stammered. "I have something extremely urgent to discuss with Mr. Tate."

He slanted his head, a pensive glimmer entering those incredible green eyes.

To her shock, Eva's heart did a tiny little flip as he once again slid his sultry gaze over her. She hadn't expected him to be so good-looking. Her uncle had told her that Tate was rumored to be a deadly warrior, and granted, he sure did look the part, but the sexual magnetism rolling off his big body was something she hadn't counted on.

"Look," she went on, "my name is—"

He held up a hand to silence her. "Let us play out this hand." With the raise of his dark eyebrows, the man she'd traveled so far to see thoroughly dismissed her and turned to the fat man. "I call, amigo."

There was a beat of anticipation as both men prepared to reveal their cards. Tate went first, tossing a pair of aces directly on the pile of cash in the center of the table. With a resounding expletive, the Mexican threw down his cards and scraped back his chair.

"Tomorrow night, same time," the little man spat out.

Tate seemed to be fighting a grin. "Sure thing, Diego."

Eva resisted the urge to tap her foot as she watched Tate reach for the money he'd just liberated from his fellow card players. To her sheer impatience, he counted it. Then smoothed out each bill—one at a time.

Just as she was about to voice her frustration, he shoved the cash in his pocket, glanced at the other men and nodded at the door. At the unspoken demand, the trio shuffled out of their chairs and practically scurried out of the room.

Eva was unable to hide her amusement. "They're terrified of you, you know," she remarked.

The corners of his mouth lifted. "As they should be."

She suspected the warning had been aimed to unnerve her, but she received a strange sense of comfort from those four lethal words. Oh, yes. This man was exactly what she needed. Her uncle had been right about him. Then again, she really shouldn't have doubted Uncle Miguel. When a San Marquez army general warned you that you'd be getting tangled up with a ruthless warrior, he probably wasn't bluffing.

"So you are Tate, then," she said bluntly.

He nodded and gestured to one of the unoccupied chairs. "I am. Now why don't you have a seat and tell me what the hell it is you want from me."

Unfazed by his short tone, she sat down, crossed her ankles together and met his stormy gaze head-on. "I have a proposition for you."

He cut her off with a low rumble of a laugh. "Proposition, huh? Well, like I said, I'm not into whores. But—" he cocked his head "—maybe I'll make an exception for you. How much, sweetheart?"

Her skin prickled with offense. "I'm *not* a prostitute! My name is Eva. Eva Dolce. And I traveled a long way to find you, so please, quit calling me a whore."

Those green eyes twinkled for a second, then hardened into stone. "How *did* you find me, *Eva?* I'm not exactly listed in any phone books."

"I heard rumors about you." She rested her suddenly shaky hands on her knees. "Someone told me you might be able to help me, so I decided to track you down. I'm… Well, let's just say I'm very skilled when it comes to computers. I studied Computer Science at Columbia and—"

"You're from New York?"

"Yes. Well, I wasn't born there. My parents decided to move to the States when I was a baby. I was raised in Manhattan, we lived on the Upper East Side and—" She halted, realizing she was babbling. She hadn't come here to tell this man her life story, damn it. "Look, none of this is important. All that matters is that I found you."

"Yes, using your trusty computer," he said mockingly.

She bristled. "I'm good at what I do. I started the search at the military base in North Carolina."

His jaw tensed.

"You're good, too," she added with grudging appreciation. "You left so many false trails it made me dizzy. But you slipped up in Costa Rica. You used the same identity twice, and it led me here."

Tate let out a soft whistle. "I'm impressed. Very impressed, actually." He made a *tsk*ing sound. "You went to a lot of trouble to find me. Maybe it's time you tell me why."

"I told you—I need your help."

He raised one large hand and rubbed the razor-sharp stubble coating his strong chin.

A tiny thrill shot through her as she watched the oddly seductive gesture and imagined how it would feel to have those callused fingers stroking her own skin, but that thrill promptly fizzled when she realized her thoughts had drifted off course again. What was it about this man that made her so darn aware of his masculinity?

She shook her head, hoping to clear her foggy brain, and met Tate's expectant expression. "Your help," she repeated.

"Oh, really?" he drawled. "My help to do what?"

Her throat tightened. God, could she do this? How did one even begin to approach something like—

"For Chrissake, sweetheart, spit it out. I don't have all night."

She swallowed. Twice.

He started to push back his chair. "Screw it. I don't have time for—"

"I want you to kill Hector Cruz," she blurted out.

Chapter 2

He was normally quite skilled at reading people, but for the life of him, Tate couldn't decide if the woman sitting across from him was for real. He also couldn't stop the blood in his veins from turning into pure ice the second she uttered those three pesky little syllables.

Hector Cruz.

Tate didn't bother interpreting the "I want you to kill" part. All it took was the sound of Cruz's name and a dose of bloodlust flooded his body, making him want to reach for the gun in his waistband and start shooting.

Before he could stop them, a barrage of grisly images burned a path across his brain. The charred woman in the brown dress. The heat of the fire. Dead rebels strewn on the ground. Cruz's coal-black glare. Will's eyes rolling to the back of his head.

Bad call.

Tate's hands curled into fists as rage consumed his body

like poison. He'd been agonizing about the botched mission for eight months now. He dreamed it. Breathed it. Fed off it. The one thing that kept him going was the thought of slashing a blade across Hector Cruz's throat and watching the bastard die.

And now this woman, this stranger who'd showed up out of the blue, was asking him to do just that.

But as tempting as it sounded, one look at Eva Dolce—if that was really her name—and all he could think was *trap*.

"I'm afraid you've been misinformed," he said, crossing his arms over his chest. "I'm not a hit man."

"I know that." Her voice wobbled. "But I also know that you want Cruz dead."

He shot her a bored look. "Says who?"

"You've been asking questions about Cruz for the past eight months, inquiring about his whereabouts, attempting to bribe the rebels who follow him. You've made no secret that you want to rid Cruz from this earth." She arched one eyebrow. "Do you deny that?"

Her matter-of-fact tone unnerved him a bit. Who the hell was this woman? And had she really tracked him down using nothing but a damn computer? She sure didn't *look* like some hacker extraordinaire. With her long black hair, sapphire-blue eyes and smooth golden skin, she belonged on the silver screen rather than in front of a computer screen. And that body... Forget movie star—those long legs and the firm breasts practically pouring out of the bodice of her yellow dress were better suited for a lingerie model.

Who exactly are you, Eva Dolce?

"I don't deny or confirm anything," Tate replied with a shrug.

She seemed annoyed. "You want Cruz eliminated, Tate. So do I."

All right. Now, *that* he might be able to believe. The

anger and disgust that entered her big blue eyes each time Cruz's name escaped her lush lips was unmistakable. But what was her connection to Cruz? Did she even have one?

Or perhaps she'd been sent here to lure Tate out of hiding. The people who were after him must be tired of slamming into the brick walls he kept placing in their paths, and he wouldn't put it past them to send in someone like Eva, a sexpot agent to seduce their favorite target into slipping up.

But…if they truly *had* found him, why send anyone at all? And one woman, to boot. Why not order an entire platoon to storm this craphole bar and riddle the place—and Tate—with bullets?

He pursed his lips, suddenly second-guessing every damn thought that fluttered into his head. Maybe they were toying with him? No, that seemed unlikely. If the people hunting him knew where he was, they'd have been here by now.

Which meant this raven-haired beauty might actually be telling the truth.

"Why do you want him dead?" Tate asked sharply.

A cloud floated across her expression. He saw more anger swirling there, but it was now mingled with…fear?

"You're scared," he said before he could stop it. He wrinkled his brow. "What are you scared of, Eva?"

"Hector," she whispered. Her chest heaved as she drew a deep breath. "That's why I want him dead. Because as long as he's alive, I'll be scared for the rest of my life." She exhaled in a rush. "He's hunting me, Tate. For three years now. I can't… God, I can't keep running anymore."

Her word choice—*hunting*—raised his hackles once more. Oh, he knew precisely what it felt like to be hunted. Was this a blatant attempt on her part to form some sort of camaraderie with him? To find common ground with the man she'd been ordered to…to what? Kill?

Battling his distrust, he pinned her down with a harsh glare. "Why don't you start from the beginning?"

She nodded, her delicate throat working as she swallowed. "Like I said, I was raised in New York, but I was actually born in San Marquez."

Tate swiftly masked his surprise. So she hailed from the same South American island nation as Cruz. Interesting.

"After I graduated from college, I decided to return to my birthplace and do some good."

When Tate laughed, her eyes narrowed. "My parents reacted the same way," she muttered. "They called me a bleeding heart. But they couldn't stop me from going. I kept seeing all this terrible stuff on the news—people dying, starving, suffering, and the government doing nothing to help them—so I joined a relief organization and began volunteering at a hospital in the mountains." She took another breath. "That's where I met Hector. Idiot that I was, I actually believed in his cause for a time."

Tate stifled a sigh. Yeah, no surprise there. According to his sources, a lot of folks had been—and were still being—duped by Hector Cruz and his ULF crazies. The United Liberty Fighters had been formed to fight the oppression of the strict San Marquez government, but over the years their freedom-fighting mentality had veered off into borderline terrorism. They were responsible for the bombing of government buildings, along with the deaths of countless politicians, and they'd even started robbing their own people—the people they claimed to be fighting for—in order to fund their activities.

"We were friends for a while," Eva went on, shamefaced, "but then he became obsessed with me. At the time, I was involved with another relief worker. John. We…we had a child together. Rafe—he's three. But Hector decided I belonged to him, and he—" she swallowed again "—he had John killed."

Tate stared at her thoughtfully.

"I ran away. I didn't want to have anything to do with that crazy son of a bitch, so I took Rafe and I ran. But Hector is always on my heels. When I found out he was thrown in prison two months ago, I thought it would finally be over, but then his men broke him out and..." She trailed off in frustration.

He could relate—that damn prison break had royally screwed things up for him, too. Two months ago, Cruz had been responsible for bombing the home of a well-known political figure in San Marquez. In a major feat for the military, Cruz had been caught and arrested, and he'd been awaiting trial when his fellow rebels orchestrated an escape and whisked their leader right out of jail.

Since then, Cruz had gone underground. Nobody had seen or heard from him in months, which made it annoyingly difficult for Tate to locate the bastard.

"For whatever messed-up reason, Hector believes that he owns me." Eva's voice jolted him from his thoughts. "Every time I think I'm safe, every time I settle down in one place, he finds me."

She grew quiet, her tale coming to a close, and an alarm went off in Tate's head. Something about that sob story didn't sit right with him. Something about it sounded... false.

"I'm tired of running," she blurted out when Tate didn't respond. "I just want that maniac to leave me alone."

As misgivings continued to course through his head, Tate met her gaze and saw that the fear had returned. Whatever lies she'd just told him, she definitely wasn't lying about her feelings for Cruz. She loathed the man. She was terrified of him.

Because he'd killed her lover? Because he'd developed a sick obsession that had sent her fleeing with her kid?

Raking a hand through his hair, Tate finally chuckled. "That was a nice story, Eva. I'm sure parts of it might even be true. But here's the thing—I don't trust you. I don't trust anyone, for that matter. So I think I'll have to pass on your proposition."

Desperation exploded in her eyes like a round of fireworks. "No! You can't. I *know* you're after him, too." Her features hardened in an expression that resembled defiance. "But you can't find him, can you? He's flown off the radar since he escaped from prison, and seeing as you're on the run, you can't exactly go traipsing around the globe looking for him, now, can you?"

He opened his mouth but she cut him off. "I don't know why you're hiding, and frankly, I don't care. I just want your help to get rid of Hector."

"Did it occur to you that I would need to come out of hiding in order to do that?" he said, rolling his eyes. "I've got my own problems, sweetheart. Like you said, I don't have the luxury of globe-trotting, and even if I did, I won't come along on a wild-goose chase for a man I may or may not want dead."

"But you *do* want him dead." Triumph crept into her voice. "And it won't be a wild-goose chase. I know where his hideout is."

Son of a bitch.

Tate faltered, unable to stop the rush of hope that swelled in his gut. She *knew* where Cruz was? He'd been trying for months to unearth the rebel's location, and he'd come up empty-handed each time.

If this woman truly knew where Cruz was holed up…

He'll kill me regardless… Forget about me, Robbie.

Like hell he would.

"And if you don't want to go to his hideout," Eva added, "all we have to do is find a way to contact him. Trust me, Hector will come to me if I make contact."

He didn't doubt her. With that gorgeous face and sexy-as-sin body, Tate couldn't see any man staying away from Eva Dolce. Hell, he was semihard just being in the same room as her. But common sense and honed instincts trumped the unfortunate desire she seemed to inspire in his body.

Trust me.

Yeah, right. He wasn't about to hand out his trust to a complete stranger. Especially not one as beautiful as her.

Not even one who can lead you to Cruz?

The nagging thought was the sole reason he didn't turn her down outright. He wasn't about to admit it, but she was right about one thing. He wanted Cruz dead. Annihilated. Wiped off the planet.

And he wanted it more than he wanted his next breath.

So…to trust, or not to trust.

Rubbing the stubble on his chin, he met Eva's pleading eyes, then rose from his chair. "Where are you staying?" he asked briskly.

She blinked. "Camino del Paraíso—it's that little motel on the east end of town. Room twelve."

"I'll contact you when I make a decision."

She shot to her feet, despair radiating from her petite, curvy body. "Please," she exclaimed. "Just give me an answer now. I *need* you, Tate."

Shrugging, he shot her a sardonic smile. "If you need me that bad, sweetheart, then you'll just have to wait." His smile transformed into a rogue smirk. "Besides, don't you know that anticipation is half the fun?"

As her eyes blazed with indignation, Tate strode out of the room without looking back.

* * *

"I don't like it," Sebastian Stone declared. "Are you sure she's not messing with you?"

Tate downed the rest of his beer and set the bottle down on the ledge. "I'm not sure of anything. That's why I'm running this by you boys."

"I think it's a trap," Sebastian said flatly. "They must have found us."

"Or they didn't," Nick Prescott chimed in. "And this chick really just wants Cruz dead."

Tate swallowed a groan. Nope, didn't surprise him that Stone and Prescott were yet again on opposite sides of an issue. Stone said up, Prescott said down. Stone wanted to go, Prescott wanted to stay. Out of all the men he'd commanded over the years, these two knuckleheads were the most difficult, stubborn and unbelievably exasperating.

But they were also loyal, intelligent and absolutely deadly when circumstances called for it.

He glanced from one man to the other, his chest going rigid with regret. Two men. Eight men had been with him on that extraction mission in San Marquez. Only two were still alive.

"Or she's dangling a carrot under the captain's nose," Sebastian grumbled in reply to Nick. "The jackasses after us have to know that Cruz is his weak spot. This is all just an elaborate trap."

"The captain's not an idiot. If it's a trap, he's not going to walk into it. But if there's a chance to get Cruz…"

With a snort, Tate held up his hand to silence them. "The *captain* is standing right here. Quit talking about me like I'm not."

They immediately went quiet, each one turning to gaze at the scenery below. Tate rubbed his temples and stared out as well, frustration gathering in his gut at the sight of the jagged brown peaks in the distance. The view, no matter how breathtaking, was just another reminder of how dire their situation was.

This isolated old fortress was nestled at the base of the mountain, and had stood abandoned for decades; apparently the Mexican government had no use for a crumbling pile of stone left over from the Mexican-American War of 1846. But it was the perfect place to lie low, and a decent stronghold with its tall watchtower and handy tunnel system. Ever since the shack in Costa Rica had been compromised, they'd been searching for a new hideaway, and this place had been a lucky find. They'd been holed up here for three weeks now, living on the mountain like a bunch of hermits.

Tate had thought the place to be safe, but clearly he'd been wrong. Because Eva Dolce had found them, and if she could, then so could the hunters.

"I think I might have to work with her," he spoke up, his voice thick with reluctance.

Sebastian's head swiveled around in surprise. "Are you nuts?"

"No, just practical." He shrugged. "I don't think she was sent here by our government, but if she was, then we can't afford to let her out of our sight. We need to find out who she is and why she's here."

Sebastian made a frustrated sound in the back of his throat. "No disrespect, sir, but…don't freaking patronize us. This has nothing to do with keeping an eye on that woman, and everything to do with avenging Will's death."

"What's wrong with that?" Nick interjected with a scowl. "Will was his *brother.* And he was my best friend. He deserves justice."

"He's dead," Sebastian said bluntly. "And wherever he

is, I doubt he's thinking about justice, and I seriously doubt he'd want us to risk our necks to get it for him."

Tate closed his eyes briefly, fighting a jolt of pain at the sound of Will's name. Had it already been eight months since he'd watched his little brother die? It felt like yesterday, damn it.

Sebastian was right. Will wouldn't have wanted them to seek revenge. The kid had always been too softhearted for his own good, constantly preaching forgiveness, even when the person in question didn't deserve a damn ounce of it. Like their old man. They'd endure a particularly brutal beating, and Will would wipe the blood off his face and say, *Don't be angry at him, Robbie. He just misses Mom.*

The memory had Tate gritting his teeth so hard his jaw twitched. Will might've been able to forgive their dad, but Tate hadn't. And he sure as hell wasn't going to let Will's murderer walk free, not if he had the chance to change that.

"You're right," he said, interrupting Sebastian and Nick's heated argument. "This isn't about Eva. It's about Cruz. Christ, Seb, I want him to die."

"What about the others who've died?" the younger man pointed out. His gray eyes blazed with anger. "What about Lafayette and Diaz? What about Rhodes and Timmins and Berk?"

An arrow of agony pierced Tate's chest. Just hearing those names made him want to pummel something.

"They were murdered, too," Sebastian went on. "Diaz and his mysterious drunk-driving accident—that kid never drank a day in his life! And Rhodes's *cancer.* Berk's *mugging.* Lafayette's—"

"Enough," Tate snapped. "I know how they died. Your constant reminders won't bring them back."

"No, but we still don't know *why* they died." Sebastian rested his fists against the dusty stone ledge ringing the watchtower. "That's what we need to be focusing on."

"The mission," Nick said wearily. "We know it has to do with the mission."

Always came back to that, didn't it? The mission that still made no sense to Tate. His orders had been to rescue an American doctor being held hostage by the rebels, but the doc was already dead when Tate's team swarmed Corazón, along with the hundred or so villagers living there, and before Tate could even begin to figure out what had gone wrong, the unit had been recalled back to the States for debriefing.

And, apparently, to systematically be killed off.

Rage and frustration coated his throat, thickening when he remembered his own close call with death. He'd been leaving his Richmond apartment at nine in the morning when a drive-by shooting had conveniently taken place out on the street. He'd escaped with a graze to the shoulder, ducking into a stairwell before the shooters could take aim again.

The police had attributed the event to a street gang who'd shot up the same area only a month before, but Tate knew better. A band of drugged-up teenagers hadn't been responsible for the attempt on his life. Oh, no, it had government-hit written all over it. Which hadn't exactly come as a shock, seeing as he'd already attended five funerals for members of his former unit.

Only Sebastian, Nick and himself were left, and the three of them had promptly disappeared after it became obvious they were being hunted down. They'd spent the past six months trying to figure out who was after them and why, but they'd struck out at every turn. Still knew squat, even after months of digging.

With so many unknowns hanging over their heads, Tate

had received great comfort from the one piece of knowledge he *did* possess.

Hector Cruz had killed his brother.

And Hector Cruz would pay for that.

"We'll figure out why they want us dead," he said, his voice low and even. "Will and I were related by blood, but make no mistake, *all* those men were my brothers. I won't rest until I know why they died."

Sebastian's silver eyes narrowed. "But…"

Tate released a breath. "But I can't let this opportunity pass me by. If Eva Dolce can lead me to Cruz, then I'll damn well be following her."

Chapter 3

Tate wasn't going to help her. Eva forced herself to accept the cold hard truth as she stared at the angelic face of her sleeping son. It had been twenty-four hours since she'd met Tate at the cantina. No phone call, no knock on the door. She'd struck out. Failed.

Back to square one.

"Mommy, that hurts."

She nearly fell off the bed at the sound of her son's drowsy voice. When she glanced down, she realized she'd been squeezing his hand so hard she'd jolted him right out of a peaceful slumber.

As her chest tightened with the shame of knowing she'd brought him pain, she loosened her grip and moved her hand to his cheek.

"Sorry, little man, Mommy didn't mean to hurt you." She stroked his silky-soft skin. "Go back to sleep, baby."

His eyelids immediately drooped, his breathing growing slow and steady as he fell asleep again. She envied him sometimes—Rafe was out like a light the second his head hit the pillow, and he could sleep through a hurricane.

Eva, on the other hand… She couldn't even remember the last time she'd slept more than two or three hours a night. Maybe before she'd met Hector.

With a sigh, she stretched out next to her son, propping herself up on one elbow to gaze down at Rafe's sweet face. When she'd been in labor, she'd wondered how she would respond to him if he inherited Hector's harsh, dark eyes and angular features. Rafe was all her, though—the blue eyes, the black hair, his grandfather's dimples.

Still, she knew she would have loved him even if he *had* resembled his father. From the day he was born, Rafe had been his own little person—strong-willed, quick to laugh, unbelievably sweet.

"You're mine," she whispered fiercely, reaching out to smooth a lock of hair off his forehead. "I won't let him have you."

She suddenly had to wonder if maybe that was why Tate had decided to refuse her. Had he known she was lying about her true connection to Hector?

When she'd come to the bar, she'd had every intention of telling him the whole truth—her relationship with the ULF rebel, the pregnancy, Hector's single-minded desire to claim his son.

But her resolve had wavered when she'd glimpsed the look in Tate's hunter-green eyes after she'd said Hector's name. There had been murder in his expression. Murder and hatred and simmering rage.

She'd realized at that moment that if she told him she was the mother of Hector's child, he might very well wrap his strong hands around her throat and strangle the life right out of her—that was how volatile his emotions about Hector Cruz were.

So she'd lied. Glossed over certain facts, made up a fake lover. She'd hoped that it would be enough to convince Tate, that he'd see how genuine her terror was, how grave her situation, and agree to help.

Looked as if she'd hoped wrong.

With a heavy sigh, she rose from the bed and glanced around the seedy motel room, growing pale when she spotted a fat black cockroach scuttling across the linoleum floor. The roach disappeared behind the dresser, officially squashing any chance of Eva getting any sleep tonight. She was *not* a bug person.

She drifted to the tiny kitchenette and sat on one of the uncomfortable chairs around the white plastic table. "Please don't crawl up my leg," she muttered, shooting a paranoid look in the direction of the dresser.

Reaching for the laptop in front of her, she opened the computer and booted it up. The motel she'd chosen was the only one in the area with wireless access, and she immediately opened the internet browser and typed in the web address for the airline. She could book flights for her and Rafe under the current identities they were using, but once they reached their destination, she'd need to arrange for new papers.

But where to go? Europe again? Or maybe Australia this time. There were hundreds of places to hide down under.

Lots of bugs, too.

Shoot, that was true. She remembered hearing that the outback had some crazy bug statistic, something like more than two hundred thousand different species of insects…

Okay, no, thank you. She promptly decided to stay far away from that part of the world. Canada might be a better bet. Find a place out west, up in the mountains somewhere.

She was in the midst of doing a quick flight search when a sharp knock rapped against the door.

Eva felt all the color drain from her face. Her first thought was that Hector had found her again—until she remembered the way his men had kicked down the door in Istanbul. Right. Hector definitely wouldn't take the time to *knock*.

Drawing a deep breath, she reached for the .45 mm next to her laptop, gripped the weapon with both hands, and made her way to the door. She left the flimsy metal chain on as she inched open the door and peered out.

A pair of vivid green eyes glared back at her.

Relief flooded her belly. *Tate.* He'd come!

"You're here," she burst out, as she fumbled to unhook the chain. She opened the door and gestured for him to enter.

He stepped inside, his muscular body vibrating with reluctance and distrust. Eva's heart did a little somersault as his scent surrounded her—spicy, woodsy and male. When she noticed the way his pants clung to his rock-hard thighs, her pulse took off in a gallop. She didn't think she'd ever seen a more virile, sexier man, and her reaction to his maleness annoyed her.

Tate's hard gaze landed on the gun in her hands, and the corners of his mouth lifted. "Do you even know how to use that thing?"

She shrugged. "Point and shoot, right?"

"Something like that."

Unable to stop herself, she found herself staring at his mouth, which was far more sensual than she'd realized. His lips were surprisingly full, and the dark stubble above his upper lip and slashing across his strong jaw painted a blatantly masculine picture.

"You done gawking at me?"

His mocking voice brought the heat of embarrassment to her cheeks. He'd caught her checking him out, but he couldn't be a gentleman about it, could he? No, he just *had* to point it out.

Gentleman? Look at him, dummy.

Yeah, she really shouldn't expect any gentlemanly behavior from this man.

Swallowing, Eva hoped she wasn't blushing and locked her eyes with his. "So can I assume you're agreeing to help me?"

Rather than respond, he gestured to the two suitcases sitting beneath the painted-shut window. "Is that your stuff?"

"Who else's would it be?"

Ignoring her sarcasm, Tate reached into his back pocket and extracted a black gadget the size of a BlackBerry. He flicked a button, then strode across the room and swept the device over her bags. A steady beeping pierced the air. Eva realized he was checking for bugs and tracking devices.

When he finished with the suitcase, he glanced in the direction of the bed, shooting a frown at her sleeping son. "You've got your kid with you." He sounded annoyed.

The remark had her own irritation flaring. "Of course I do."

Tate's biceps flexed as he crossed his arms. "He can't come with us."

"He has to. I have nobody to leave him with."

He slanted his head. "What about your parents?"

"I haven't seen my parents in three years," she said in a dull voice.

Still looking irritated, Tate grumbled something unintelligible and marched toward her. "Spread your legs, arms out to the side."

Indignation seized her insides. "Pardon me?"

"I'm checking you for wires. Same goes for the kid."

Eva's eyebrows soared. "You honestly think I'd put a wire on my three-year-old child? Who would do that?"

"You'd be surprised." Those green eyes watched her expectantly, and when she didn't move a muscle, he gave a low chuckle. "You're not going anywhere with me unless I'm sure you're clean, so either you let me pat you down, or I walk right out the door, sweetheart."

Her cheeks grew hot again. Pat her down? God, she didn't want this man touching her. Not one bit.

But what other choice did she have?

Swallowing down her humiliation, she widened her stance and lifted her arms.

Two seconds later, Tate's big, rough-skinned hands were roaming her body as if they owned it.

He started from the south, gliding those callused palms up each of her legs, the heat of his touch searing through the fabric of her leggings and making her skin tingle. Her pulse quickened when his hands neared her midriff. He patted her belly, her back, her shoulders, while she stood there, cheeks scorching, heart pounding.

Why did this man affect her this way?

Four years of celibacy will do that to a girl.

Right, that had to be it. It wasn't Tate. Every human being had basic, carnal urges, and she'd been depriving her body for so long it was no wonder the mere proximity of a member of the opposite sex was getting it all excited.

Tate's hands suddenly cupped her breasts, and Eva squeaked in protest. The sudden contact confused her nipples as much as it confused her brain, because those two buds puckered at once and strained against the front of her T-shirt.

"No bra," Tate remarked, those green eyes glinting with approval. "Convenient."

Outrage and mortification mingled in her blood. "I'm

not wearing a bra because it's not comfortable to sleep in, not because I anticipated you taking it off me."

The corners of his mouth twitched as he dropped his hands from her chest. "I meant convenient in another sense, sweetheart. The best place for a woman to stash a wire is in her bra—either the straps or beneath the cups. Saves me time, not having to search your undergarments."

"Oh." She nearly apologized for assuming the worst but stopped herself at the last second. Why on earth should she apologize to this man? *He* was the one who'd just felt her up, for Pete's sake.

"That your laptop?" he asked, gesturing to the silver MacBook on the table.

She nodded.

"Unplug it, shut it down and take the battery out."

Her nostrils flared. "No."

"Do it or I walk out of here."

It was obvious he wasn't going to budge. Grumbling her displeasure under her breath, Eva followed his instructions. After she slid her computer into its plush case, she looked over at Tate with a frown. "What now?"

"Gather your stuff. We'll talk in the car."

Getting her things didn't take more than a minute. She hadn't bothered unpacking her bags—living out of a suitcase had become second nature after being on the run for three years. She collected a few of Rafe's toy trucks off the floor and threw them into one of the bags, then reached for the storybook on the nightstand, which she'd read only two lines of before her son had conked out.

She zipped up the suitcase and headed for the bed, tossing Tate a dark look over her shoulder. "Are you still intent on searching my son?"

"Sorry, but yes."

Eva bent down to scoop Rafe into her arms, then gritted her teeth as Tate stalked over and patted her son down with those rough, warrior hands. The little boy stirred, then burrowed his head against her breasts, made a snuffling sound and continued sleeping.

"Shocking," she muttered after Tate deduced her kid was "clean."

He ignored the barb. "Ready to go?"

Holding her son tight, she gestured to the suitcases and laptop case on the floor and shot Tate a pointed look. "Can you carry those?"

Without a word, he picked up the bags as if they weighed nothing, then marched toward the door.

The parking lot of the motel was dark and deserted when they stepped outside. Tate headed for a beat-up Jeep Cherokee that had more rust than paint and flung open the back door to toss the suitcases inside. While he slid into the driver's seat, Eva buckled Rafe in the backseat, then joined Tate up front.

After she was settled, the engine roared to life and then they were pulling out of the lot and heading for the main road. Eva briefly glanced out the window, watching the derelict buildings whiz by before turning to study her companion's hard profile.

He must have felt her gaze on him, because he gave the sharp swivel of his head and pinned her down with a scowl. "The kid's not coming with us," he muttered. "We'll have to leave him with my men."

Panic trickled through her. "I'm not going anywhere without him."

"And I won't take a child on a potentially dangerous op."

She chewed on her thumbnail, seeing his point. When she'd fled Istanbul and made the decision to find Tate, she hadn't exactly thought through all the logistics. The only thing on her mind had been getting rid of Hector once and for all, but now she realized they did indeed have a problem. They couldn't take Rafe to San Marquez.

But she couldn't leave her son in the hands of a stranger, either.

"Meet my guys and then decide," Tate added with a shrug.

"And if I don't trust them?"

Sarcasm dripped from his gruff voice. "I suppose we could research reputable day cares in the area."

Her nostrils flared. "Don't be a jerk." She tilted her head. "You don't have any children, do you?"

"None that I know of," he said with a crooked grin.

She rolled her eyes. "If you were a parent, you'd understand my apprehension about leaving my son."

"Well, I'm not a parent, and I don't give a damn what you do with the kid—but he's not coming with us."

His tone brooked no argument, so Eva smothered a sigh and fell silent. She would decide what to do with Rafe after she met Tate's "men." Until then, she would just have to be grateful that Tate was even helping her at all.

Twenty minutes later, Eva gulped as the Jeep ascended a dirt road that snaked its way up the mountain. It was pitch-black out. She couldn't see a thing, save for the two pale yellow beams provided by the headlights. Tate obviously knew where he was going, though. He sped along the barely visible road with confidence, not bothering to reduce his speed.

When he finally slowed down, she exhaled a rush of relief, then wrinkled her forehead when a foreboding gray fortress came into view, a structure she'd expect to see in a war documentary or history textbook. Shaped like a square, the fort looked old and unstable. Walls were crumbling away, and up above, the watchtower looked ready to tumble over, boasting several gaping holes where there should have been stone.

"Nice place," she murmured.

"Safe place," he corrected. He stopped in a small dusty courtyard and killed the engine. "It has a pretty complex tunnel system, leading out to various parts of the mountain. Lots of useful escape routes."

"Hector's hideout is in the mountains, too," she found herself saying. "The entrance is carved right in the rocks, almost completely hidden from sight."

His green eyes narrowed. "I see."

It took her a second to register the expression on his face as surprise. "You didn't believe me," she accused. "When I told you I knew where he was."

Tate shrugged. "I half believed you."

"And now?"

Another shrug. "Three-quarters."

Eva almost laughed. She couldn't quite figure out this man. One second he was as cold as ice, a lethal warrior who could probably kill her without breaking a sweat, and in the blink of an eye, he was a charming rogue, ready with a sarcastic remark, a mocking joke, a sensual grin. He completely unnerved her—yet at the same time, he made her feel oddly safe.

"I'll get your bags, you carry the kid," he barked, back to business.

She bristled. "His name is Rafe."

"Like I said, the kid."

As she hopped out of the Jeep to get Rafe, she ordered herself not to be annoyed that Tate viewed her son as a hindrance. What had she expected? That he'd welcome the idea of being saddled with a three-year-old? That he'd toss Rafe on his shoulders and parade him around with pride? Tate wasn't Rafe's father, for Pete's sake.

Oh, no. That honor belonged to a monster.

Holding Rafe tight, she stuck close to Tate as they approached the old fort. They paused in front of a narrow door, and Tate rapped his knuckles against the rusted metal in what sounded like a secret code. There was an identical resounding knock, then a grating sound, and the door swung open.

A shadow loomed in the doorway.

Eva instinctively recoiled when a man stepped out of the darkness, but she relaxed once she got a better look at him. He was in his late twenties, with a handsome face, shaggy brown hair and warm, amber-colored eyes.

"That was fast," the man remarked.

Tate gave that careless little shrug she was beginning to think of as his trademark. He gestured at Eva and said, "Eva, Nick. Nick, Eva."

Before she could greet the other man, Tate was ushering them all inside. She blinked a few times, trying to adjust to the dark as she followed the two men deeper into the fort. She stumbled after them toward the faint glow coming from the end of the corridor. A moment later, they entered a large chamber illuminated by dozens of candles that rested on the floor and various ledges.

She studied the room, taking in the squalor with a frown. There were makeshift tables, a couple of metal chairs, the skeleton of a couch. She spotted a few sleeping bags, along with several big black duffels and a crooked wooden table littered with canned food. Another table in the corner housed a whole lot of laptops. A tall man with dirty-blond hair was bending over one of the computers, and his shoulders stiffened at their entrance.

"This her?" the third man muttered, turning to examine Eva with a pair of suspicious gray eyes.

She nearly flinched under his impenetrable gaze. This

man couldn't be considered classically handsome like his cohorts, but there was something very magnetic about him. His features were hard, angular, and his nose wasn't quite straight, as if he'd broken it a time or two. He was sexy, though. Extremely sexy, in a stark, masculine kind of way.

"Eva, this is Sebastian," Tate told her.

Wary, she met the other man's angry eyes. "It's nice to meet you."

"So you want to kill Cruz," he said in lieu of a greeting.

She lifted her chin in resolve. "Yes."

Sebastian grumbled something under his breath, then cursed when he zeroed in on the bundle in her arms. "Is that a kid?"

Jeez, what was it with these men? Had they never seen a child before?

"Eva's son, Rafe," Tate filled in, sounding as disgruntled as Sebastian looked.

"Here, let me take him," Nick said with a genuine smile. He beckoned his arms at her. "He can sleep over here until we figure things out."

Warmth spread through her body. Finally. Someone who didn't act like Rafe had the Ebola virus.

"Thank you," she said gratefully. "He's getting a little too heavy for me to carry these days."

Smile widening, Nick plucked Rafe out of her arms and took him toward one of the sleeping bags. Eva watched in wonder as he tenderly smoothed out her son's hair before placing him down on the cushy bag.

"I love kids," Nick said over his shoulder, covering Rafe with a thin wool blanket.

"Do you have any?" she asked.

"No, but my older sister has three little ones. Her twin girls are two, and their big brother is five." He paused.

"They're probably enormous now—I haven't seen them in six months."

It was hard to miss the melancholy chord in his voice, which had her wondering, why were these men on the run? She hadn't given it much thought when she'd been tracking Tate—as far as she was concerned, his problems were none of her business. All she'd wanted from the man was his assistance in dealing with Hector, but now she couldn't fight her curiosity.

She swept her gaze from Nick, to Sebastian, to Tate. All three were clearly military, and all wore the same uneasy expressions, as if her presence had raised each of their guards.

"If we do this, we'll be leaving your son with Nick and Seb," Tate said. He glanced at her as if seeking her approval.

After a moment of hesitation, she nodded. "Okay. I think that could work."

Sebastian wouldn't have been her ideal choice of babysitter, but Nick had won her over. Anyone who looked at a child with such tenderness couldn't be a threat, right?

Still, her chest tightened at the thought of leaving Rafe behind.

"I'll take good care of him," Nick said, evidently sensing she needed the reassurance.

She nodded again, the thick emotion clogging her throat making it hard to speak.

"All right, so we've got babysitting duties out of the way," Sebastian said rudely. "Can we focus on more pressing matters now?" He threw Tate a pointed look. "Like why the hell are we working with this woman and how do we know she won't get us killed?"

Eva jerked as if she'd been struck. Sebastian's hostility rippled through the air like an invisible storm cloud. As indignation swirled in her belly, she shot a quick look at Tate in an unspoken request for backup.

To her dismay, he merely offered her a sardonic smile and said, "Yes, Eva, tell us why we can trust you." His smile went feral. "Tell us why I shouldn't kill you right where you stand."

Chapter 4

The woman was fearless, Tate had to give her that. Rather than cower under his and Sebastian's deadly stares, Eva crossed her arms over her chest and scowled at them both.

"You shouldn't kill me because then you won't get Hector," she answered coolly. "And if you do kill me? With my three-year-old son sleeping less than ten feet away? Then you'd be the most coldhearted bastard on the planet."

Tate lifted a brow in challenge. "Who says I'm not?"

Those big blue eyes flashed with defiance. "Fine, you want me to call your bluff? Go ahead and kill me, then."

Their gazes locked for several long moments, and Tate couldn't help but chuckle. He didn't trust this woman, not in the slightest, but he did appreciate her steely fire.

"Sit down," he finally said. "Let's talk details."

Eva's shoulders remained stiff as she primly sank into a chair. Her black hair was twisted in a messy knot atop her head, and a few wispy strands slid out as she sat down, framing her beautiful face.

She crossed her ankles together, drawing his gaze to the shapely legs covered by tight black leggings. Her gray V-neck T-shirt was loose but couldn't hide the full, high breasts beneath it, and Tate's mouth went dry as he remembered how firm those breasts had felt when they'd filled his palms earlier. He almost wished she *had* been wearing a bra, just so he could've watched her remove it.

Down, boy.

Yeah, he definitely needed to control this rush of desire. For a man whose libido hadn't seen any action in eight months, a woman like Eva Dolce was the ultimate temptation. The perfect combination of vulnerable and gutsy, not to mention far too attractive for her own good. Sex appeal oozed from her pores, yet she seemed oblivious to it, which was either an act or she truly didn't know the effect she had on the males in her vicinity. Even Stone, who clearly didn't approve of Tate's decision to team up with the woman, kept eyeing her in a purely masculine way.

Ignoring the zip of heat moving through his veins, Tate lifted his gaze from Eva's chest and focused it on her cagey blue eyes.

"I suppose you want to talk money, right? I'll pay whatever you want. Well, within reason," she added hastily.

He waved a dismissive hand. "I don't want your money."

She looked surprised. "No?"

"No. But if we do this, I want to leave as soon as possible." He grabbed a chair, turned it around and straddled it. "Are you good to travel or do we need to set you up with documents?"

"I've got papers." She paused, her gaze drifting to the sleeping child across the room. "If you don't want me to go with you, I could always stay here with Rafe. I'll give you the exact location of Hector's camp, and you can—"

"No," he cut in. "You're coming with me."

Her dark eyebrows knitted in a frown. "No need to snap at me. I'm just thinking in practical terms—I don't want to slow you down."

He flashed her a cheerless smile. "I've got all the time in the world, sweetheart. If I'm going to San Marquez, you'll be coming with me. That's a deal breaker."

"Why is that— Oh, I get it," she said, understanding dawning on her face. "You still think I'm not being up-front with you."

"Do you blame me?"

"No, I guess not." She bit her plump bottom lip. "I'm not, by the way."

He arched his brows. "You're not being up-front with me?"

"I'm not leading you into a trap." Exhaustion lined her face as she released a sigh. "I want him dead, Tate. I can't keep running for the rest of my life."

Sebastian, who'd been leaning against the wall, stepped forward with a frown. "And why *are* you running?" he asked with a bite to his tone. "Are we seriously expected to believe that Cruz developed an obsession with you and is now spending his time and resources to locate you? That he's wasting his hard-earned money to track down a piece of ass?"

Eva didn't even flinch. Again, rather than back down, she met Sebastian's skeptical gaze head-on. "Are you friends with Hector?" she asked mildly.

Sebastian blinked. "What? Of course not."

"Did you spend a year working in San Marquez and talking to him nearly every day?"

"No," Sebastian said, his jaw going rigid.

"Did he ever share his hopes and dreams with you? Pursue you romantically? Call you his 'heart and soul'?" Eva's features hardened. "I'm going to assume the answer to those questions is also no. So, really, what makes you qualified to presume what Hector deems important enough to spend his time and money on?"

Seeing Sebastian's cloudy expression, Tate hid a grin, but Eva wasn't done.

"Maybe I *am* a piece of ass to Hector, but you know what? Clearly my ass is a big deal to him, because he's been after it for the past three years. He's hired investigators, sent men to tail me, has my parents watched, and every time I manage to disappear, he finds me." Her voice wobbled. "I'm sick of being on the defensive. I want him *dead,* goddamn it."

"Mommy?"

Eva's face went stricken. Cursing softly, she hopped off the chair just as her son stumbled groggily off the bed platform Nick had arranged for him, clutching a small stuffed elephant against his chest. Her outburst had woken the kid up, and Tate stifled a groan as he watched the little boy dash into her arms.

As Eva scooped the kid up, elephant and all, the boy peered past her shoulder, his blue eyes going as big as saucers when he spotted the three men.

"Mommy, who are *they?*" the kid whispered.

Eva's tone was unbelievably tender as she answered, "These are some friends of Mommy's. See the big one sitting over there? That's Tate." She crossed the room, stopping in front of Nick and Sebastian. "And this is Nick, and Sebastian."

"Hey, kiddo," Nick said warmly, leaning in to ruffle the boy's hair. "It's way past your bedtime, huh?"

"I had a scary dream."

Eva's expression strained as she carried her son to the chair and sat down again. The little boy instantly wrapped his arms around her neck and his legs around her waist, clinging to her like a monkey.

She rubbed his back in a soothing manner and planted a kiss on the top of his head. "You want to tell Mommy about it?"

Tate smothered a curse.

Jesus. What a messed-up situation. He wanted Cruz eviscerated, but saddling himself with this raven-haired sexpot and her snot-nosed kid? Not exactly his cup of tea.

Well, all right, Prescott and Stone would be the ones wiping the kid's snot, but Tate almost found that preferable to embarking on this journey with Eva Dolce.

He didn't trust her. It came back to that, and always would.

Did. Not. Trust. Her.

She's going to lead you to Cruz.

Tate held on to that reminder as he watched Eva kiss her son's forehead. "Come on," she coaxed when the boy didn't answer. "Tell me about your dream."

"The bad men were there and you were screaming and then the booms got really loud and..." The kid trailed off and snuggled deeper into Eva's breasts.

Tate frowned. Why did he get the feeling that was a lot more than a dream?

Over the top of her son's head, Eva sought out Tate's gaze and held it. "Cruz," she said, barely audibly. "His men came after us in Istanbul last month."

She rose from the chair and carried the kid back to the sleeping bag. "Give me a few minutes," she told the men.

As Eva tended to her son, Tate strode toward the table where Sebastian had set up the laptops. Both Stone and Prescott were damn good with computers, but so far, neither of them had managed to uncover why their own government was determined to kill them.

"I don't trust her," Sebastian muttered.

"Preaching to the choir," Tate mumbled back.

Nick spoke up in a quiet tone. "Her story checks out." He gestured to one of the laptops. "Orlando just got back to me about the info request we put in."

Tate leaned down and scrolled through the documents on the computer screen. His gaze flicked over the birth certificate, school transcripts, the application she'd filed with the Helping Hands relief foundation.

The documents backed up the story Eva had fed them, but then again, that meant absolutely nothing. Any agency worth its salt would produce the paperwork needed to corroborate an agent's cover story. *If* Eva Dolce was an agent.

"You're good," came her grudging voice.

He glanced over to see Eva standing next to Nick, peering at the screen. He shifted his gaze and saw that her kid was sound asleep again, curled up on the sleeping bag.

"I made contact twenty-four hours ago and you've already got your hands on my high school transcripts," she remarked.

"The credit's due elsewhere," Nick admitted sheepishly. "Our information dealer compiled all this."

"Information dealer, huh?" She sounded bemused. "Maybe I should've gone into that line of work." Her tone took on a cocky note. "Because I'm pretty sure I had *your* high school transcripts in much less than twenty-four hours."

It took Tate a second to realize she was talking to *him*. "Bull," he shot back.

The corners of her mouth lifted. "D-minus in tenth-grade English. What's the matter, Tate? Can't read? Were you one of those kids who slipped through the cracks?"

Nick snorted, and even Sebastian managed a reluctant smile.

"Funny," Tate grumbled.

Tenth-grade English... Yep, that was the year he'd missed three months of school after his old man broke both of Will's legs. Someone had needed to stay home and take care of his little brother.

He decided not to mention that. Let Eva think he was a dumbass. Playing stupid was never a bad strategy, and he could use it to his advantage if needed.

Eva's blue eyes abruptly turned somber. "But I can see from your expression that my background check doesn't convince you of anything, does it? You still don't trust me or believe I'm telling the truth."

He shrugged and moved away from the computer. "I'm more of a gotta-see-it-to-believe-it kind of man."

"So you won't believe I can lead you to Hector's camp until you see it with your own eyes?" Without waiting for his answer, Eva gave a determined nod. "Fine. Let's make you a believer, Tate. When do we leave?"

"Dawn," he said briskly.

"Are we flying direct?"

Scrubbing a hand over the stubble coating his jaw, Tate turned to Nick. "Air traffic's still being monitored by the San Marquez military, right?"

Nick nodded. "Ever since the ULF started running drugs using the relief foundation planes. If you don't have government clearance to land on the island, they'll shoot you right outta the sky."

"We could fly commercial," Eva pointed out.

Tate rolled his eyes. "Sure, sweetheart, why don't you go ahead and do that. I'll take the route that *doesn't* leave a trail, and we'll rendezvous later."

"No need to be snarky about it."

"We'll fly to Colombia," he decided, ignoring her muttered reply. "Hire a boat from Tumaco. Bribe someone at the port to look the other way."

Eva looked dismayed. "But the harbor is in the east. It'll be easier if we come in from the western mountains—that's where Hector is. Otherwise we'll have to trek through the jungle for days."

Tate once again ignored her. "Get in touch with Hastings," he told Sebastian. "Tell him we might need his cabin, depending on which route we take to the west."

"Who's Hastings?" Eva asked, her tone distrustful.

"An ally," Tate said vaguely.

He didn't elaborate, and wouldn't have even if she'd pushed. These days, allies were hard to come by, and Ben Hastings was too valuable an asset to lose. An expat living in San Marquez, Hastings was former military with a list of connections longer than the Nile. Tate had first met the man in basic training, and they'd kept in touch in the fifteen years since. Other than Stone and Prescott, Ben Hastings was the only other person in the world Tate trusted implicitly.

As his brain snapped into business mode, he barked out some more orders. "Prescott, grab Eva's gear from the Jeep. She and the kid can bunk in one of the cells tonight."

"*She* is standing right here," Eva announced. "And what the hell do you mean, one of the *cells?*"

"That's what we call the rooms in this place," Nick explained with a twinkle in his eyes. "Either that, or closets. They're all so small, which is why we usually just crash in this room." He swept his arm around the enormous chamber before ambling off to do what Tate ordered.

Sebastian drifted off, too, a satellite phone pressed to his ear. Once both men were gone, Eva turned to Tate. Her blue eyes flickered uneasily in the glow of the candles.

He couldn't help but notice that she looked annoyingly beautiful in candlelight, and he had to force his gaze away from all that smooth, honey-colored skin, the incredibly vivid eyes, the lush, sensual mouth.

Heat promptly flooded his groin, making him stifle a curse. Crap. He seriously needed to get a grip on this attraction. Lust had a way of fogging a man's brain, and foggy brains led to mistakes. He couldn't afford to make a single mistake around this woman.

"Is this fort really habitable?" she demanded, those big eyes narrowing as she examined her surroundings. "I don't know if I feel comfortable leaving Rafe here. What if the ceiling collapses or something?"

"We assessed the structural integrity before making this our base. The place is solid."

Her teeth dug into her bottom lip. "What about food? And, um, washroom facilities? And—"

Tate cut in. "We've got an outhouse, plenty of wild game in the mountain, a clean well, freshwater spring half a mile from here, and the town isn't far away if my men need more supplies."

"He'll have a blast," came Nick's reassuring voice. The younger man reappeared in the doorway, lugging Eva's two big suitcases, which raised a cloud of dust as he dropped them on the stone floor. "Seb and I will treat your son to a real wilderness adventure."

"What about security?" she asked in a sharp tone. "We just drove right up to the door, and a secret knock isn't much of a safety precaution."

"There are cameras and motion sensors all over the place," Tate said with a shrug.

She looked surprised. "Really?"

He gestured to the laptops scattered on the tables. "We'll see or hear anyone coming from a mile away. The tunnels provide half a dozen escape routes. Oh, and the whole mountain is rigged to explode. Anyone tries anything, Nick or Seb push a button and kaboom."

"Rafe will be safe here," Nick said gently.

To Tate's irritation, moisture welled up in Eva's eyes as her gaze drifted to her child. "I've never been away from him for more than a few hours."

Before Tate could make a quick escape—dealing with female tears were *not* his strong suit—Eva recovered from her emotional moment in an impressive display of self-control. "I guess I should get some sleep, then. You said you wanted to leave at dawn?"

He gave a brisk nod. "Oh-dark-hundred hours. That's the only way I operate."

Her lips twitched. "Fine. Wake me up when it's time to go. Now can someone show me and my son to our cell?"

A few hours later, a gruff voice jolted Eva awake. Her eyelids snapped open to find Tate's aggravated face staring down at her.

"We've got to move," he ordered.

She blinked a few times, oriented herself, then relaxed when she registered the heat of her son's body, snuggled close to her side. Careful not to wake Rafe, she slid out from beneath the scratchy wool blanket Nick Prescott had given her and stumbled to her feet.

The men hadn't been kidding about the size of the room. It couldn't have been more than eight by ten feet, with a dusty floor and oppressive stone walls that lent the space a claustrophobic feel. A tiny square window allowed a patch of moonlight inside; that silver light had been shining directly on her and Rafe, yet somehow she'd still managed to fall into surprisingly deep slumber.

"Now?" she said, wiping the sleep from her eyes.

Tate nodded. Shadows obscured his face, but that little shard of moonlight made his dark green eyes glitter like gems and emphasized the strong line of his jaw.

Her heart did an involuntary flip, and she hated herself for it. She couldn't remember the last time she'd responded to a man on such a primal, sexual level. The dark, heady scent of him stirred her senses, and his long, lean body brought prickles of feminine awareness to her skin.

This man was far too attractive for his own good.

And ruthless. Oh, yes, there was no doubt in her mind that he had a ruthless streak a mile long running through that warrior body of his. He wanted Hector dead, and he'd use anyone and anything at his disposal to make that happen. Including her.

But she'd known that going in. It was why she'd chosen Tate in the first place—that kind of single-minded determination was exactly what she needed if she wanted to get rid of her monster.

"Say goodbye to your kid," Tate said gruffly.

Her heart promptly sank to the pit of her stomach, and then she looked at her son and a jolt of panic blasted through her. Oh, God. She couldn't do it. She couldn't leave Rafe.

As her hands began to shake, she sucked in a deep breath and forced herself to calm down. No, it had to be done. She couldn't bring a toddler on a mission to kill his *father,* for God's sake. Rafe would be safer here, guarded by Tate's men.

Men you don't even know.

Her anxiety doubled.

"I don't know if I can do this," she blurted out.

At the shrill sound of her voice, Rafe stirred on the sleeping bag.

She quickly lowered her voice and shot Tate a miserable

look. "I don't trust you," she whispered. "I don't trust your men. How can… I… God, I can't leave him with strangers."

A muscle jumped in Tate's strong jaw. After a beat, he planted his hand on her arm. "Come into the hall."

The rusty iron door creaked as he pushed it open and led her into the corridor, which was lit by a single candle in a candelabra hanging on the wall.

"We both seem to be having trust issues," Tate said in a tone tinged with equal parts humor and aggravation. "I won't apologize for not trusting you, and I don't expect an apology from you, either. But your kid? He's an innocent. You understand what that means?"

She furrowed her brows.

"It means that my men and I don't use innocents as leverage, or pawns, or to further our agendas," he said roughly. "This world is a messed-up place, sweetheart. Bad people, bad situations. We've gotta preserve whatever innocence we have left, so trust me when I tell you that Prescott and Stone will protect him with their lives."

She certainly hadn't expected *that* from Tate, and some of the tightness in her throat eased. "Really?"

He nodded.

A wry smile played over her lips. "So I should trust you when it comes to my son, but not about anything else?"

"Pretty much." He tipped his head, a mocking glimmer entering his eyes. "Just like I won't trust anything but your desire to see Cruz dead."

"So that much you believe."

"Yes." He donned a contemplative look. "You want the man out of your life, but don't think for a second I bought the story you told me."

She worked hard to keep her face expressionless. He was absolutely right—she'd lied through her teeth about who Hector was to her and Rafe. But she didn't regret her decision to keep the truth from Tate. No way would he have agreed to help her if he knew she'd once been Hector's lover.

"You don't believe my story, yet you're still coming to San Marquez with me," she pointed out.

"Indeed I am."

She fixed him with a contemplative look of her own. "You'll take the risk that I'm playing you, all for a shot at Hector. Why is that, Tate? What did he do to you?"

A laugh escaped his lips, low and harsh. "Nice try, sweetheart. Now say goodbye to your kid. Come to the main room when you're done."

Eva watched as his tall, powerful body disappeared into the shadows. She wished she could figure him out. Rough, calculating, charming, indifferent, sensual—barely a day of knowing him and he'd shown her so many sides of himself she had no idea who he truly was.

He's the man who's going to set you free, that's all you need to know.

Wrenching her gaze off Tate, she walked back into the tiny room and knelt down beside her son. Hot emotion flooded her chest as she watched him sleep. When she noticed the way his bottom lip stuck out a little, she smiled and blinked back tears, wishing she didn't have to leave him.

It was funny how apprehensive she'd been about having Rafe. She'd been twenty-two years old and trying to find a way to escape the tyrant she'd foolishly gotten involved with, only to discover she was pregnant with the tyrant's child. She'd always wanted children, but not then, and certainly not with Hector.

Yet the moment she'd seen Rafe's sweet face, the moment she'd held that tiny infant in her arms, she'd fallen head over heels in love with her son—and she'd vowed to protect him at all costs. Theirs hadn't been an easy life so far—six moves in three years was exhausting—but Rafe was such a resilient child, well-adjusted, intelligent and with such a sweet disposition.

"Mommy has to go away for a few days," she whispered, gently stroking his silky hair.

She decided it was probably best not to wake him. It'd only upset and confuse him.

Then again, wasn't that precisely how he would react when he awoke to find her gone?

Guilt seized her insides. It was a good thing she'd already introduced him to Nick and Sebastian—Rafe would have been terrified to wake up and find himself with someone he didn't recognize.

"I promise you, I'll be back as soon as I can," she went on, her throat so tight it hurt. "I'm going to make sure that monster doesn't come anywhere near you. He'll never hurt us again, baby."

Blinking away the tears that welled up in her eyes, she planted a soft kiss on Rafe's forehead, breathing in his sweet, little-boy scent. It took all her willpower to force her legs to carry her out of the room.

Her heart throbbed with guilt and pain as she walked down the dark corridor in the direction of the main chamber. Angry voices wafted from the open doorway, and she instinctively ducked to the side, not feeling the slightest bit bad about eavesdropping. The more insight she had about these men, the better prepared she'd be.

"I won't stay behind."

She immediately recognized the gravelly voice as belonging to Sebastian.

"I'm giving you an order, Seb." Tate, sounding extremely irritated. "I need you here with Nick."

"You need me watching your six."

"Don't push this. You're not coming, Sergeant. That's an order." Tate paused. "I know you're out there, Eva. Get in here."

Eva's cheeks heated as she entered the room. "Wow. Do you have superhearing or something?"

"No, you're just very loud." Tate stalked toward her, stopping to swipe a pile of clothes from a nearby chair. "Change into these," he ordered, shoving the items into her hands.

She glanced down, and a frown marred her mouth. Jeans, T-shirt, socks, panties, bra and hiking boots—all belonging to her.

"Did you go through my suitcases?" she demanded.

Unfazed by the outraged expression on her face, he shrugged and reached for the black backpack sitting on the floor. "Yeah. I also took the liberty of packing you a bag. We only take what we can carry on our backs."

Although she was inwardly stewing over his presumptuous—and, frankly, nosy—behavior, she choked down her annoyance and stepped back into the hall to change her clothes. When she reentered the room a few minutes later, she headed for one of the tables and scrounged up a pen and scrap of paper. She scribbled down a few details before handing the paper to Nick Prescott, who raised his brows.

"What's this?" he asked.

"The address and phone number for my parents in New York." She swallowed. "If anything happens to me…if for some reason I don't come back…take Rafe to them, all right?"

Nick's brown eyes softened. "All right."

"And if you can, read to him before bedtime—his storybooks are in my suitcase. And don't give him too much sugar, he turns into a little terror if you do. Um, what else? He hates bath time. He can sleep through anything. He doesn't like to be yelled at, so quietly telling him he did something wrong is more effective than yelling. Um, he—"

"Any allergies or medical conditions we should be aware of?" Nick interrupted.

She shook her head.

He grinned. "Then that's all we need to know. Your son will be in good hands."

With an impatient breath, Tate strode across the room and picked up a nylon backpack, same style and color as the one he'd given her. He slid one strap over his shoulder, then bent down to retrieve a navy blue duffel bag from the floor.

"Eva and I'll take the Jeep," he told his men. "I'll stash it at the airfield. That leaves you the Rover and dirt bikes— you good with that?"

Sebastian still looked angry as hell, nodding stiffly to Tate's question. "We'll be fine."

Tate's gaze shifted to Eva. "You ready?"

She let out a shaky breath. "As I'll ever be."

Sebastian waited ten minutes after the captain left with Eva Dolce before springing to action. He stripped off his ratty jeans and threadbare T-shirt and replaced them with cargo pants and a muscle shirt made of lightweight, breathable fabric. Combat boots went on next, and then he shoved a handgun in his waistband and started putting together a go bag. Rifle, pistols, extra clips, grenades. Canteen, MREs, power bars, flashlight, poncho… He tossed in anything he might need for a potential trek, jungle or mountainous.

The entire time, Nick watched from the door. "Why am I not surprised that everything the captain said went in one ear and out the other?"

Sebastian ignored him. He swept his gaze over a table piled with enough weapons and gadgets to launch an assault on a small country, all courtesy of a black ops community that hadn't turned its backs on them even when their own government had.

"You actually think you can follow them without the captain making the tail?" Nick sounded highly amused.

He zipped up his bag and shot the other man an irritated look. "You saying I don't know how to be invisible?"

"No, I'm saying Tate's got superhuman senses. If you tail him, he'll know."

"That's a chance I'll have to take."

Nick ran a hand through his brown hair, suddenly looking very, very tired. "Maybe she can be trusted."

Sebastian snorted. "And maybe the Easter Bunny comes over for Sunday brunch every year."

"She might really lead him to Cruz."

"Or right into an ambush." He zipped up his bag. "Either way, I'll be around to make sure the captain walks out of this alive."

He slung the strap of the duffel over his shoulder and approached Prescott, extending a hand. He and the lieutenant might not always get along—fine, they argued like cats and dogs—but Sebastian had nothing but the utmost respect for Nick Prescott. They'd become brothers the moment they joined Captain Tate's command, and that bond had been tested and become stronger after years of death and bloodshed.

With six of their brothers already under six feet of dirt, Sebastian was even more determined to protect the two that remained. That meant Nick and Tate—no matter what his damn orders were.

"Contact me on the sat phone if you need me," he said gruffly, still holding out his hand.

After a moment, resignation settled in Nick's amber-colored eyes. He leaned in for the handshake. "Don't do anything reckless."

"Same goes for you." His lips twitched. "You just stay here and hold the fort. Literally."

Nick snickered. "I'll do that." His expression promptly sobered. "Be careful, Seb. I'm not in the mood to attend another funeral."

"Don't worry, Nicky. Nobody's dying."

Except for Eva Dolce, if she made even one wrong move toward the captain.

But Sebastian kept that thought to himself.

Chapter 5

"Why didn't you want Sebastian to come with us?" Eva asked, as Tate steered the Jeep down the mountain.

Because only one of us needs to die on this wild-goose chase.

Rather than voice his dour thoughts, Tate just shrugged in response and focused on the road ahead. The sun had yet to set, but faint ripples of light hovered over the horizon line, hinting that dawn was near. Gomez was already waiting for them at the airfield, and Tate couldn't wait to get on the damn plane and get this over with.

Best-case scenario? Eva was telling the truth, they would infiltrate Cruz's hideout, and Tate would exact his revenge.

Worst case?

Jeez, there were so many of those he didn't even know where to start. Even if Eva was on the up-and-up, that didn't guarantee they'd make it in and out of Cruz's camp alive. Tate couldn't formulate a plan until he saw the place for himself, and who knew what he'd find in San Marquez? Cruz's lieutenants and followers continued to fight for the cause while Cruz was holed up underground, but for all Tate knew, the majority of Cruz's men were protecting that camp. An entire army might be waiting for him when he got there.

And if Eva *was* lying, Cruz might not be the pot of gold at the end of this messed-up rainbow. The people who wanted Tate dead might off him long before he even got close to the ULF leader.

That was why he didn't want Stone anywhere near this. Killing Cruz was *his* crusade, *his* albatross. If for some reason Tate didn't make it out of this alive, at least Stone and Prescott would survive and live another day to figure out why they'd become targets.

Twenty minutes later, he pulled up at the dusty airfield, which consisted of two dirt runways, a large hangar with a sagging tin roof, and two armed guards at the rusted gate out front.

The guards waved Tate through without batting an eye. No surprise. He was well-known here in Paraíso—and not for being an upstanding citizen.

His first night in town, he'd had a run-in with a lowlife drug dealer in the cantina, and it hadn't ended well for the dealer. That night he'd earned both the fear and respect of the townsfolk, most of whom were criminals or, like Tate, on the run for one reason or another.

"Is that even a real runway?"

Eva's uneasy voice jarred him back to the present. He glanced at the passenger seat and shot her a crooked grin. "Sweetheart, does this look like a real airport to you?"

"Can your pilot at least fly a plane?" she grumbled, tucking a strand of silky black hair behind her ear.

"Don't worry. He'll get us to Colombia safe and sound."

Tate parked the Jeep and hopped out without another word. He rounded the vehicle, grabbed his go bag and the two backpacks, then tossed one to Eva just as she jumped out of the Jeep. She caught it against her chest with a thud.

"Heads up," he said dryly.

She scowled at him. "You're supposed to say that *before* you throw something at someone."

"I wanted to see if you're quick on your feet. You passed. Come on, follow me."

He strode off, his tan-colored boots kicking up clouds of red dirt. Inside the dilapidated hangar, he found Manuel Gomez tinkering with the propeller of an older-model single-engine Cessna. The stocky bald man lifted his head at Tate's approach.

"Good. You're here," Gomez said in Spanish. His dark eyes flicked in Eva's direction. "Who's the woman?"

"Eva." Tate didn't elaborate, and Gomez didn't push, but the Mexican did arch his eyebrows knowingly before nodding hello at Eva.

"We all set?" Tate asked, gesturing to the plane.

"Good to go." Gomez tossed his wrench into the metal toolbox on the floor. "Throw your gear in the baggage hold."

As Gomez conducted his preflight check, Tate stowed their bags, then extended a hand to help Eva into the small plane.

She hesitated before accepting his hand, and the second his fingers made contact, a jolt of heat sizzled right down to his groin. Everything about this woman turned him on. Her silky jet-black hair, her centerfold body, the graceful curve of her neck. And her scent…talk about addictive. A flowery aroma, with a hint of orange blossoms and something uniquely feminine.

Damn, it had been way too long since he'd had a woman.

Eva was the first female he'd spent more than five minutes with since he'd fled Virginia. The whores at Juan's cantina didn't count—they held no appeal to him, and besides, Tate hadn't paid for sex a day in his life.

Then again, he could probably trust those prostitutes more than he could trust Eva Dolce. At least Juan's whores made their agendas clear.

He saw Eva's pulse throbbing in the hollow of her throat as she shrugged her palm out of his grip. She settled in one of the tattered seats in back of the plane, and he noticed her hands trembling as she buckled up.

"Everything okay?" Tate drawled.

Her jaw tightened. "I don't like the way you look at me."

A chuckle slid out. "And what way is that?"

"You know what I mean."

He pressed his lips together to keep from chuckling again, then climbed up beside her.

A moment later, Gomez slid into the cockpit, flicked some switches, and the little plane shuddered to life. As they taxied toward the makeshift runway, Gomez peered at Tate over his shoulder.

"Should be a smooth ride," the pilot said. "Flight will be a little over four hours."

He leaned back against the chair's headrest and shot Gomez grim look. "Did you file a flight plan?"

The man flashed a grin, revealing his crooked front teeth. "Why, of course, Mr. Tate. We're taking a day trip to Panama, remember?"

Tate grinned back. "Of course."

The engine hummed as the plane picked up speed, and five minutes later, they were in the air. Eva jumped when the landing gear retracted with a thump, but then she relaxed and shifted her gaze out the window. She stared at the clouds for a long while before finally turning to shoot him a perplexed look.

"How do you have so many connections?" she asked. "When I tracked you down, I got the feeling the U.S. government isn't exactly looking out for you."

He shrugged. "Uncle Sam might have disowned us, but we've got a whole lotta cousins watching our backs."

She wrinkled her forehead. "Cousins?"

"Mercenaries, expats, active duty operatives, retired operatives, you name it. The spec-ops community looks out for its own. And when you work Special Forces, you develop a network of contacts that aren't always on the legitimate side."

"So you were Special Forces," she mused.

"You didn't already know that?" he said sardonically.

"No, I couldn't gain access to your military file. It was classified. But your status listed you as honorably discharged."

His shoulders tensed. "Are you telling me you actually managed to hack into the army database?"

Eva smirked. "Like I said, I'm good with computers. I had help with that one, though. I have this hacker friend— he can break into any system, and I mean *any* system. Anyway, we got off topic. How do you pay all these connections of yours?"

"Hasn't anyone ever told you it's rude to ask strangers about their finances?"

She rolled her eyes. "Seriously, how do you have enough money to sustain yourself on the run? I checked your financial statements, and no way was your military pension enough to pay for the kind of expenses you've got—the security measures, on-call pilots, all those weapons I saw back at the fort. When you cleaned out your savings account, it only had five grand in it, so how are you paying to stay hidden?"

He wanted to be insulted, but truth was, her tactics impressed him. It was exactly what he would do, research the hell out of a potential ally—or enemy. Still, it grated that this woman had been privy to the sorry state of his savings.

"All my funds were tied up in the house I bought a few years back," he admitted. "I didn't have time to sell it and cash out. We kind of skipped town without much warning." He smiled dryly. "But Seb and I had no idea how fat Prescott's wallet was. He cleaned out his savings account, too, and I'm talking seven figures here. Cash."

"You didn't know Nick was wealthy, even though you served in the same unit?"

"Another thing about us Special Forces guys—we don't like to talk about ourselves. I know Stone and Prescott better now than I did when they served under me." Tate narrowed his eyes. "What about you? You mentioned you've been running from Cruz for a while. How is it you can afford new identities each time you and your son haul ass? I saw your documents—they're flawless. Which means pricey."

"The first time we ran, my parents gave me money. Rafe was still a newborn, and I had just left San Marquez and moved back to New York. Hector showed up and demanded that I go back with him." Bitterness dripped from her tone. "It didn't seem to faze him that I kept saying no. He was determined to have me."

Rubbing her temples, Eva stretched her legs, drawing his attention to the way the faded blue denim hugged her firm thighs. He forced his gaze back to her face, ordering himself to concentrate on her words rather than her body.

"He got violent when I refused to leave with him. He told me he'd give me twenty-four hours to come to him willingly, and after that, he'd use extreme measures. So that night, my dad gave me fifty thousand dollars from his private safe. I said goodbye to my parents, took Rafe and disappeared. That fifty grand paid for our first identities and a house in Thailand."

"What happened when the money ran out?"

Her blue eyes grew veiled. "I became more resourceful."

He studied her, strands of suspicions coiling in his gut. "You stole what you needed," he said slowly. An alarm dinged in his head. "Oh, hell, you stole from *Cruz*." Now he felt a burst of triumph. "Is that why he's after you, Eva? Is that the real reason?"

"No. I told you why he's after me. He's obsessed." Her mouth relaxed as a smug little smile tugged at it. "He has no idea I stole money from him. There's no way he could ever trace it back to me."

"You sound certain of that."

"I am." She ran a hand through her hair, sending another wave of her intoxicating aroma his way. "The ULF stores their funds in dozens of bank accounts across the globe. Caymans, Switzerland, Dubai—name the country, and the ULF has a numbered account there."

He raised a brow. "And you managed to hack into all of these accounts?"

"Not all, but my friend helped me out and we managed to gain access to some of the accounts."

She proceeded to explain how she'd dipped into various accounts and transferred funds under the guise of commissions, banking fees and administrative charges; that way, if the ULF suspected or noticed something fishy, the wrongdoing would trace back to the person who oversaw that particular account, making it look as if that person had stolen the funds.

Tate let out a low whistle as he grasped what she'd

said. "You do realize that if Cruz or his lieutenants believe they're being cheated, these bankers will get their heads chopped off?"

There was zero remorse on Eva's beautiful face. "The men who cook the books for the ULF are not innocent. Accountant, banker, manager, I don't care who handles that money. They're as responsible for all the deaths the ULF causes as the rebels themselves. These people sit in their cushy offices and move blood money around and pocket it to look the other way. I have no sympathy for them. None."

He cocked his head. "Interesting."

"What?" she said defensively.

"You are far more ruthless than I would have imagined."

"Ruthless? No. Sick and tired of the corruption? Yes." Her expression grew stony. "I came to San Marquez four years ago to make a difference and all I got out of the experience was disillusionment. The ULF doesn't care about the country's people any more than the government. The only things anyone concerns themselves with are money and bloodshed."

"Says the woman who spent a considerable amount of time and energy to track me down—so I could kill a man for her."

"You're not killing Hector for me. You're killing him for *you*. I'm just giving you the means with which to do it."

"Win-win, then?"

"Murdering a man… Sure, Tate, it's win-win," she said flatly, and then she fixed her gaze out the window and promptly put an end to the conversation.

Eva was a bundle of nerves by the time they arrived in the small port city of Tumaco. Tate's pilot had taken them as far as Cali, Colombia, where they'd boarded another plane piloted by another nefarious-looking character from Tate's network of shady associates. Less than an hour later, they'd landed in Tumaco and taken a taxi to the harbor, where Tate was now haggling with the captain of a small cargo vessel.

It had only been six hours since they'd left Paraíso, but Eva was already exhausted. She felt as though she'd run a marathon followed by two triathlons and a decathlon thrown in for good measure. Probably the heat. March in South America could be brutal, and today was no exception. Only eleven in the morning, and the temperature must be nearing ninety-seven degrees already. The sun's merciless rays beat down on her head—her wide-brimmed straw hat was doing nothing to protect her scalp from the heat— and the air was so muggy it felt as if she was inhaling fire each time she took a breath.

She hoped it would be cooler on the water, but if the stifling breeze rolling off the ocean was any indication, the impending boat ride probably wouldn't offer much relief.

Her gaze moved in Tate's direction, and she couldn't help but notice the way his sweaty white T-shirt clung to every hard angle and corded muscle of his broad chest. With the brim of his baseball cap pulled low, she couldn't see his expression, but his body language displayed unmistakable irritation. He towered over the captain of the cargo ship, a slight, dark-skinned man who seemed determined to bleed Tate dry, judging by the second stack of bills he shoved in the man's palms.

A few moments later, Tate stalked over to where she waited, dodging dock workers on his way. "He'll take us. We leave port in thirty minutes."

"What did you tell him?"

"That we're American, here to volunteer with one of the relief foundations. I said we missed our flight and decided we wanted a nautical adventure rather than wait for the next plane."

"How long to San Marquez by boat?"

"Four, five hours. We'll get there late afternoon."

Eva glanced over at the fruit stands a hundred yards from the dock, a sight that elicited a grumble from her stomach and served as a reminder that she hadn't eaten a thing since last night.

"Do we have time to grab some food for the ride?" she asked.

Tate nodded and took her arm as they fell into step with one another. She didn't know if it was a protective gesture, or if he wanted to make sure she didn't run off, but the heat of his fingers as they curled lightly over her biceps made her heart to do a little flip.

Lord, her heart had to quit doing that. She had no business being attracted to this man. To any man, for that matter. After her experience with Hector, a result of her own naïveté, she had no desire to get burned by a man ever again. Her son was the only male she wanted—or needed—in her life now.

Banishing the awareness rippling over her hot skin, Eva filled a cloth sack with fresh mangoes and a bushel of bananas, paid the plump Colombian woman and then followed Tate back to the dock. At their approach, the captain impatiently gestured for them to come aboard, announcing in Spanish that it was time to go.

Lugging his duffel, Tate took the lead and strode up the gangplank, his boots thudding on the creaky main deck of the vessel. Eva scampered after him and accepted his hand as he helped her on board.

Not long after, they were heading due west, the balmy breeze slapping their faces and the salty ocean mist stinging their eyes. Thankfully, it *was* cooler on the water. As

Tate stood by the railing, watching the waves, Eva sank on a metal crate and gave her rumbling stomach some nourishment. She devoured two bananas, then cut open a mango with the small switchblade she found in her backpack, unruffled by the sticky juices that stained her hands. Lord, she was hungry.

"Mango?" she asked Tate between mouthfuls.

His rugged profile shifted in her direction. "Toss one over."

She dug a mango out of the sack and lobbed it his way. He caught it easily, then slid a lethal-looking blade from the sheath on his hip and sliced a piece of the ripe fruit. He flicked it up to his mouth with the tip of his knife, bit and sucked the fruit, then tossed the peel into the water.

She was oddly fascinated as she watched him eat. His every movement was done with military precision, from the way he handled the knife to the way he threw away the peels. Even the way he chewed seemed carefully planned.

"Can I ask you something?" she asked, as she uncapped a bottle of water. It would probably be the last "luxury" drink she'd have in a while—once she and Tate reached the river, they'd only be able to drink water that they'd purified first.

"You can ask," he replied, "but there's no guarantee I'll answer."

She took a sip, then rested the bottle on her knee. "How come you don't go by the name Robert? At first I thought it was a military thing, using your last name, but Nick and Sebastian both used their first names when they introduced themselves."

His expression darkened. "I prefer Tate."

"Clearly. But why?"

"Robert was my old man's name," he said tightly. "I

didn't want to have anything in common with that man. Sharing a surname was bad enough."

An unwitting rush of sympathy filled her chest. "Bad childhood?"

"If you consider getting the crap kicked out of you on a daily basis for ten years *bad,* then yeah."

Her breath caught. She studied his harsh face, but there was no hint of humor, no sign that he was messing around with her. Instantly, her heart constricted with pain for everything he must have suffered growing up.

"I'm sorry," she said softly. "That must have been difficult."

"I survived."

She released a frustrated breath. "Do you always do that? Brush everything off like it's no big deal?"

"Only when it really *is* no big deal." He rolled his eyes. "Don't look at me like that, sweetheart, with those big pitying eyes. I dealt with my crap years ago. The past is the past."

God, she wished she could think like that. But for her, the past *wasn't* the past, not when it threatened her future. Her son's future. She'd made a mistake when she'd fallen for Hector four years ago, but Rafe didn't deserve to pay the price for it.

The wind picked up and snaked underneath her ponytail, blowing the ends of it into her mouth. She shoved the hair away and adjusted her hat, then glanced at Tate, still trying to make sense of him. "So your father, is he still alive?"

Tate moved his gaze back to the horizon line. "He died eleven years ago. DUI."

"I guess it would be too optimistic to think you mourned him."

He chuckled. "I was tempted to throw a damn parade."

"That's sad."

"What, that I didn't grieve for the bastard?"

"No, that you had him for a father in the first place," she said quietly.

He sliced off another chunk of mango and chewed slowly, shooting her a what-can-you-do look. "Luck of the draw. Some kids are just destined to have crappy parents, I guess."

Didn't she know it. Her son had drawn the short stick, too, when he'd gotten Hector Cruz for a father, but Eva was determined to protect Rafe from the man who'd sired him. Not only was Hector a violent, sadistic killer, but nothing was sacred to him, not even youth. The ULF frequently recruited child soldiers for its cause, a horrifying truth she hadn't realized until much later. Hector had even bragged to her that he'd personally trained some of the children in the movement.

Well, she refused to let Hector corrupt her little boy. Solving violence with violence had never been a philosophy she'd subscribed to, but in this case, she would make an exception. Hector had to die. It was the only way to keep her son safe, the only way to—how had Tate put it? Preserve innocence.

Eva rose from the crate and approached the railing. She gazed out at the greenish-brown dot in the distance. The island of San Marquez. Her birthplace, her son's birthplace. In a few short hours, she'd be back in the place she'd vowed never to return.

"You haven't been back since your kid was born?" Tate asked gruffly, following her gaze.

She shook her head.

"Where exactly does the name Dolce come from? I figured you'd have a Latin American name since you were born in San Marquez."

"My dad's Italian," she explained. "He met my mom

when she was vacationing in Italy as a teenager. She was from San Marquez, and Dad was too smitten to say goodbye to her, so he followed her all the way to another continent and they lived here for a couple of years. He worked in the capital, but then his firm transferred him to the States right after I was born, so we moved to America."

A cloud of smoke wafted in her direction, making her wrinkle her nose. Glancing over, she spotted a tanned deckhand standing by the stern, one arm resting on the steel railing ringing the deck, the other holding a hand-rolled cigarette. He inhaled again, then blew out another puff of the sweet, potent flavor unique to the tobacco produced on San Marquez.

The scent brought both a wave of nostalgia and a rush of dread to her belly. The latter feeling increased the closer they got to the island. Funny, how such a small, beautiful place could harbor so much ugliness.

San Marquez was smaller than the countries on the mainland but larger than most of the island nations dotting the continent. To the west sat the Marqueza Mountain range, looming over a coastline that offered nothing but boulder-ridden white sand and jagged cliffs with steep drops. Merido, the capital city, was centrally located, a crowded metropolis with a struggling tourism industry thanks to the strife with the ULF. The eastern region of the island featured an array of coastal towns and villages, along with a harbor that served as the base of the country's fishing and trade industry.

"Damn," Tate muttered, as the ship neared its destination.

Eva immediately understood the source of his unhappiness. The telltale navy-blue-and-gold uniforms stood out among the throng of people bustling in the harbor.

"I don't remember there being much of a military presence on the coast before," she remarked with a frown.

The deckhand she'd been eyeing ambled over, sucking hard on his cigarette. "Smuggling happen," he said in garbled English. "Drugs, weapons, hide on boats."

"ULF?" Tate said sharply.

The man nodded. "They be getting reckless lately. Cruz gone, rebels fighting each other."

Eva's frown deepened. Dissent within the ULF. Hector was probably fuming about that. Would he come out of hiding to take care of the problems? She prayed he wouldn't, at least not before she and Tate reached his hideout.

The closer the cargo vessel got, the more uneasy Eva felt. The port wasn't overflowing with soldiers, but she spotted at least a dozen posted at various points of the harbor, their hawklike eyes sweeping over the people milling the area.

By the time the ship reached the dock, her pulse was racing. She didn't want to attract any undue attention, but she might not be able to help it once they disembarked. The dockworkers were mostly male, and as a female, she'd stand out like a sore thumb.

Tate evidently concurred because he lowered his voice and said, "When we get off, keep your head down. I don't want anyone getting a good look at our faces."

She nearly said "mine more than yours" but quickly bit back the words. If anyone was the more recognizable of the two, it was her, the former lover of the ULF's *leader*.

Panic tugged on her belly as she realized that everything could go up in smoke if anyone connected to Hector recognized her. If Tate found out she'd been involved with his enemy, he'd either kill her or abandon her. Unfortunately, neither of those outcomes was desirable.

She nearly fell overboard when she heard a loud metallic thump. She relaxed when she realized it was the gangplank being lowered, but then she noticed Tate picking up his duffel bag and her anxiety returned. She didn't exactly know what was in that bag of his, but she had a pretty good idea that most of the contents weren't legal.

"What if we're searched?" she murmured.

"Taken care of," he murmured back.

She didn't have time to question that statement, but she found out soon enough. The customs official that greeted them on the walkway barely even glanced in their direction—or at the passports they handed him. He scribbled something on his clipboard, stamped their passports, then stalked off.

"How'd you manage that?" Eva asked as she watched the burly man's retreating back.

"All that cash I handed our captain in Tumaco? That was so he'd put in a good word for us with his brother." Tate hooked a thumb in the direction the customs clerk had gone in. "That was his brother."

She grinned. "How lucky for us."

After bidding goodbye to their captain, she and Tate maneuvered their way through the busy harbor, heading for the road several hundred yards away. The odor of fish, salt and earth hung in the air, along with that sweet tobacco that every male within ten feet seemed to be smoking.

Eva angled the brim of her hat and kept her head down as they walked, doing her best not to make eye contact with anyone. People jostled them, some pushing past using their hands, and she squeaked in objection when a particularly aggressive dockworker bulldozed past her, nearly clipping her in the side of the head with his elbow.

"You okay, baby?"

Tate's sandpaper-rough voice made her blink in surprise. *Baby?*

"Uh, I'm fine, he just bumped—"

She almost jumped out of her own skin when Tate slung an arm around her shoulder and dipped his head to nuzzle her neck. Despite the hundred-degree temperature, goose bumps rapidly rose on her skin.

What the hell was he—

His husky voice interrupted her thoughts. "I cannot wait to get you alone," he rasped. "Just you and me. On a bed. All night long."

Chapter 6

Shock and arousal coursed through Eva's body like an electrical current. Her heart pounded, nipples puckered, core ached. She couldn't remember ever getting this turned on this fast.

Beside her, Tate seemed as cool as a cucumber. He rubbed his stubble-covered cheek on her neck, the prickly beard growth abrading her suddenly feverish skin. And he didn't even slow his pace—nope, just kept walking, practically dragging her beside him even as his lips closed over those sensitive tendons in her neck and sucked gently.

"What are you doing?" she stammered.

"You taste incredible." He swiped his tongue over her heated flesh then took a teasing nip with his teeth.

Before she could even attempt to figure out what had gotten into him, he abruptly straightened his shoulders and slid his hand to the small of her back, resting it there in a casual but possessive pose.

What on earth? Up until now, Tate hadn't shown an overt amount of sexual interest in her, but all of a sudden he was a different man. His smoldering green eyes, the sensual lift of his mouth, the dangerous seduction radiating from his masculine frame.

"Easy," he murmured, rubbing circles over her tailbone. His voice lowered to a scarcely audible pitch. "Play along, sweetheart."

Understanding dawned fast and hard, becoming clearer when she caught a flash of navy blue and gold in her peripheral vision. Soldiers. Two of them. They must have been walking directly behind her and Tate, but now they veered to the right and hurried off in a brisk march toward a group of unruly boys who looked to be in the middle of a full-out brawl.

As the soldiers shouted and raised their guns, the fighting boys broke apart and took off like bats out of a cave, disappearing in all directions.

Eva and Tate took full advantage of the soldiers' distraction, picking up their pace as they made their way to the road. It wasn't until they were out of sight that she allowed herself to dwell on the completely inappropriate response she'd experienced back there.

She'd wanted Tate.

In that moment, when his warm lips had met her skin and his big hand slid under the hem of her shirt to stroke her lower back, she'd wanted him more than she'd wanted her next breath.

His kiss. His touch. His powerful body crushing hers as he moved inside her. She'd wanted it all, damn it.

Even now, those wicked images caused that spot between her legs to tingle. God, this was wrong. Having sex with Tate would be a bad idea. A *terrible* idea.

And not even a viable idea, considering he'd faked that

entire flirty, seductive exchange. While she, idiot that she was, had believed every second of it.

"Sorry about that," he muttered. "They were staring at us too long for my liking."

She swallowed the embarrassment lining her throat. "How do you know they were staring? They were behind us. Do you have eyes in the back of your head or something?"

"Sensed it. Fifteen years in the military will do that to you." He shrugged. "I can sniff out a threat from miles away, even if it's behind me."

"Yeah? What kind of threats are around us right now?" she couldn't help but challenge.

"Other than the government soldiers crawling over every inch of the harbor? Well, there's the ULF rebel trying to blend in over there by the loading dock. The pickpocket that's already robbed two fishermen, which is damn impressive because the kid can't be older than five or six. That woman standing by the fruit cart is packing heat— AK, judging by the size and bulk, but I suppose it could be a lower-caliber ri—"

"I get the point," she cut in, unable to fight a smile. "You know your threats."

He tipped his head and shot her an ironic smile. "I sure do, Eva. And the biggest threat of all happens to be right beside me."

She bristled with insult, but she couldn't exactly fault him for being distrustful. This man was risking a lot to be here. He'd come out of hiding, and now he was taking a gamble that Eva could lead him to Cruz. Well, fortunately for him, the gamble would pay off because she planned on delivering Tate right to Hector's door.

And watching while he killed her son's father.

A shiver ran up her spine. Did it make her a coward, for

not doing the job herself? Or a monster, for actively seeking out a man's death? Maybe both. Maybe neither. All she knew was that her son would never have a normal life as long as Hector was alive.

"You'll realize soon enough that I'm not a threat," she said quietly. After a beat, she offered a dry smile. "Until then, try not to kill me in my sleep, okay?"

His lips twitched as if he were fighting laugher. "Deal."

"This is as far as I go."

The driver of the ancient truck they'd flagged down let the engine idle, which made the entire vehicle chug like a steam engine. Tate was happy to get out of the truck; he and Eva had been crammed in the front seat for the past three hours, and his body desperately needed a reprieve. Sitting there with Eva's firm thigh pressed against his had been pure torture.

He'd tried to distract himself by focusing on the scenery, but the green hills and soil-rich fields that made up the island's eastern landscape hadn't succeeded in making him any less aware of Eva Dolce. The woman smelled like temptation, all sweet and spicy and orange-blossomy, and she tasted like heaven—he knew that for a fact now, seeing as he'd had his lips buried in her neck earlier.

Christ, this unfortunate attraction to a woman he didn't trust was liable to drive him insane.

"Thank you so much for the ride."

Eva's melodic voice jolted him from his thoughts. As he pushed on the broken door handle of the passenger side, Eva leaned in to squeeze their driver's shoulder in thanks. Which was kind of impressive because Tate wouldn't have touched the man with a ten-foot pole. Long, greasy hair, bushy gray beard with what looked like pieces of food stuck in it, dirty fingernails and several missing teeth. The guy looked like a cartoon hobo, for Chrissake.

But hey, in the hobo's defense, he'd stopped to pick them up when he'd spotted them on the side of the road, and Tate was compelled to offer a thank-you of his own before he hopped out of the truck.

He rounded the vehicle and grabbed his duffel from the truck bed, which was piled high with wooden crates over-flowing with oranges. The citrus scent filled his nostrils and made him think of Eva, who came up beside him, tight-ening the straps of her backpack. The moment he slung the duffel over his shoulder, the truck driver revved the engine and sped off in reverse, raising a cloud of moist brown dirt that nearly blinded them both.

Tate wiped the dust off his face, watching as the driver executed a rapid U-turn that made the vehicle lurch and chug harder. After the truck disappeared, he glanced at Eva. Her blue eyes were apprehensive as she gazed at the landscape up ahead, where the road became impassable.

Thick vegetation awaited them, and the scents emanat-ing from the tangle of greenery were ones he'd recognize anywhere—damp earth and wildflowers and acrid rot. Even from where he stood, he heard the din of the jungle, the familiar noises of the wildlife, the buzzing of insects and rustling of trees, and he drew great comfort from it all. This was his element—out in the wild, hunting down his prey, a silent, shadowy predator. *This* was what he'd been trained for, not hiding away in a stone fortress like a coward.

"I hate the jungle," Eva remarked in a glum voice.

"Well, start loving it, because we've got a long walk ahead of us. Three days, barring any unforeseen compli-cations, and that's factoring in only a few hours' sleep a night. If you want more sleep time, it'll take longer."

She made a grumbling sound. "Trust me, I won't be sleeping at all."

He had to grin. "Scared of what bumps in the night?"

"More like what *crawls.* I do not like bugs." Her tone was flat and emphatic. "At all."

"Then the jungle ain't gonna be your friend, sweetheart," Tate said with a chuckle.

They moved into the thick canopy of trees, and immediately, the temperature became more humid, the air muggy and moist. Clinging foliage and dense vegetation blocked the sun, but shafts of light found their way through gaps in the trees, making the dew sparkle on the colorful flora that cropped up all over the area.

And everything was so damn noisy. Mosquitoes buzzing past Tate's ears, a macaw squawking from somewhere high in the trees, the unmistakable bark of a spider monkey followed by a sudden rustling of branches. The jungle was a whole other world, a living, breathing entity pulsing with life and activity.

A sense of peace washed over Tate, ironic considering that danger lurked in every corner, from the decaying matter underfoot to the trees up above and everything in between.

He unzipped his duffel and grabbed a few necessities, including a razor-sharp machete, a handgun, his favorite Bowie knife and his trademark M-16 rifle.

"Planning for an assault?" Eva asked wryly.

"Always." After a beat, he removed a 9 mm from the bag and extended it to her. "Here. We might as well both be prepared."

She looked surprised, but handled the gun with ease as she checked the clip then stuck the weapon beneath her waistband at the small of her back.

Tate sheathed his knife, shoved the H&K in his belt and

slung the strap of his rifle over one shoulder. The machete he kept on hand.

"No mosquito netting," he muttered, as he peered into the duffel. Damn. Prescott must have forgotten to shove it into the go bag. Ah, well. He'd remembered the bug repellent, at least.

Tate quickly transferred the remaining contents of the duffel into his backpack, then shoved the duffel beneath a pile of rotting palm fronds; he'd only needed the bag to carry and conceal his weapons. Now it was time to travel light.

Palming the handle of his machete, he stood up and appraised Eva, pleased by what he saw. Her jeans would protect her from the bugs, and she could put on the white button-down tied around her waist if her arms started to get bitten. Her hiking boots were sturdy—he'd checked back at the fort—and that hat ought to protect her from the sun.

He gave a satisfied nod. "Ready?"

She nodded back.

"Good. We'll follow the river," he said briskly, his boots crunching over the dense undergrowth that made up the jungle floor.

Hope lit in her blue eyes. "If we're sticking to the river, why not just raft it?"

"Too risky. The river patrols have increased since Cruz went underground. Every member of the military is hunting him."

She sighed. "Fine. Then let's go. I want this to be over as soon as possible." As if to punctuate that, she slapped the mosquito that had the misfortune of landing on her neck and flicked the dead insect away with a grimace.

"Stay behind me," he ordered.

"I plan on it. In fact, if we get attacked by a crazed

monkey or something, I'm fully prepared to use you as a human shield."

A laugh escaped his mouth, and he quickly had to berate himself for it. Eva was gorgeous—no denying that. She was also far more intelligent than he'd previously thought, not to mention entertaining, thanks to that wry sense of humor.

But she was still a potential enemy.

He needed to remember that before he did something stupid—such as starting to actually *like* the woman.

They traveled at a vigorous pace for the next several hours. Tate used the machete to hack a crude path in the vegetation, while Eva trailed after him. To her credit, she didn't complain once during the trek, except to voice her annoyance with the relentless mosquitoes that refused to let up.

Tate could hear the river from the east, water gurgling and lapping the riverbank, but he didn't stick too close to it. He set a parallel course, one that kept them hidden in the event a river patrol cruised by. He and Eva stopped only to refill their canteens at a freshwater pool they happened upon, then scarfed down a couple of MREs while they waited for the purification tablets to do their job and make the water safe to drink.

By the time the sun dipped toward the horizon line, they'd made damn good time, and he was pleased with their progress. Eva didn't seem to be tiring, which impressed the hell out of him.

"You're in good shape," he remarked, as he hacked away at the low-hanging vines blocking his path.

"I work out at night when Rafe is asleep." She paused. "I don't sleep much. Especially not since Istanbul."

He used the blade of the machete to shove aside some moss-covered branches; you never used your hands if you knew what was good for you, as there were lots of nasty surprises in all that greenery.

"What happened in Istanbul?" he asked carefully.

"Two of Hector's men—"

The jungle drowned out the rest of her reply. Screaming monkeys, a breaking branch, the swoosh of wings as a macaw soared right above their heads.

Eva's soft laughter broke through the din. "Noisiest place on earth, huh? I can barely hear myself think. Anyway, as I was saying, two of Hector's men tracked me to the house I rented in Istanbul."

"Did they hurt you?"

"Almost. They broke down the door while I was feeding Rafe his dinner. They were armed, and they lunged at us. I grabbed Rafe and ran into the bedroom at the back of the house. I found my gun, and…and when they burst into the room, I fired." Her voice shook. "I unloaded the entire clip."

Tate halted, lowering his machete as he turned to face her. The torment in her eyes was hard to miss, and he noticed that her hands were trembling.

"I murdered two men," she said softly.

He let out a breath. "You were defending yourself and your son."

"But they weren't trying to kill us." Agony clung to her tone. "They were hired to bring me to Hector. They wouldn't have hurt me."

"Taking you somewhere against your will *is* hurting you. You did what you needed to do to survive."

Bitterness slashed across her face. "Is that how I should justify it?"

He shrugged. "Justify it however you like. All I'm saying is, you didn't murder two men in cold blood, Eva. You can let yourself off the hook."

"I've tried." Her teeth dug into her bottom lip. "He didn't

see it. Rafe, I mean. I shoved him under the bed just before the men burst into the room, but he heard the gunfire and…he must have heard their screams."

"He's three. I doubt he can truly grasp what happened that day."

"He has nightmares about it."

"They'll go away."

"You really believe that?"

No.

"Sure," he said lightly, before taking a step forward. "Let's keep moving."

She followed him without protest, sticking close as they forged a path through the jungle. "How come you don't have any kids?" she asked.

"Never wanted any."

"Why not?"

"Just not interested."

A branch snapped overhead, and Tate immediately looked up, seeking out the source of the disturbance. Critters had a habit of dropping right on top of your head out here. The way he saw it, if you weren't alert, you deserved whatever you got.

"Don't want the responsibility, huh?" Her voice held a note of amusement.

"I'm fine with responsibility, sweetheart." He paused. "I don't think I'd be much of a role model for a kid, okay?"

Now she sounded surprised. "Army captain, black ops supersoldier…you're like a real-life hero. Kids eat that stuff up."

Discomfort welled in his chest, and he was glad Eva was behind him so she couldn't see his face. He suspected his expression was as broken and empty as the rest of him. With Will gone, he had absolutely no reason to pretend anymore. Pretend to give a damn, pretend he had any humanity left.

Truth was, he'd shut down a long time ago, but he'd been putting up a pretense for his little brother's sake. Now there was nothing stopping him from embracing the anger burning inside him, nothing to stop him from giving the finger to a world that had constantly and unfailingly turned its back on him.

"I'm no hero," he said gruffly. "And I wouldn't wish my own company on any child."

Her tone softened. "I wasn't sure I'd be a good mother, either, but after I had Rafe, those maternal instincts just reared up out of nowhere. He's made me a better person, I think. He's my entire life now."

Tate chopped at some vines, then ducked through the opening he'd created. "Your entire life, huh? That can't possibly be healthy. No room for a man in your life?"

"Nope."

"What about in your bed?"

"What about it?"

He couldn't control the husky note in his voice. "You don't get lonely sometimes, Eva? Late at night, when you're lying alone in bed?"

"No." He couldn't see her face, but he felt the heat of her gaze on his back. "Why, you offering to relieve some of my loneliness?"

A bolt of arousal sizzled down his spine and settled in his groin. Damn, just the thought of burning the sheets with this woman got him harder than concrete.

"Because if so, I'd have to decline," she went on. "I kind of prefer it when the men in my bed actually like and trust me. Otherwise, it feels like—"

A high-pitched shriek sliced through the air.

"Holy hell, what was *that?*" Eva burst out. She slapped

her shoulder in a panic and proceeded to hop around as if the ground was on fire. "What was that *sound?* What the frickin' *hell?*"

Tate instantly drew her to his side and dragged her a few yards away. He ran his hands up and down her torso in a hurried inspection, then examined her shoulder, lifting up the sleeve of her T-shirt to take a look.

"Lucky girl," he told her. "You didn't get bitten."

"Bitten by what? What was that shrieking noise?"

She looked so utterly freaked out he stifled a laugh. "Bullet ants."

"That five-inch thing that pounced on my shoulder while screaming like a banshee was an *ant?*"

"Yes, and five inches is an overexaggeration—those things only grow about an inch or so. And for some messed-up reason, they make that noise when they attack you." Satisfied she'd been spared, he dropped his hands from her shoulders and took a step back. "You're damn lucky. Bullet ant bites are painful as hell."

She shuddered in revulsion. "Oh, my God. Why do insects like that exist? *Why?* And don't give me the whole food-chain, circle-of-life crap. I understand that everything needs to eat, okay?" Another shudder overtook her curvy frame. "Oh, man, I can't erase this creeped out goosebumpy feeling."

This time he laughed out loud. "Wow. You weren't kidding about hating insects."

"I never kid about bugs. Ever." She sighed, then removed her hat so she could fix her ponytail, which had come undone during her meltdown.

As he watched her, Tate's hands tingled with the urge to slide through all that long black hair. To twine those silky strands around his fingers and angle her head so he could lean down and capture that lush mouth with his. A groan lodged in his throat as he imagined that moment when their tongues would meet, when Eva would arch her back and press her firm breasts against his chest while he kissed her, slowly, deeply, until she was begging him to take her.

"Why are you staring at me?"

He met her gaze. Noticed the knowing gleam in her blue eyes, mingled with the flicker of unease. "You know why," he said huskily.

Her lips parted in surprise. She swallowed, her delicate throat dipping.

Silence stretched between them, but their eyes stayed locked. His pulse kicked up a notch, and he cursed himself for it. What was he doing, standing there having eye sex with the woman?

Disgusted with himself, he broke the eye contact and shifted his grip on the machete. "It'll be dark soon," he muttered. "Let's find a place to set up camp."

She nodded a few times, as if trying to clear her head. "Sure."

They didn't say much as they resumed walking, and it was another mile or so before Tate found a suitable place to set up camp. Close enough to the river that he could hear its soft babbling, but far enough that they weren't in danger of being swept away in a flash flood. He cleared some of the undergrowth with the machete, probing beneath the snarled jungle floor with a branch to make sure the area was free of snakes and other menaces.

As he strung up the hammock, he felt Eva's blue-eyed gaze on him, and finally glanced over to frown at her. "What?"

"Did you only bring that one hammock?"

"Yes." He arched an eyebrow. "Something wrong with that?"

"So we're, um, sharing it?"

"Uh-huh. Unless you'd prefer to sleep on the ground with the snakes, ants, scorpions, termites and pretty much any other insect or reptile you can name."

Her cheeks took on a green tinge. "Oh. Well. Then I'd *love* to share the hammock with you, Tate."

He fought another burst of laughter. Damn it. This woman was testing his control—each time he raised his guard, she knocked it right down with her dry remarks, or her self-deprecating smiles, or her fear of bugs. She was not at all what he'd thought she was, and she'd been throwing him for a loop from the moment she'd walked into the back room of the cantina. A woman as gorgeous as this one often tended to be arrogant, strutting around with a pampered sense of entitlement. Either that, or ditzy and self-indulgent. But Eva was none of those things, which made it all the harder not to like her.

"I'm allotting us four hours of shut-eye," he said once the hammock was secured.

If it was up to him, they'd operate on less sleep than that, but Eva's fatigue was evident, even if she wouldn't admit it. She had dark circles under her eyes and smudges of dirt on her cheeks, and when she dropped her backpack on the ground and reached up to massage her shoulders, Tate knew the heavy load had gotten to her.

"I'm going to wash up in that stream we just passed." She tossed her hat on top of her bag, then lifted her arms over her head for a deep stretch. "I can't sleep if I feel grimy."

She bent down and rummaged through her pack, removing her canteen, a washcloth, and a fresh shirt and socks. "Also, would it have killed you to pack some tissues or something?" she asked. "I have to pee again and I really don't like using leaves."

He rolled his eyes. "The texture is too rough for your delicate parts?"

"No, I spend too much time examining the leaf to make sure there's no bugs on it."

He laughed and reached into his own bag for the package of tissues he'd noticed in the front zipper pocket. When he tossed the packet to Eva, she looked at him as if she'd won the lottery.

Then she scowled. "You had these the entire time? Holding out on me, were you?" She moved toward the trees before he could respond. "I'll just be a few minutes."

She'd just taken a step when Tate saw the flash of brownish-gold amid the greenery.

"Eva, stop," he hissed.

"But I want to wash up before it gets any darker—"

"Eva. *Don't move.*"

The lethal pitch to his voice didn't go unnoticed.

Eva froze on command, and her sharp intake of breath revealed the exact moment her gaze collided with the broad head and rounded snout of the pit viper dangling right in front of her face.

Chapter 7

Eva was actually pretty proud of herself. She wasn't screaming her lungs out. Wasn't running for her life. Wasn't throwing up or passing out.

Then again, she wasn't doing any of those things because she was utterly and completely paralyzed with fear.

Her gaze locked with the hypnotic, catlike pupils of the deadly snake eyeing her down. The bushmaster—she recognized the species from the survival course she'd taken before joining the relief foundation five years ago. With its brownish-pink coloring and black diamond-shaped markings along its back, the deep pits on either side of its face and a terrifyingly long body, the snake was undeniably beautiful, in a predatory kind of way. The shape of the head gave its deadliness away—slightly triangular, a clear warning that this species was poisonous.

Her heartbeat accelerated, thudding out a frantic rhythm against her ribs. She was tempted to drop the canteen and clothes she was holding and run like hell, but she knew pit vipers were deceptively fast. And their bites were fatal. One wrong move and she'd be full of snake venom.

"Stay still, sweetheart."

Tate's voice was low, barely a whisper.

She opened the corner of her mouth a crack. "Should I try to grab it and whip it away?" she whispered back.

"God, no." She heard a soft rustling, and then, "I mean it, Eva. Don't move a goddamn muscle. If I miss..."

"Miss what? What are you—"

Something hissed right by her ear, slicing the air with a high-pitched whistling sound and ruffling the loose strands of hair at the side of her face.

A second later she heard a sharp smack and the viper was gone.

Shock, relief and adrenaline streamed through her blood, bringing a rush of light-headedness. Gaping, she stared at the wooden handle of the knife that had pinned the bushmaster to the tree—by its head. The snake was still alive, body undulating wildly and fangs exposed as it thrashed around, but the blade of Tate's knife made it impossible for it to escape.

"Go wash up." Tate came up beside her with another knife in his hand.

Her pulse continued to shriek in her ears. "Wh-what?"

"Wash up. I'll take care of this."

She felt dazed, unable to do more than just gawk at him. After a beat, he made a frustrated sound and forcibly moved her away from the tree. He cupped her chin with one strong hand, his thumb sweeping over the edge of her jaw. "Go to the stream and get cleaned up, Eva."

His rough command snapped her out of her fear-induced trance and suddenly she became aware of Tate's hand on her face. Her pulse raced, and this time it had nothing to do with fear or lingering adrenaline and everything to do with the sexy man standing so close to her. With his square jaw covered with dark stubble and his green eyes glittering with fortitude, he made a seriously imposing picture.

She sucked in a breath, only to inhale the spicy, masculine scent of Tate. Wow. Even after trekking through the jungle all day, the man smelled great.

Uh, deadly poisonous snake pinned to a tree?

The reminder nearly made her laugh. "Okay. Um. I'll be right back," she said, while the pit viper continued to thrash on the moss-covered tree bark.

Avoiding Tate's eyes, she stumbled through the trees toward the small freshwater pool ten yards away, where she stripped off her sweat-soaked tee and kicked off her boots. She quickly splashed water on her face, then washed her hands, feet and underarms before slipping into a loose long-sleeved shirt and fresh socks. She went to the loo with a tissue gratefully on hand, then filled up her canteen and dropped an iodine tablet inside to purify the water.

By the time she returned to the clearing, she felt calm and relaxed, her near-death experience with that pit viper nothing but an unpleasant memory. She glanced at the tree. No snake. Then she glanced warily at Tate, who was lying in the hammock with his arms propped behind his head.

"What'd you do to the snake?" she asked, as she shoved her things into her pack.

"Cut his head off and gave him a nice burial."

She blanched. So that was why he'd sent her away. He hadn't wanted her to see him brutally decapitate that poor fellow.

Tate gazed up at the green canopy high above their heads. Barely any light got through the trees, and everything around them was bathed in shadows now.

"No fire?" she said.

"No point. We'll be on the move again in a few hours." His voice became husky. "Better come up. It'll be pitch-black soon."

She knew he was right; it got dark scary-fast in the jungle.

She scampered over, then hesitated as she stared at the big body sprawled in the netting of the hammock.

With a knowing, slightly mocking smile, he shifted and held out his arm.

There was a lot of swaying and rustling as she climbed in next to him. The swinging motion had her falling against Tate's broad chest, and his arm quickly came out to steady her. His strong grip and warm touch caused her heart to do an annoying somersault.

It took a few moments to find a comfortable position— she ended up sandwiched next to Tate, her cheek pressed against one of his defined pecs, while his arm wrapped tightly around her.

By the time they were settled, darkness had completely fallen. She couldn't see a foot in front of her, and as Tate covered them with a thermal blanket, she was grateful to be above the treacherous ground and sheltered in Tate's arms.

After a moment's reluctance, she draped her arm over his chest and snuggled closer, taking advantage of his body heat and the comfort of his body. When her fingers brushed over something cold and hard, she lifted her head with a frown. "Are you holding your gun?"

"Yes. I never sleep without one."

His revelation was disconcerting, but oddly comforting at the same time.

"By the way, you did good today," he added.

She couldn't hide her surprise. "How so?"

"You kept up with my pace, you didn't complain, you wolfed down that MRE like it was a juicy steak."

She smiled in the darkness. "Eating it quickly was the only way not to focus on how bad it tasted."

"Regardless, you impressed me today. You didn't strike me as a fan of the outdoors."

The answering rush of warmth that rippled through her was unwelcome. She shouldn't care what this man thought of her. Yet…she did. For some reason, his approval and respect meant a lot.

"I love the outdoors," she confessed. "So do my parents. When I was growing up, we rented this cabin in Vermont every summer, right in the middle of nowhere, and we'd spend all day fishing and hiking and swimming. And Dad would take a few weeks off work every year so the two of us could go on an adventure together. An African safari, fishing trips, mountain climbing—pretty much whatever kept us outside." Her voice cracked. "When I was pregnant, Dad used to talk about all the adventures he wanted to have with his grandson…."

She trailed off, the lump in her throat making it difficult to continue. Lord, she missed her parents. She called or emailed them whenever she thought it was safe, but she hadn't seen them since Rafe was just a baby.

"What do your parents do?" Tate asked.

"Dad's a lawyer, he mostly does tax and estate stuff. Mom was an event planner, but she does volunteer work now, planning charity benefits, running committees, that sort of thing." She smiled in the darkness. "Neither of them was happy when I decided to help out with the San Marquez relief efforts after college. I'm an only child, so they've always been a tad overprotective."

"Must be nice," he murmured. "Having someone worry about you."

Eva saw right through the flippant response. The sad,

haunted note in his voice told her he was thinking about his own upbringing.

After a beat of hesitation, she said, "You told me about your father, but what about your mom? Why wasn't she around to stop your dad from…from hurting you?"

Now his voice dripped with bitterness. "My mother left when I was seven, but by then, we were all happy to see her go. She had a raging heroin problem, OD'd twice right in front of me and survived both times. I'm sure she's dead by now."

Each word was spoken in a flat monotone, and Eva's heart ached. She suddenly remembered a detail from the background search she'd conducted on him, but wasn't sure if she ought to bring it up. Tate hadn't volunteered that piece of information, after all.

Then again, he hadn't volunteered *any* information since she'd met him.

"Your basic file, the one I was able to access, mentioned you had a younger brother," she said carefully.

She immediately felt him stiffen.

When he didn't respond, she raised herself up again and studied his face. She couldn't make out his expression in the darkness, but the tight line of his mouth revealed a lot. "The file said he died."

A muscle in his jaw twitched. "Did it say how he died?"

"In the line of duty."

The low, cheerless laugh that slipped from his throat sent a cold shiver up her spine. "That's not true, is it?" she said.

"No, it's true. Technically."

"So he *did* die in the line of duty?"

"He was murdered." Three words, popping out in harsh bursts like bullets from a pistol.

Eva's breath caught. "Oh. How did—" Something suddenly clicked. "Hector. Hector killed your brother, didn't he, Tate?"

He didn't respond.

"That's why you're so set on killing him," she said slowly. "I knew your reasons for wanting Hector dead had to have been personal, but I wasn't able to find any connection between the two of you. I'm right, aren't I? He's responsible for murdering your brother."

"If you say so." His evasive tone gave nothing away, and yet told her everything.

"The American government was providing assistance to San Marquez in dealing with the ULF. Your unit was sent here, wasn't it? That's how you encountered Hector. It all makes sense now." She furrowed her brows. "Except for one thing—why are you in hiding now? What happened after you left the military? Or maybe I should be asking, what happened to *make* you leave the military?"

"Anyone ever tell you that you ask a lot of questions?"

Her eyes were beginning to adjust to the darkness, and she was able to make out the amused glimmer in his mossy-green gaze. "Anyone tell you that you don't provide a lot of answers?"

"I'm not in the habit of confiding in strangers."

"I don't think you confide in *anyone,* strangers *or* friends."

"True," he said, relenting.

A smile tickled her lips. "Well, I don't see the harm in telling me, considering you already think I'm here to lure you out of hiding."

His eyes narrowed. "Who says I think that?"

"Oh, come on, of course you do. That's why you don't trust me. A part of you suspects I'm an agent sent by the government to bring you in. Which is kind of absurd, because if I was supposed to arrest or kill you, wouldn't I have done it by now? And why would I bring my three-year-old son along on the assignment? Face it, Tate, your theory doesn't hold up. You have no reason to doubt me."

Liar.

All right, that wasn't entirely true. She'd kept a very huge detail from him when she'd solicited his help, but she refused to dwell on the lie she'd told. Besides, the fact that Hector was the father of her son had nothing to do with this mission. She and Tate *both* wanted Hector dead, and they each had their own reasons for it. So what if she'd given Tate a fake motive by claiming Hector had killed Rafe's father? As long as their endgames aligned, wasn't that all that mattered?

She'd never been a fan of the "ends justifies the means" mentality, but right now she was its biggest advocate. And no matter how guilty she felt about lying to the man who'd agreed to help her, she hadn't been able to take the risk that he'd turn her down, which he might've done if he'd known the truth.

Now, after realizing that Hector had killed Tate's brother, she was even more certain of her decision to tell that little white lie. She'd been romantically involved with the man who'd murdered Tate's brother. She'd given birth to that man's son, for Pete's sake.

Tate would probably kill *her* if he found out.

"You raise a good point." His grudging voice drew her from her thoughts.

"So you don't think I'm a government agent anymore?"

"I didn't say that." He shrugged, and the hammock swung a little. "But if you *are* government, my reasons for hiding out wouldn't be a surprise, so I guess there really ain't much harm in telling you."

With a pleased grin, she lay back down and settled her

cheek against his chest, but when Tate didn't speak immediately, she didn't push him.

She listened to the racket of the jungle instead. Even at night, the noise levels didn't abate by much. The clicking of insects as they scuttled along the jungle floor, the harmonic buzzing of cicadas, the drone of insect wings, the croaks and bellows of nearby amphibians. It was kind of peaceful, as long as she didn't focus too much on the bug noises, which reminded her that she was surrounded by, well, *bugs*.

"People want me dead."

His raspy confession brought a mock gasp to her lips. "No, really? Here I thought you were hiding out in Mexico for the fun of it."

"You know, your sarcasm doesn't make me want to confide in you."

"Sorry. Go on."

He let out a strangled laugh. "Anyway, for some reason I haven't been able to determine, my own government wants to kill me."

Her brows knitted in confusion. "You really have no clue why?"

"None. All I know is that it's related to the last op my unit was involved in."

"Which was?"

He hesitated for a long moment, then cursed under his breath. "Hell, no point in worrying about security clearance anymore, huh?" he said in a wry voice. "We went in to rescue a hostage. Richard Harrison, an American doctor who was doing research at a small medical clinic in the mountains. The ULF ambushed the village and kept the doc captive. They tried to negotiate with the U.S.—they'd release the doc if we called off the alliance between our governments."

Eva wasn't surprised—the ULF made no secret of the fact that they resented American interference in San Marquez's affairs. "But rather than negotiate, the States sent your unit instead," she guessed.

"We were ordered to extract the doc, but he was already dead when we got to the village. So were all the villagers."

Her lips tightened. "Hector?"

"Yep." He paused. "So we went home for debriefing, and a couple months later, nearly every man on my unit was dead, all from various bogus causes. When someone tried to blow my head off out on the street in broad daylight, I contacted Stone and Prescott and we got the hell out of Dodge."

As he went silent, Eva chewed on the inside of her cheek, trying to make sense of everything he'd told her. A monkey howled from somewhere in the tree tops, and its cry was answered by several matching wails.

"I don't get it," she finally said.

"Join the club."

"You have *no* idea why they want you guys dead?" She chewed on her bottom lip in thought. "Did you see something you weren't supposed to? Hear something?"

"I don't have a goddamn clue, Eva. All I saw in that village was a hundred dead bodies, burned to a crisp."

She flinched at the gruesome image he brought to mind. "Well, maybe—"

"Maybe it's time we go to sleep," he cut in, an edge to his voice.

She closed her mouth, then opened it to release a heavy sigh. "Fine."

She probably shouldn't push her luck, anyway. Tate had revealed more in the past five minutes than he had in the two days she'd known him. Might as well leave it at that and try again tomorrow.

Try again?

The puzzled voice in her head raised a good question. Why was she going out of her way to get to know Tate? Why did she care about his past or his motives or the reason he lived as if he had a target painted on his forehead?

All she needed to know about the man was that he was going to help her get rid of Hector.

Shifting, she tried to get comfortable again, but no matter where she put her head or arms or legs, she was still plastered against Tate like plastic wrap. His intoxicating scent, pure man, teased her senses, and the rock-hard chest beneath her palm was pretty much inviting her fingers to stroke it. Resisting the urge, she curled those fingers into a tight fist and slid her hand down to his belly so she wouldn't have to feel those defined pecs rippling beneath her fingers. But his washboard abs were just as tempting, and her hand being so close to his waistband meant her forearm now rested directly on his groin.

Which boasted the unmistakable bulge of arousal.

Heat scorched her face at the same time Tate's mocking voice broke the silence. "Are you finished feeling me up?"

"I wasn't feeling you up. I was just trying to get comfy," she sputtered.

"Uh-huh."

"I was," she insisted. Then she felt a spark of irritation. "And why am I the one defending myself? You're the one lying here with a *boner.* Jeez, Tate."

His husky laughter increased her annoyance. "Sweetheart, I'm a man. A man who's lying in a hammock with a beautiful woman—what else did you expect would happen?"

Eva swallowed. "You think I'm beautiful?"

He paused before releasing a ragged breath. "Yes. I think you're beautiful." His tone became sardonic once more. "So now, unless those busy hands of yours plan on unzipping my pants, let's get some damn sleep."

Desire pulsed between her legs, hot and persistent. His words were a challenge if she'd ever heard one, and for a moment, she almost did exactly what he'd taunted her about—unzipped his cargo pants, slid her hand inside and discovered if he was as big and hard down there as he was everywhere else.

But she fought the impulse, bringing her hand up and tucking it against her own belly.

"Good-night it is," he murmured wryly.

Gulping, Eva slammed her eyes shut and tried to pretend that she was alone. That she wasn't sharing a hammock with this sexy, magnetic man. That he didn't intrigue her. Didn't excite her. Didn't make her feel the first spark of attraction she'd felt in years.

She didn't want a man in her life, or her bed. Maybe someday, once she got the bitter taste of Hector out of her mouth, and only if she met someone worthy of her heart. Someone kind and gentle, someone she could trust with her son, someone who would *love* her son. Tate was neither kind nor gentle, and from the way he'd dismissed Rafe on sight, he would never be a part of her son's life.

As those thoughts cemented themselves in her head, the little pulses of lust shooting up and down her body dissipated, much to her relief. With Tate's steady heartbeat thudding against her ear, she fell into a soundless sleep.

He wanted Eva Dolce.
No, you don't.
Ah, hell. He did. He really, really wanted her.
Dangerous thoughts, buddy.
As one conflicting thought after the other wreaked havoc on his brain, Tate tried to focus on chopping a path

through the jungle. With all the voices throwing opinions around in his head, he was beginning to feel like a damn schizophrenic.

Not to mention that last night had done a real number on his groin—his entire lower body actually *ached,* though four hours in a hammock with a sexy woman plastered against him would do that to a man. He'd been lying with a hard-on the entire time, and it was a miracle he'd gotten any sleep at all.

When they'd woken up before dawn and set off, he'd hoped that the novelty of Eva would wear off on the second day of their journey, or that the attraction would taper to a level he might be able to tolerate, but that had been damn naïve thinking on his part.

As they walked at a brisk pace, he was painfully aware of Eva. The way she walked. The sound of her breathing. The squeaky little noise she made whenever a mosquito flew in her face.

Christ, he wanted her.

No, you don't.

Stifling a sigh, he hacked at a particularly annoying vine that refused to get out of his way. The machete finally sliced the thick diameter and the vine hit the jungle floor at the same time a flash of lightning lit up the sky.

"Oh, crap," Eva mumbled. "This is *not* gonna be fun."

Her words proved to be prophetic. Within seconds, the patches of sky that were visible through the trees turned black, a boom of thunder cracked in the air, and the rain began to fall in earnest.

It happened so fast neither of them had time to do anything but exchange rueful grins.

That reaction alone upped his opinion of the woman. Rather than shriek about getting soaked, Eva seemed completely unruffled. In fact, as sheets of rain drenched her clothes and plastered her hair to her head, she started to laugh, the melodic sound mingling with the loud pattering of the rain.

As the thunder rolled and the treetops shook, he grabbed her hand and pulled her toward a cluster of enormous banyan trees. They ducked beneath the dangling moss-covered branches and rootlike shoots, which provided instant shelter from the downpour.

Tate leaned his rifle against the tree trunk, stuck his machete in the dirt and wiped the moisture from his face with the back of his hand.

"Next time we decide to kill a man, let's do it during the dry season," Eva remarked in a facetious tone.

He had to chuckle. "Agreed."

She lifted her ponytail and wrung the water out of it, then shoved wet black strands off her forehead and tucked them behind her ears.

He couldn't help but admire her beautiful features, perfectly symmetrical, flawless, a touch exotic thanks to her olive coloring and sparkling cobalt-blue eyes.

"You're doing it again," she murmured.

"Doing what?"

"Staring at me. Every time we've taken a rest break today, you've been staring at me."

"Have I?" His voice came out hoarse, seductive, and he had to clear his throat before continuing. "Well, we already established that I think you're beautiful. I guess I like looking at you."

Surprise registered on her face. "I don't understand you."

"How so?"

"Since we met, you've made it clear you don't trust me. And yet…"

Her cheeks grew pink, but he couldn't be sure if it was

due to embarrassment or the humidity thickening the air. "And yet what?" he pressed, his voice low.

"You act like you want to go to bed with me," she murmured. "You would have done it last night, wouldn't you? If I'd given you the green light?"

Arousal, hot, thick and relentless, traveled down his body and hardened his cock. "Yes," he admitted.

"And that's what I don't get."

Her naïveté both surprised and appealed to him. "Oh, I see. You think sex and trust go hand in hand." When she nodded, he couldn't help but chuckle. "Oh, sweetheart, how wrong you are."

She frowned. "So you're saying you don't need to trust me in order to sleep with me?"

"That's exactly what I'm saying."

Eva fell silent, her gaze shifting from his face to the opening in the branches. She watched the rain hammer the vines and shrubs and decaying matter littering the jungle floor, looking perturbed as her teeth dug into her bottom lip.

"I couldn't do that," she said, her voice soft and distressed. "I can't sleep with a man I don't trust."

He took a step toward to her, bringing a wary glint to her eyes. "So if *I* gave *you* the green light, you would turn me away?"

Her breath hitched.

He moved even closer. Only a foot separated them. Her long-sleeved shirt was unbuttoned, so he had a clear view of the tight white tank top she wore beneath it. White wasn't a color you wanted to wear in the rain—in Eva's case, the wet fabric had become transparent, revealing her flesh-colored bra and the unmistakable puckering of her nipples.

"You're turned on," he said silkily, making no attempt to hide the focus of his gaze.

"I'm cold. From the rain."

"The rain is as hot as the air, sweetheart." Tate brought his hand to her cheek, enjoying the spark of heat that flared in her eyes.

His hand took on a life of its own. Even if he'd tried, he wouldn't have been able to stop himself from stroking Eva's smooth skin, from dragging his fingers to her mouth and tracing the seam of her lush lips. He didn't trust her, but damn, how he wanted her.

When he eliminated the final inches of distance between them and gripped her slender waist, her blue eyes widened.

"Tate." Her voice was throaty, lined with apprehension and…need.

It was that needy pitch that snapped the last thread of his control.

With a desperate growl, he took possession of her mouth and kissed her.

Christ, she tasted so damn good, and her body, lush and supple, felt like sheer heaven pressed against his. Curling one hand over her hip, he raked the other one up her body, grazing the side of one firm breast before traveling higher to cradle the back of her head.

He came up for air and searched her gaze, satisfied by the glaze of passion he glimpsed. Then he slanted his mouth over hers again and deepened the kiss, pushing his tongue inside without waiting for permission.

Eva's moan tickled his lips and quickened his pulse. Her hands clung to his shoulders, her blunt, unpolished fingernails digging into the fabric of his T-shirt and stinging his skin. When their tongues met, shock waves pounded into him, scorched his nerve endings and made him groan in desperation. Shoving his hands underneath her tank top, he stroked her flat belly, then moved higher to cup her breasts over her bra.

"Tate." His name left her lips, half a whimper, half a moan.

He couldn't remember ever being this hard. Ever wanting a woman this badly. Mindless with lust, he slid his hands out from under her shirt, brought them to her ass and hauled her up against him.

"Oh, *God,*" she choked out when her core came in contact with his unmistakable erection.

Her legs wrapped around his waist, hands clinging to his neck as Tate backed her into the trunk of the tree. Driving the kiss deeper, he rubbed his lower body into hers, thrusting his hips in time to the thrusts of his tongue in her mouth.

Screw it. Keeping his hands off this woman clearly wasn't gonna be an option. He craved her on a dark, primal level he couldn't explain, and nothing short of dying could stop him from claiming her.

No sooner had the last thought entered his head than his instincts began to hum.

Tate froze. His mouth lifted, hovering over Eva's lips.

"What's wrong?" she murmured. "Why did you—"

He pressed his index finger to her lips to silence her.

Cocking his head, he willed his heartbeat to steady, letting pure instinct take over. The rain had stopped—he'd been so consumed with lust he hadn't even noticed—but the abrupt silence wasn't the reason for his raised hackles.

Very slowly, he set Eva on her feet and peered through the tangled roots that surrounded them like a canopy. He didn't see anything out of sorts, but his ears compensated for what his eyes couldn't perceive.

He heard the same familiar noises that gave life to the jungle—monkeys and birds and insects, clicks and wails and hoots and squawks. Branches snapping and leaves rustling and wind blowing.

And footsteps.

"Son of a bitch," he hissed out, his arm snapping out to grab his rifle.

"What's going on?" Eva demanded.

"We've got company." With a grim look, he propped the rifle up on his shoulder. "Get down on the ground and stay here. Don't come out unless I tell you."

"Tate—"

Locked and loaded, he slid out and into the open—just as six armed men burst out of the brush.

They took one look at Tate and started shooting.

Chapter 8

As a bullet missed his temple by an inch and a half, Tate hit the ground, rolled and took cover behind a gnarled tree trunk. The telltale *rat-tat-tat* of an assault rifle echoed in the air. Pieces of bark and branches flew over his head and landed on the ground with sharp smacks. The creatures that called this jungle their home didn't appreciate the sudden uproar—a chorus of bird cries joined the gunfire and created a deafening cacophony that made it hard for him to hear himself think.

His attackers were military. San Marquez military, to be precise, but not an elite unit, if their uncoordinated assault and disorganized formation were any indication. Bottom-of-the-totem-pole soldiers, then. Sent to...well, kill him, judging by the next round of bullets that slammed into the tree he'd taken cover behind.

Gritting his teeth, Tate raised his rifle and ducked out for a second, pulling the trigger to unload a round at his attackers. Two blue-and-gold uniforms went down, lifeless bodies tumbling to the twisted undergrowth. He didn't have time to high-five himself because the four men he *hadn't* hit were closing in on him.

He popped out again and sprayed bullets until his rifle clicked and emptied. Crap. Spare clips were in his backpack—which was sitting, oh, a yard away, with Eva, in the tree.

Looked as if he'd have to make do with the pistol. Dropping the rifle, he swiped the H&K from his waistband and took a steadying breath. Two more soldiers had gone down during his last sweep. Two remained, unless there was a second military unit somewhere, ready to attack on command.

Tate didn't question why these soldiers had been dispatched. All he knew was that they were a threat. To him. To Eva. And he'd be damned if a bunch of poorly trained grunts took him down before he got his shot at Cruz.

The gunfire had ceased. Only the sounds of the jungle remained now, to a civilian, anyway.

To Tate, the presence of the enemy was clear as a cloudless blue sky. Soft breathing, the swish of pant legs as the soldiers attempted to move soundlessly.

They were nearing the tree.

Adrenaline spiked in his veins. He tightened his grip on the pistol. Said a prayer. Then burst out from behind the tree—only to get his gun knocked right out of his hand by a soldier who turned out to be much closer than Tate had realized.

A gun fired, cracked in the air. He felt something hot whiz by his ear, which immediately began to ring, but despite the sudden loss of hearing, his equilibrium wasn't affected. Grunting, he brought his elbow to the jaw of the man who'd nearly shot his head off.

The soldier—lanky, black-haired and dark-skinned—made a guttural sound thick with pain and stumbled backward. Tate took advantage and did a leg sweep, knocking the soldier off balance. The man staggered, but before he could fall over, Tate grabbed him by the cuffs of his uniform shirt, spun him around and used him as a human shield.

The remaining soldier growled with fury as he watched his comrade absorb the impact of the bullets he'd been aiming at Tate.

"Se va a morir!" the man shouted. *You will die.*

Tate kept a steady grip on the dead soldier he still had in a chest lock. "I don't think so," he said coolly.

Before the enemy could react, he whipped the handgun from the holster secured to the lifeless man's hip and fired at the last surviving soldier.

He hit his intended mark—the soldier yelled in pain as the bullet sliced into his shoulder.

Tossing his human shield away, Tate lunged for the remaining man. He knocked the AK-47 out of the soldier's hand and tackled him to the ground. As the other man cursed and struggled, Tate pinned him down by jamming a knee into his chest and a forearm against his neck.

"Who sent you?" he demanded, speaking in Spanish so his demand didn't get lost in translation.

A pair of brown eyes shot daggers at him. "Screw you" was the harsh reply.

He bared his teeth in a mocking smile. "You want to live? Then you'd better answer the question."

This time he got a wad of spit that splashed his chin.

"Suit yourself." With a shrug, he pressed the barrel of his gun to the soldier's temple and pulled the trigger.

Silence.

For a split second, the jungle actually went eerily silent, as if someone had pressed Pause on a heavy-metal CD.

And then the play button clicked on, and the noise decibel returned to normal.

When he heard the unmistakable sound of leaves snapping beneath boots, he drew his weapon and bounced to his feet, but it was just Eva, stepping out from behind the long, dangling branches.

"That was…" Her gaze traveled over the six bodies strewn on the jungle floor. "Efficient."

Like Eva, he swept his gaze over the dead soldiers littering the ground. Taking them out had been no difficult feat; military training in San Marquez was far inferior to the rigorous training endured by members of the American armed forces, which was probably why the ULF rebels continued to wreak such havoc on the country—and why the San Marquez government had been relying more and more on its Western allies to help them contain this revolution.

Tate eyed the dead men again, one by one. Mediocre soldiers, sure, but damn good trackers. Not a surprise, seeing as this jungle was their native turf; they knew every square inch of the place, every leaf, every tree, every vine and speck of dirt.

"Were they following us the whole time?" Eva asked, her face going pale.

"They probably picked up our trail back at the road, but they were smart. They must have hung back and covered ground when we camped for the night." His jaw tensed. "They knew I'd sense them if they got too close, so they waited for a distraction, the right moment to close in."

"The rainstorm," Eva mumbled.

Suspicion clouded his face as he met her blue eyes. "How did they find us?" he asked in a low voice.

She blinked. "What? You just said—"

"I mean, how did they know we were on this island to begin with?"

Her dark brows drew together. "I don't know. Maybe someone spotted us at the port."

"That's what I suspect, but that means someone was on the lookout for us. *Expecting* us to show up." His eyes narrowed. "Why would anyone be expecting us, sweetheart?"

Exhaustion washed over her beautiful face. She'd been hugging her own chest since she'd stepped out of the tree, and her hands seemed to curl tighter over her upper arms.

"Who knew we were coming?" he demanded.

Her cheeks took on an ashen hue, and she began swallowing repeatedly. "Tate…"

He fixed her with a deadly glare. "Why were we expected?"

"I don't know," she stammered. Gulp. Gulp.

He moved even closer. "What's the matter, Eva? Why do you suddenly look so nervous?"

"I…"

Another gulp. Her cheeks grew paler. And then her hands dropped from her chest and he saw the bright spot of crimson on her left sleeve.

Blood.

She'd been shot.

"Tate, I don't feel—"

Her sentence died abruptly, and Tate lunged forward just in time to catch her as she fainted.

Someone was holding an open flame to her flesh.

Or at least, that was the only explanation Eva had for the excruciating burning sensation in her upper arm, for the pulses of hot agony and the feeling that someone was poking a knife underneath her skin.

When her eyelids fluttered open, she realized that was *exactly* what was happening.

Tate was *literally* digging through her flesh with a pair of tweezers.

As a wave of nausea scampered up her throat, she passed out like a light.

When she came to the next time, she got the foggy impression that Tate was threading a needle.

Cue the black dots flashing in front of her eyes.

The third time, she managed to stay conscious, which earned her a rueful smile from Tate. "See if you can pass out again, sweetheart. This is gonna hurt."

He was right. It did. In fact, it hurt so much she was actually quite stunned that she *didn't* pass out. Getting stitched up without a numbing agent was no picnic. Each time the needle sliced into her skin, she experienced a sharp throb and fiery pinch. Tears sprang to her eyes, but she didn't scream in pain. She bit her bottom lip instead, until she tasted the coppery flavor of blood in her mouth.

Unhinging her jaw, she glanced at Tate's intense green eyes and croaked out, "Am I going to live?"

"Yes. Doesn't seem to be any arterial damage. I got the bullet out and gave you a shot of antibiotics. You'll have to take a dose every six hours if you want to ward off infection."

She felt another painful pinch in her arm, and her stomach rolled.

Gulping down the rising queasiness, she shifted her gaze skyward and tried to distract herself by counting the veins on a leaf above her head. Tate cleaned and dressed the wound, taped the stark white bandage down with clear tape, and by the time he muttered a quick "All done," she was close to throwing up.

Stumbling to her feet only increased the nausea; pins

and needles pricked her hands, and her vision grew so blurry she had to blink several times before everything came back into focus.

"Sit down," Tate said roughly.

She drew in a slow breath, not answering him until she managed to fight the overwhelming need to empty the contents of her stomach.

"No. We should go," she insisted once the nausea passed. "We don't know if those soldiers called for backup before—"

She halted when she noticed that the six bodies were gone. For a second she wondered if she'd imagined the whole thing. Maybe nobody had rushed out of the trees. Maybe the bullet that had slammed into her upper arm while she'd been hiding had come from a rare breed of bullet-shooting monkey or something.

But no, Tate must have carried her away from the scene of the assault, because the tree they'd sought shelter under was gone, too, and that cluster of sweet-smelling orchids definitely hadn't been here before.

"Thank you," she said quietly. "I know the only reason you didn't leave me to die back there was because you need my help to find Hector, but I still appreciate it."

"That's not the only reason I didn't leave you."

For a second she thought he was implying it had something to do with the kiss. That hot, explosive kiss that had set fire to her body and robbed her of all common sense.

But the edge to his voice spoke otherwise. As did the suspicion clouding his green eyes.

Confused, Eva met his gaze head-on. "What is it?" she asked warily.

He hooked his thumbs in the belt loops of his cargo pants. "It's time we finished our conversation."

"And what conversation is that?"

"The one in which you explain why anyone would be expecting me to show my face in San Marquez." His jaw moved as if he were grinding his teeth together. "Who've you been in contact with?"

Shock traveled up her spine and slackened her jaw. "Nobody."

"Oh, sweetheart, please don't give me the wide-eyed innocence routine right now. I just killed six men and then performed jungle surgery on your damn arm when I could've just let you die."

"Then why didn't you?" she snapped. "Clearly you think I'm responsible for those soldiers ambushing us."

"Aren't you?"

Anger skidded up her spine. "No, I'm not. Obviously someone recognized one of us at the port and tipped off the military. Which makes no sense, because why would the San Marquez military be after either of us? You're being hunted by *our* government, and me? I've done nothing to piss off San Marquez. Besides, my uncle would never—"

He cut in sharply. "Your uncle? What are you talking about?"

"My uncle Miguel. He's the one who suggested I track you down."

The expression on Tate's face frightened her. So did the way he began pacing in front of her, one fist clenched to his side, the other hovering over the butt of the gun poking out of his waistband. He could draw that weapon in a nanosecond and blow her brains out, and from the rage burning in his eyes, she got the feeling that outcome wasn't so farfetched.

"You never told me about this *uncle*." He strode toward her, assuming an aggressive stance.

"It wasn't important," she said defensively. "Miguel is my mom's older brother. He lives in Merido. He had heard the rumors about a man asking about Hector, and he's the one who told me your name."

"Why would your uncle know my name?" Tate demanded, his voice colder than an Arctic ice cap.

She swallowed. The menace rolling off his big body sent a shiver up her spine. "Because he knows pretty much everything that goes on in his country." She licked her dry lips. "He's a general with the San Marquez army."

If the jungle weren't so damn loud, the silence that followed would have been of the hear-a-pin-drop variety.

A combative gleam ignited Tate's eyes, along with a dose of ire and a splash of betrayal. And then, before she could blink, he whipped up his gun and aimed it directly at her chest.

Chapter 9

"What are you going to do, Tate? Shoot me?" Eva's blue eyes were heavy with resignation.

Tate clenched his teeth so hard his jaw hurt. Damn it. Goddamn it. This entire op had turned into one giant, screwed-up mess. The ambush, Eva getting shot, finding out her frickin' uncle was a frickin' *general*.

He knew without a shred of doubt that Eva's uncle had used her to lure Tate out of hiding. The only question was, why?

He had no beef with the San Marquez government, no connection to this godforsaken country aside from one botched mission that went down eight months ago. He'd been back to San Marquez a few times since, talking to rebels, asking around about Cruz, but that was no reason for the military to target him. If anything, the government ought to be *happy* he was here—they wanted the leader of the ULF dead as much as Tate did.

Really, giving Tate free rein to kill Cruz was probably this country's best course of action.

So why try to kill him just now? It made no sense. Unless...

"Well, are you going to shoot or what?" came Eva's flat voice.

His gun was still aimed at her heart, but after a second, he lowered the weapon and let out a savage expletive. Frustration punched him like a pair of fists. Nothing made sense. Absolutely *nothing* made sense.

In front of him, Eva's scowl faded, her expression taking on a sympathetic light. "Talk to me, Tate," she said softly. "Tell me what you're thinking."

He scrubbed a hand over the thick stubble darkening his jaw, unable to put a single thought into words. He walked over to his pack and grabbed the canteen, then took a long swig of water.

Eva's sigh hung in the late afternoon air. "My uncle couldn't have sent that unit after us. Well, technically he *could* have, but I don't think he did."

He raised his eyebrows in challenge. "Yeah, and why not?"

"Because I could have been killed, too. He knew that if you showed up in San Marquez, I would be traveling with you. Miguel would *never* put me in harm's way."

"You weren't," Tate said darkly. "Not a single one of those soldiers pointed their weapons at the tree where you were hiding, or made an attempt to go after you."

"Uh, hello?" She gestured to her bandaged arm. "I was *shot*."

"By accident," he replied with confidence. "I think you got hit by a stray bullet."

She huffed out a breath. "So what are you saying? That

my uncle *did* send that unit and ordered them not to hurt me, but to kill *you?*"

"That's exactly what I'm saying." He took another sip of water, then reached up to pinch the bridge of his nose, hoping to ward off an oncoming headache.

None of this made sense. If Eva's uncle, the *general,* had indeed dispatched the attack squad, then that could mean two things—either someone in San Marquez also wanted Tate dead, or the U.S. had enlisted San Marquez's help in tracking Tate down.

"The government here hates the ULF," he spoke up thoughtfully.

Eva looked confused. "Yes. They do. Hector has been on the most-wanted list for years now." She tilted her head. "Where are you going with this?"

"Your uncle, I assume he knows what happened to your kid's father?"

For a second, she looked even more confused, but then she gave a quick nod. "Right. Yes, Miguel knows about Rafe's dad."

"And he knows you want Cruz dead?"

Another nod, and then she offered a triumphant look. "See, that's another reason why Miguel couldn't have ordered that ambush. He knew I was going to you for help in getting rid of Hector, and Miguel hates the ULF as much as everyone else. He wouldn't have tried to stop us from killing Hector, which means he couldn't have tried to kill you just now."

Tate didn't share her conviction. "Are you sure old Uncle Miguel isn't playing you, sweetheart? That he's not on Cruz's take?"

Her blue eyes flickered with indignation. "No way. Miguel can't be bought."

Again, he didn't feel much conviction about that, but

he dropped the subject. Truth was, he didn't care if Eva's uncle was in cahoots with Cruz. He was more concerned about the notion that San Marquez was in cahoots with the Americans, and the ramifications of that.

"Damn it," he mumbled, so frustrated he felt like tearing his own hair out. "What the *hell* happened on that mission?"

He suddenly wished that Sebastian or Nick were here so they could talk this out, but they weren't, and his only sounding board was a woman he didn't trust.

At the thought of Seb and Nick, he muttered another curse, realizing it was now imperative he check in to make sure they hadn't had to deal with an ambush of their own.

Bending down, he rummaged through his pack until he found the satellite phone.

Eva immediately dashed to his side. "Are you calling Nick?" she demanded.

He nodded, dialing.

"I want to talk to my son."

Ignoring the request, he listened to the dial tone, growing uneasy the longer he waited. When Nick finally picked up with a quick "Prescott," Tate experienced a burst of relief.

"It's me," he said brusquely. "Checking in."

Nick sounded as relieved as Tate felt. "Is it done?"

"Not even close. Still making our way there. We hit a snag a while ago."

"What kind of snag?"

"The easily taken-care-of kind. Just wanted to make sure everything is all right on the home front."

"Everything's good here, Captain. Don't worry about us. Rafe is having a blast."

"And let me guess, Stone dumped all the babysitting duties on you."

"Something like that," Nick said in a rueful tone.

He chuckled before going somber. "Stay alert, Prescott. If you catch even a whiff of trouble, get yourselves and the kid outta there."

"Yes, sir."

"Now put the kid on the line. Eva wants to talk to him."

As a shuffling sound came over the extension, Tate handed the phone to Eva, who grabbed it as if it were a winning lottery ticket. She lifted the phone to her ear, and a moment later, absolute joy flooded her eyes.

"Hey, little man," she said, her voice softer and warmer than Tate had ever heard it. "Are you having fun?"

Keeping his ear on the one-sided conversation, he began gathering up the supplies he'd used to tend to Eva's arm and shoving them back in the first aid kit.

"Mommy misses you, too....I know, baby, I know.... You *did?*" Her tone grew incredibly amused. "Well, that's amazing! Maybe if you ask Nick very, very nicely, he'll take you again tomorrow."

Zipping up their packs, Tate stood up and headed over to Eva. He handed her the backpack, then made a gesture for her to wrap up the call.

"I've got to go now, little man." Her voice wobbled a little. "I'll be home soon, okay? And when I come back, I'll take you out for ice cream and then—" Now that voice downright cracked. "And then we'll go to New York to see your grandparents....Uh-huh....Yep....I promise. Love you, baby."

A moment later, she hung up and handed him the sat phone. He didn't miss the moisture that sparkled in her eyes and clung to her long, sooty eyelashes.

"The kid's doing good?" he said gruffly.

She reached up to wipe her eyes. "He sounds like he's having a lot of fun. Nick took him on a hike this morning, and apparently last night they ate hot dogs." A fresh batch of tears welled up. "I miss him."

Uncomfortable, he slid his arms into the straps of his backpack, then made sure all his weapons were secure. "We should go," he said.

Surprise flickered across her face. "You mean you want to go on?"

"As opposed to what?" he cracked. "Turn back, thus making these past few days a total waste?"

Without waiting for a response, he shifted his rifle to his other arm and found a more comfortable grip on the machete handle. Then he headed toward the trees.

"You can trust me, you know."

Soft and even, Eva's voice rang with confidence.

Slowly, Tate turned to face her. "Whatever you say, sweetheart."

"You can," she insisted.

Tightening the straps of her pack, she strode toward him, and he couldn't help but notice the way her firm breasts swayed beneath that tight white tank top. Her long-sleeved shirt was tied around her waist, and when he caught sight of the bloodstained sleeve, he bit back another string of obscenities, knowing he was reaching the end of his rope.

He had no frickin' idea what to make of this woman. An hour ago, he'd dug a *bullet* out of her flesh, then stitched her up while she'd been conscious, and now here she was, standing in front of him with her shoulders set high and her eyes glittering with conviction. He didn't doubt she was in pain—he could see it in her eyes, in the way she'd flinched when she'd slid her arm through the backpack strap. Yet she refused to give up or slow down, and that impressed the hell out of him.

"When I tracked you down, I knew you were hiding from something," Eva went on, "but I promise you, I had no idea what it was. I don't know why people want you dead, I don't know if my uncle used me to lure you out of hiding—but I highly doubt that—and I don't know who's working with who."

He rolled his eyes. "Sounds like you don't know much of anything."

"At the moment, no." Steel hardened her blue eyes, making them glint like cobalt. "But I'll find out."

He arched a brow. "Oh, really."

"I'm making you a promise right now, Tate. See this through with me, kill Hector for me, and in return, I'll do everything in my power to figure out why you're being hunted."

Doubt washed over him. "What, you think you'll hack into some magical spec-ops system and find a file labeled Why We Want to Kill Tate?"

She scowled at him. "Obviously it won't be that easy. And I can't promise that I'll be able to find the truth all wrapped up in a tidy little bow, but I will try."

Her assurances didn't do much to appease him. Eva might have tracked him to Mexico, but that didn't mean she was a miracle worker.

"So what do you say?" she asked. "Can we agree to trust each other, at least until we see this through? Like, 'no more pointing guns at me' kind of trust?"

An unwitting smile tugged at his mouth. "I'll see what I can do."

Swiveling on his heel, he started to set out once more, only for Eva's voice to stop him again.

"And, Tate?"

He half turned. "Yeah?"

"That kiss…" Her cheeks turned pink. "I'm not sure why you kissed me, but I don't want to play games."

Games? He decided not to mention that kissing her had

been the furthest thing from a game. He hadn't been trying to unnerve her, hadn't been manipulating her, hadn't been doing a damn thing but satisfying the craving that been plaguing him from the moment they'd met.

"So." She cleared her throat. "It can't happen again. I don't *want* it to. Okay?"

He swept his gaze over her tousled black hair, rumpled clothing and bandaged arm, and decided that he'd never seen a sexier sight.

But she was right.

That one kiss had distracted him to the point where he'd nearly allowed a military unit to blow his head off. No matter how much he craved Eva, it was time to drag his head out of the gutter. Focus on revenge rather than sex.

And keep his hands—and lips—to himself.

Twenty-four hours later, Eva exhaled with relief as she and Tate finally put the jungle behind them.

The little community they stumbled into was a welcome sight. A small marketplace took residence in the center of the village, and the smell of cooking meat and rich coffee wafted through the air. Everywhere she looked, she saw people milling around, talking, laughing, haggling.

A group of tanned, dark-haired women stood by a booth offering brightly colored scarves, holding plump, toothless-grinning babies in their arms. The sight evoked a pang of longing. Hearing Rafe's voice yesterday had been pure torture. She'd wanted so badly to abandon this mission and go home to her son, and it had taken all her willpower to refrain from doing that.

Rafe would never be safe as long as Hector lived. She simply had to remind herself of that every time she missed him.

Lifting the tin cup to her lips, Eva swallowed her coffee, enjoying the way the rich flavor teased her taste buds. Coffee was one of San Marquez's main exports; it was in high demand, in fact, which didn't surprise her one bit. The coffee here was to die for.

She would've liked to spend a few more hours in the village to rest, wash up, call her son again. But Tate wasn't having it. For the past twenty minutes, he'd been in deep conversation with one of the male villagers who owned the rusted pickup truck Tate had been eyeballing ever since they'd arrived.

Ten minutes later, when he strode over with a set of keys in his hand, she didn't even raise an eyebrow. Given his penchant for pushing people around, it wasn't at all surprising that he'd persuaded the driver to part with the truck. With his big, hard body and that intense glare he'd perfected, you felt compelled to give the man anything he wanted.

Anything?

The inner taunt made her frown. It also brought a jolt of heat straight to her core.

No, darn it. She had to quit thinking about that kiss. How firm his lips had been, the seductive swirl of his tongue, the strength of his arms as he'd lifted her up and rubbed his lower body all over her aching core.

A groan lodged in her throat. God, this was *not* the time to be lusting over a man. Especially one as ruthless and enigmatic as Robert Tate.

"Let's go," Mr. Ruthless and Enigmatic ordered. "I want to make it to Valero before nightfall."

Taking one last swig of coffee, she rose from the splintered wooden bench and followed Tate toward the pickup truck parked on the dirt several yards away.

"Why Valero?" she asked, wrinkling her forehead as she pictured the rustic mountain town. She'd spent some time in that area when she'd worked with the relief foundation, and she remembered all the towns around there being rather isolated.

"The associate I mentioned, Hastings, has a cabin there."

"So?"

"So we'll bunk there until I figure out the best way to infiltrate Cruz's camp. I won't go into this half-cocked."

Of course he wouldn't. Sliding into the passenger seat of the truck, she resigned herself to the possibility that it could still be days before they closed in on Hector. Tate would probably plan this attack to the last detail.

He turned the key in the ignition, and the truck's engine chugged to life. Since her seat belt was broken, Eva ended up bouncing and sliding in the front seat as Tate sped down the bumpy dirt road leading out of the village. Both the windows were rolled down, and the air was cooler here near the mountains. Still humid, but not as suffocating, and the breeze that met her face when she peered out the window was quite refreshing.

Tate expertly shifted gears as the manual transmission truck traveled along the two-lane road that eventually turned from dirt to gravel. "How's the arm?" he asked, shooting her a sidelong look.

She gingerly touched the bandage covering her upper arm, a tad impressed that she'd completely forgotten all about her bullet wound. She'd been diligently changing the dressing, shooting herself up with antibiotics and popping Tylenol every few hours to alleviate the pain, and the dull throb was nothing more than background noise now. She felt the pain only when Tate reminded her of it.

"It's fine," she replied. Then she grinned. "I've never been shot before. Now I'll have a cool story to tell Rafe." She paused. "When he turns eighteen, maybe."

Tate chuckled.

The husky sound made her heart skip a beat, a reaction for which she quickly berated herself. "I assume you've been shot before," she said wryly.

He shrugged. "A few times."

Shifting her gaze, she focused on his chiseled profile. "What made you decide to enlist in the army?"

"It was my ticket out."

She didn't have to ask *out of what.* "What about your brother?" she said carefully. "He was, what? Five years younger than you?"

The air in the pickup cab grew cold, something she hadn't thought possible in this sweltering South American climate. From the way Tate's stubble-covered jaw went tighter than a drum, he clearly didn't appreciate the mention of his younger brother.

"Yes," he said stiffly.

"So he would have been thirteen when you enlisted." She frowned. "Did you leave him behind?"

His head swiveled, and the look of revulsion on his handsome face caught her off guard. "You honestly think I'd leave my kid brother in the clutches of our abusive bastard of a father?"

Eva faltered. "I don't know what to think. I have no idea what you're capable of, Tate."

And yet she *didn't* believe he'd do that to his brother, which he confirmed with his next words. "He came with me when I left Boston," Tate muttered. "We had an aunt in North Carolina, and I convinced her to let Will stay with her while I went through basic training."

"That was nice of her."

He snorted. "Sure, Auntie Carol was a real saint. That arrangement cost me every penny I had."

Sorrow thickened her throat. "Your aunt demanded you pay her to take care of her own nephew?"

"Yep."

"What happened when Will came of age?"

"He enlisted, too." Tate's voice went hoarse. "When I was asked to head up a spec-op unit, I requested that Will be assigned to my team."

"So the two of you stayed close over the years."

"He's—*was*—the only person I've ever been close to."

She choked down a lump of sadness. "I'm sorry for your loss, Tate."

He offered another one of those careless shrugs, which she was beginning to see right through. "S'all good, sweetheart. I've made my peace with it."

An incredulous laugh slipped out. "No, you haven't. You're currently risking your neck just to exact revenge on the man who killed your brother."

He laughed right back. "Talk about the pot and kettle. You're here for revenge, too."

"Maybe," she agreed, "but I'm not pretending to be at peace with what I've lost."

"My brother's dead, Eva. I *have* made peace with that."

"Okay." She tilted her head. "What happens after you avenge Will? You go back to hiding?"

"Yes. At least until I figure out why I'm a wanted man."

The reminder had her biting her lip in thought. "I still don't get it," she murmured, her brain kicking up a gear. "You *must* have seen something during that mission. It's the only thing that makes sense."

"Nothing makes sense," he grumbled. "And I didn't see a damn thing."

"Tell me again what happened."

He released a sigh, his green eyes focusing on the road ahead. The brown peaks of the mountains loomed in the horizon, making a seriously pretty picture against the cloudless blue sky and shining yellow sun. But there was nothing pretty about any of this. What awaited them in those mountains was ugly. Very, very ugly.

"Tate?" she prompted when he still didn't answer.

"I already told you," he said in a tone overloaded with frustration. "When we infiltrated the camp, the doctor was dead and—"

"How did he die?"

"Bullet between the eyes, courtesy of Cruz's rifle."

She flinched. "Okay. And the villagers?"

"The rebels burned the bodies." His jaw set in a grim line. "Hopefully they all got bullets between their eyes, too. I'd hate to think that son of a bitch burned them alive."

Queasiness churned in her belly. Banishing the horrifying images Tate had brought to mind, she gulped down the acid lining her throat and said, "Why?"

"Why what?"

"Why would Hector kill the doctor and burn the villagers?"

"Who knows. Maybe he knew the U.S. would never negotiate with him and decided to cut his losses. Or maybe someone alerted him that a military force was closing in on him, so again, he decided to cut his losses. Trust me, I plan on asking Cruz the very same questions before I slit his throat."

A chill skidded up her spine. God, that cold, blunt statement terrified her, and as much as she hated doing it, she couldn't help but compare Tate to the very man he was itching to kill. Hector had no qualms about slitting throats, either, and just like Tate, he considered it his duty to exact revenge on his enemies.

The sad truth caused a sense of weariness to wash over her. Men were ruthless creatures. Honor, loyalty, vengeance, justice—sometimes she wondered if the male sex just used those concepts as excuses to be violent, tried to give some legitimacy to their primal desire to kill and destroy.

"And afterward?" she said quietly. "After you kill Hector and confront the people who want you dead, what will you do then?"

"Disappear."

"And live the rest of your life alone?"

"Yes."

"That's very sad, Tate."

He went quiet for a beat before letting out a husky laugh. "Don't waste your sympathy on me, Eva. I want to be alone. I prefer it. Hell, if it weren't for Will, I would have waved goodbye to the world a long time ago."

She gasped. "You mean, *killed* yourself?"

He laughed again, sounding far more amused this time. "Of course not. I definitely would've left civilization behind, though. Built a cabin in the woods or a shack on the beach, and lived the rest of my life in peace and quiet. On second thought, I still might do that."

"That's…sad," she said again.

"You know what they say, one man's hell is another man's heaven."

The cabin was actually cozier than Eva expected it to be. Made of weathered logs, the A-frame structure was nestled in the trees, almost entirely hidden from view, and a good ten miles outside of Valero, the little town where Tate had stashed their pickup truck. They'd trekked it to the cabin on foot, reaching it just as the sun set and the air grew considerably cooler.

Eva sighed in relief as she followed Tate toward the front door. The past four days had been nonstop walking, and though she was in good shape, she looked forward to the rest. Tate had said the cabin even had indoor plumbing, and she could not wait to take a shower.

"Stay out here," he ordered, swiftly bringing his rifle up as he approached the door.

Although she was dying to immerse herself in some semblance of civilization, she patiently waited for Tate to assess the interior of the cabin. A few minutes later, she heard a soft whistle, then his gruff voice saying, "We're good, sweetheart. Come in."

Sweetheart. She didn't know why, but her heart did a dumb little flip whenever the endearment left that man's lips.

Make that *mocking* endearment, she had to amend. But still, even knowing that those two syllables were most likely a taunt didn't squash the desire that hearing them inspired.

As they entered the small main room, Eva dropped her backpack on the hardwood floor and glanced around. Her gaze encountered sparse furnishings, bare walls and no personal touches—the place looked uninhabited, which apparently wasn't the case since Tate said his former army buddy had been living here for years.

"Where is this Hastings?" she asked warily, continuing to inspect her surroundings. A minuscule kitchen took up the other side of the room, and she deduced that the narrow corridor behind her led to the bedrooms.

"Picking up some supplies for us," Tate replied.

Right. She remembered something of that nature being discussed when Tate contacted his buddy via the sat phone. Nevertheless, she didn't particularly trust Tate's mysterious colleague. All she knew was that he was a former Green Beret turned expatriate who now lived in a cabin in the middle of the wilderness. Needless to say, she wasn't sure how comfortable she felt about any of this.

Tate must have sensed her hesitation. "Relax. Ben is a good guy. He can be trusted."

"I'll decide that for myself, if you don't mind."

"Not at all." He shot her a crooked grin. "The jury's still out on how much *we* trust each other, so what's one more untrustworthy companion?"

"I'm really starting to hate that word," she grumbled. *"Trust."*

"Deadliest word in the English language," he said with a shrug.

Tate leaned his rifle against the back of the ratty polyester couch, then slid his pistol from his waistband, and he made such a sexy, imposing sight that Eva couldn't tear her gaze off him. Everything about him excited her—the muscular body, clad in cargo pants and a snug white T-shirt streaked with dirt. The thick beard growth covering his strong jaw, lending him a lethal air. The ease with which he held his weapon, the soundless way he moved despite the heavy boots on his feet.

The dark, seductive smile he flashed when he caught her eyeing him...

"Oh, sweetheart, if you keep looking at me like that, I *will* kiss you again. You know that, right?"

Heat danced through her body, bringing a flush to her cheeks and an ache to her core. "We already agreed that wasn't going to happen," she reminded him.

He set his pistol on the uneven table next to the sofa, his eyes downright predatory as he made his way toward her. "We agreed to no such thing," he said, that hot gaze glued to her mouth.

Eva's pulse raced. "I told you I didn't want it."

"You lied," he countered.

She gulped. Hard.

Tate's gaze continued to eat her up as if she were a juicy

steak he couldn't wait to dig his teeth into. "I have no idea what to do with you, Eva," he said after a moment.

His voice came out rough and rueful, and the odd glimmer of apprehension she saw in his gorgeous green eyes was absolutely puzzling.

"What do you mean?" *Her* voice came out as a squeak, which was super annoying.

"I mean… Ah, hell, I don't know *what* I mean." His massive chest heaved as he released a breath. "All I know is that I'm going to kiss you again."

Her words came out squeaky again. "I don't want that."

"Liar."

And then he called her bluff and slanted his mouth over hers in a deep, unapologetic kiss.

Yep, she'd lied. She *did* want this. She wanted it desperately, and as his sensual mouth coaxed and teased and kissed her into oblivion, she realized she'd never, ever wanted to kiss anyone more than she wanted to kiss Tate.

His spicy, intoxicating scent enveloped her senses, and the persistent strokes of his tongue unleashed a rush of pleasure that heated every erogenous zone in her body. With one strong hand, Tate yanked at the elastic band holding her ponytail and let her hair loose, tangling his fingers in her long tresses and angling her head so he could kiss her deeper, harder, more possessively.

He slid one hand to her throat, swept his thumb over the pulse point there, then chuckled.

"Your heart's beating fast," he murmured, his warm breath tickling her lips. Both his hands traveled down to her chest. "And your nipples are hard."

Eva gasped as he squeezed her breasts. When he toyed with her nipples over her shirt and bra, she nearly passed out from the wild pleasure that rocketed through her.

"So who's playing games now?" he rasped. "You want this as badly as I do. At least have the guts to admit it."

He was right.

She wanted him.

She *craved* him. Like heroin. Or something equally addictive.

"Fine," she choked out. "I want this. I want you. God, I want—"

Click.

She froze midsentence, as the unmistakable sound of a gun being cocked echoed in the room.

Battling the tingle of fear, she shifted her gaze to the door and found herself staring down the barrel of the gun.

Chapter 10

Despite the fact that a gun was currently being aimed at him, Tate didn't feel threatened in the slightest. If anything, he was just annoyed by the interruption.

"Nice to see you, too, Ben," he grumbled without turning around. "And your timing sucks."

"Gee," came the deep, sarcastic voice, "sorry to interrupt, Robert. Next time I'll be more considerate in my own home."

Chuckling, Tate stepped away from Eva and strode over to his old friend. He'd seen Ben a few months ago when he'd come to San Marquez to do some digging about Cruz's whereabouts. Ben had taken him in without question then, just as he did now.

"It's good to see you," Tate said, holding out his hand.

Ignoring the hand being extended to him, the beefy African-American pulled Tate in for a hearty hug, then slapped his shoulder and released him.

"Still alive, I see," Ben remarked, sounding pleased. "How're the boys?"

Tate hid a smile. Stone and Prescott hated being called "boys," but neither of them had voiced a single complaint when Ben had referred to them as such during that last visit. With his shaved head, harsh features and black goatee, not to mention the roped muscles and barrel chest, Ben Hastings was one mean-looking SOB. And it wasn't all for show—the man really was as lethal as they came.

"The boys are also alive," Tate answered.

Ben's dark eyes drifted to Eva. "This her?"

Tate nodded. "Ben, Eva. Eva, Ben."

With visible wariness, Eva walked over to shake Ben's hand. At six-five, Ben towered over her petite frame, and for some reason Tate felt the oddest urge to move to her side in a gesture of protectiveness.

Brushing off the strange thought, he glanced at Ben and said, "Mind if Eva uses your shower?"

The request brought a blush to Eva's cheeks, which made him roll his eyes. "You keep longingly looking at the corridor, as if you're dying to find out if there's a bathroom there."

"There is," Ben confirmed. "And it's yours for the taking. Spare towels in the cabinet below the sink. Soap in the medicine cabinet."

Although Eva's expression perked up, she didn't make a move to go. Rather, she looked from one man to the other, then frowned. "You're trying to get rid of me, aren't you?"

"Yep," Tate confirmed.

After a second, the frown faded. "Fine. Whatever. Talk behind my back all you want. As long as I get to shower, I'm cool with that."

Tate noticed Ben's lips twitching as Eva dashed off toward the hallway. Once she disappeared from view, his buddy let the grin show. "That is one fine woman."

Tate couldn't disagree.

"But, dude, is it really a good idea for you to be hitting that?" Ben continued, heading to the kitchen. "Or have we decided she's trustworthy?"

"We haven't decided a damn thing," he admitted.

"Beer?"

Before he could answer, a longneck bottle sailed in his direction. He caught it with ease, making a face as he studied the label. The local beer sucked, but for some reason, Hastings seemed to love it. Whatever. After three days of traveling through the jungle with the ultimate temptation by his side, he deserved a reward, even if it came in the form of watery beer.

Twisting off the cap, he brought the bottle to his lips and took a long swig. "Thanks." He arched a brow. "What's for dinner?"

"If you think I'm gonna cook for you, you're seriously delusional."

Tate stared at his buddy.

"Fine. We're having lamb stew," Ben said grudgingly.

He barked out a laugh. Ben Hastings might be strong, dangerous and downright frightening, but the man did love to cook. And he was damn good at it, too.

The sound of creaking pipes wafted from the corridor, followed by rushing water, and the second Tate pictured Eva stepping under the shower spray and getting all nice and wet, his mouth went utterly dry. Christ. She would look spectacular naked. No doubt about that.

Pushing aside the wicked images, he took another sip of beer, then said, "So tell me what's been going on around here. ULF seems to be causing even more trouble since Cruz went underground."

Ben's expression darkened. "Let's talk outside." The silver dog tags hanging around his neck clinked together as he headed toward a door off to the right.

Tate followed the other man to the back porch. The wooden slats beneath their boots creaked as they walked to the pine railing, where both men set their beers. The back of the cabin offered a view of the mountains in the distance, as well as the narrow creek visible through the trees.

"There's been more riots," Ben began, as he tapped his long fingers on the railing. "A couple of assassination attempts on high-ranking officials. Cruz's second in command, Luego, is flashier than his boss—he goes for shock and awe, big explosions and loud noises to get his point across."

"Always an effective strategy."

Ben snickered. "Yeah, well, it's not working. Military presence has gone up a hundred percent—"

"I noticed that at the harbor. There were a lot more soldiers compared to only a few months ago."

"Like I said, Luego has been causing some trouble."

"So Cruz still hasn't shown his face," Tate mused.

"Nope. Ever since he pulled off the Great Escape, he's been MIA."

Tate stifled a curse. Crap. That meant he had no choice but to go forward with this potentially suicidal mission. Cruz sure as hell wasn't going to come to *him*.

"Your girl really knows where Cruz's hideout is?" Ben asked, reading his mind.

He made a gesture of frustration. "She claims to, but who the hell knows if she's telling the truth?"

"I *am*," came Eva's sharp, yet earnest, voice.

Both men turned to see her standing in the open doorway. She wore a fresh pair of jeans and a tight black T-shirt. With her black hair loose, feet bare, and face pink and glowing from the shower, she looked absolutely incredible, and as usual, Tate's body responded to her nearness.

As his groin stirred, he banished the rising arousal and focused on Eva's blue eyes. "So you keep saying," he said vaguely.

A sigh left her lips. "I thought we agreed to the whole trust thing." Without letting him answer, she turned to Ben. "Do you have a computer I can use?"

Ben arched one bushy black eyebrow. "And what do you need a computer for?"

"I made our friend *Robert* a promise," she replied, shooting Tate a pointed look. "You still want to figure out why you're being hunted, right?"

As much as he didn't enjoy giving Eva the upper hand, he couldn't deny how tempting her offer was. If she could truly discover the truth behind the past eight months from a few keystrokes, he'd be a fool to stop her.

With a resigned breath, he turned to Ben and said, "If you've got one, give it to the lady."

Looking intrigued, Ben nodded and headed back to the door. Tate trailed after him, beer bottle in hand, as he watched the bulky African-American stride toward the tall wooden cabinet in the corner of the living room. Ben unlocked the cabinet with a set of keys he unclipped from his belt, opened the doors and removed an older-model Dell that he placed on the coffee table.

It was hard to miss the way Eva's entire face lit up at the sight of that laptop. The resulting rush of jealousy that burned his gut was downright laughable. Jeez. He was jealous of a damn *computer?* Because it had put that look of rapture on her face?

Wow. Clearly he had some problems.

Eva flopped down on the shabby sofa and opened the laptop. "Password?" she asked Ben.

"No password. I hardly ever use that thing."

A perplexed groove dug into her forehead. "You don't? Where do you store all your personal information?"

Ben tapped his temple with his index finger. "Everything I need is right in here."

She grinned. "You're an old-school kinda guy, huh?"

"You know it, baby-cakes."

Baby-cakes?

Tate resisted the urge to shake his head in bewilderment as he listened to their exchange. Ten minutes ago, Ben had been eyeing Eva like she was a threat to national security, and then one good-natured wisecrack on her part and they were best buds?

Yet somehow that didn't surprise him one damned bit. Eva Dolce, he'd come to learn, was incredibly easy to be around. Too damn likable for her own good.

"I can't believe you get wireless here," she commented, as her fingers moved over the laptop's track pad.

"San Marquez isn't a total failure in the technology department," Ben agreed.

Eva's face set in intense concentration as she studied the screen, her long, delicate fingers flying over the keyboard. "Mind if I explore your hard drive? I need to get a sense of what I'm working with here."

"Explore away."

It didn't take long before Eva mumbled a string of aggravated curses that had Tate and Ben exchanging a look.

"This computer sucks," she announced, lifting her head with an expression of disgust.

Ben held up his meaty hands in surrender. "Like I said, I'm old-school."

"I'm serious. I cannot emphasize how much this computer *sucks*. Not enough RAM to run any of my software.

Hell, even the internet browser takes an eternity to load." She huffed out a breath. "It's not fast enough."

Ben didn't look at all bothered. "I told you, I barely use that thing. Only to check my email every now and then."

Tate noticed that Eva now looked distraught. Catching his eye, she bit her bottom lip, then said, "I can't help you. At least not using this system."

He shrugged. "It's fine, Eva." He neglected to add that he hadn't expected her to find anything of use anyway.

"No, it's not. I promised I'd find out why people want you dead." Her mouth tightened in determination and when she looked at him again, he glimpsed that same fortitude in her big blue eyes. "Let me contact my friend, Tate."

"No way," he said instantly.

"I promise you, he's discreet. And he's good, even better than I am. He can hack into any system without being detected."

Tate remained doubtful.

"I'm serious," she insisted. "He's the one who helped me get into the army database, and so far, the military police haven't come knocking on either of our doors, so clearly nobody knew we got in."

"And how *do* you get in?" Ben spoke up, sounding intrigued.

"Depends on what we're trying to do."

She ran a hand through her hair, and Tate's fingers itched to slide through those long, damp tresses. And the way she kept chewing on her bottom lip...it made his own lips tingle with the urge to kiss her again. Christ. Why the hell couldn't he stop thinking about kissing this woman?

Shaking the cobwebs from his head, he tried to focus on the words coming out of Eva's mouth rather than on that sensual mouth itself.

"Most people think hackers are evil, looking to stick it

to 'the man' and infect the world with virtual viruses, or to steal from corporations and hardworking folks, or simply to cause trouble for the hell of it. But that's not what hacker culture is about," she said, sounding so animated Tate fought a smile.

Ben looked equally amused. "So what *is* it about?"

"Challenge. Curiosity. We're visionaries. Pioneers. Sure, there are some hackers who have malicious intentions, but the majority of us don't do what we do to hurt anyone. We embrace the challenge of getting into a system nobody else can, or one that programmers brag can't be breached."

"Doesn't make it any less illegal," Ben quipped.

"No," she agreed, "but sometimes it ends up helping the people whose privacy we violated. Like my friend, for example, he breaks into systems and then creates programs that implement better security measures, which he sells to the companies that utilize the vulnerable security pathways he breached in the first place."

Ben grinned. "But I bet he doesn't tell them that."

She grinned back. "No, not usually." The smile faded and her features grew serious again as she glanced at Tate. "If I had my computer with me, I could run my own software, but you made me leave my laptop behind." She punctuated that with a scowl. "But if you let me contact my friend, he can do the grunt work for us."

"Let me guess, for a price," he said sardonically.

"Actually, no. He owes me one." That sassy grin played over her lips again. "He owes me tens of thousands, in fact."

Because she'd stolen from the ULF, Tate remembered. With the help of this "friend," whom she'd no doubt monetarily rewarded for his troubles. From what he was starting to know of Eva, she was all about returning favors. He got the feeling she didn't like owing anyone anything, and that was a mindset he totally understood. Outstanding debts had no place in his life, either.

"He can be trusted, Tate. Just say the word, and I'll contact him and get the ball rolling."

Indecision washed over him, but he couldn't bring himself to turn down the offer. Nick and Sebastian were good with computers, but they weren't first-class hackers or anything. That honor had gone to Berkowski, the tech specialist of their unit.

Bitterness clogged his throat. Unfortunately, Berk was dead, and unless Tate got some answers, he'd never be able to know why Berkowski had died.

"Fine," he said gruffly. "Contact your friend."

When her features brightened, he held up his hand and fixed her with a toxic look. "But if this *friend* double-crosses me, make no mistake, I'll be holding *you* responsible, sweetheart."

She rolled those beautiful blue eyes. "Shocking. Just add it to the list of all the other negatives you attribute to me— I'm a secret government agent, I'm a liar, I'm in cahoots with my uncle…anything else I'm forgetting?"

Tate's only response was a hard frown.

Next to him, Ben chuckled. "I think I like her."

Dinner consisted of a lamb stew prepared by Ben, and after three days of eating Meals Ready to Eat, Eva devoured the delicious home-cooked meal like a starving woman. As the trio sat around the lopsided table in Ben's small kitchen, she surreptitiously studied the men and tried to make sense of their unlikely friendship.

Ironically, neither man behaved in a way that corresponded to his appearance. While Tate was ruggedly handsome and sinfully sexy, his personality was thorny, brooding and sarcastic—which was what she'd have expected from Ben, whose harsh features and enormous body were incongruous with his laid-back charm and easy laughter.

Ben had explained that the two of them had struck up a friendship during basic training in the army, but while Tate had remained in the military, Ben only completed one tour before moving to South America to "retire." Eva suspected Tate's friend was involved in shady enterprises, but she'd yet to figure out what he actually did for a living.

After dinner, she helped Ben clear the table, then accepted the beer he handed her. Once again, the two men drifted onto the back terrace. This time she joined them, refusing to let them shut her out again. She knew they intended to discuss the plan for taking out Hector, and she'd be damned if she didn't have a say in how it went down.

Tate frowned as she leaned against the wooden railing, but he didn't order her to leave, a fact for which she was grateful.

"I can't see you walking out of this alive. Either one of you."

Ben's frank remark brought a spark of panic to Eva's gut. She met the man's dark eyes, then turned to Tate. "Do you think he's right?"

"Probably." He shrugged. "But I knew from the start that there'd be a fifty-fifty chance I'd end up dead."

She was not expecting to hear *that*.

"Then why did you agree to come with me?" she demanded, baffled.

Although he didn't respond, his silence spoke volumes.

He'd agreed to this mission because he didn't *care* if he died. As long as he got to kill Hector, Captain Robert Tate was perfectly willing to give up his life.

The realization intensified her panic. No. This couldn't

be a suicide mission. Tate might be okay with dying, but she refused to die. She had a three-year-old son to live for.

"I get it," she said evenly. "You want Hector eliminated and you don't care if you die trying. But *I* care. I will do anything in my power to go home to my son, which means you can't half-ass any of the planning for this."

Ben grinned at her. "You tell him, honey."

Without cracking a smile, she lifted her beer to her lips and took a long sip. When she felt a little calmer, she glanced at Tate again. "So how are we going to do this?"

"You tell me." His green eyes twinkled briefly with amusement before going hard. "You're the one who's familiar with Hector's camp."

"Should I draw you a map of everything I remember?" She was already moving to put down her beer, but Tate waved a hand. "Later. Right now I just want a general overview. You said he's hiding out in the mountains?"

Eva nodded. "In an underground bunker. The entrance is carved right into the rocks. You'd walk right past it if you're not looking for it."

"Only one entrance?" He sounded dubious.

"Two that I know of. The main one in the rocks, and another way out through the western foothills. There's one tunnel running beneath the bunker, leading out to the hills."

She halted, noticing that both men were staring at her. "What?" she said defensively.

"How exactly are you privy to these details?" Ben asked before exchanging a look with Tate.

"You never said you've been *inside,*" Tate added, a suspicious cloud traveling over his face.

She gulped. "I told you, I supported the ULF cause at one time."

"Enough for Cruz to bring you to his secret lair?"

"I—*we*, Rafe's father and I—were close with Hector.

We were attempting to find a way to move supplies to the needy areas of the region using the relief foundation's resources. We held a lot of strategy sessions in that bunker."

The lies slid from her mouth, smooth as cream, but she couldn't afford to feel guilty about it. Besides, the fiction sounded so much nicer than the reality of it all. Strategy sessions in Hector's bunker? She *wished* their association had been that benign.

She spoke before the men could question her previous remarks. "The main entrance is guarded, but the one in the hills isn't."

"You sure about that?" Tate said sharply.

"It's Hector's secret escape route. He doesn't draw attention to it. Inside the tunnel is another story—there's a guard posted at the exit door, and a couple more by the ladder that leads up to the bunker."

Tate glanced at Ben. "Thoughts?"

The African-American looked pensive. "Clearly the entry point will be the foothills. Getting in will be easy, Robert, you know that. It's getting out that'll be the problem."

"I know," Tate said grimly. "What if we create some chaos? Draw the guards to one entrance and make sure they stay there, giving me enough time to sneak in through the tunnel, take out Hector and then get out the way I came."

"What do you mean, *you?*" Eva said in confusion.

He spared her a brief look. "Once we reach the camp, you're out of this, sweetheart. I go in and take care of Hector alone."

Surprise spiraled through her. "But why?"

"You said it, Eva. You have a son to go home to. I don't." He met her eyes, looking vaguely embarrassed before he wrenched his gaze away. "Once I'm convinced you've led me to the right place—and that I'm not walking into an ambush—Ben and I will handle it from there."

She turned to Ben. "Wait—you're coming, too?"

"Of course. Who else is gonna create the chaos? Speaking of which, I should head out." The big man polished off the rest of his beer before tossing the empty bottle into the plastic bucket by the door. "There are a few more items I need to procure. It might take all night, so don't wait up."

As Ben lumbered off, Eva furrowed her brows. "What exactly does he *do?*" she blurted out. "What items is he *procuring* and why will it take all night to get them?"

Tate chuckled. "Ben's what you'd call a middleman. If you need something, he hooks you up with someone who can provide it for you."

"Something?" she echoed warily. "Like weapons? Drugs?"

"He has the strings to get you anything you want, but weapons and information are his specialties."

Again with the whole information-as-a-commodity thing. Eva made a mental note to look into that when all this was over. With her skill on a computer, she might actually be able to make a darn good living selling information, but that was an idea for another day. Right now, she had to focus on the task at hand.

"Why don't I draw that map now?" she suggested. "Maybe if you see what the interior of the bunker looks like, it'll help you come up with a plan."

Tate nodded in agreement. He threw his head back and drained his beer, then followed her inside and watched as she rummaged around in the kitchen for some scrap paper and a pencil.

Rather than join her at the table, he edged toward the doorway. "I'm gonna hop in the shower while you do that," he said, scrubbing a hand over the beard covering his jaw.

"Okay," she said absently, already sketching the basic outline of the bunker.

After Tate left the room, she tried to focus on constructing a detailed map for him, but it wasn't long before the sound of the shower distracted her.

Eva lifted the pencil from the page, feeling her cheeks go hot as she listened to the water running. She couldn't help herself—she pictured Tate, big and hard and naked beneath the spray, soapy water coursing in rivulets down his broad chest, gliding over rippled muscles and hard sinew.

I knew from the start that there'd be a fifty-fifty chance I'd end up dead.

His words continued to haunt her. Did he really not care if he died? Because if that was the case, why was he bothering to hide out at all? Why not just let himself be killed by the people who were after him?

For his men.

The answer flew into her head, making her sigh. Of course. Tate wasn't trying to figure out the truth about that failed mission for *his* sake. He was doing it for Nick Prescott and Sebastian Stone.

Chewing on the inside of her cheek, Eva set down the pencil and stood up, too wound up to focus on the map. She knew Tate and Ben wouldn't leave this cabin until they had a solid plan in place, but she wished they could just go after Hector tonight. Now, even. She missed her son, and she was tired of feeling so…edgy.

Tate made her feel hot and uncomfortable and…well, *edgy,* damn it. The sexual awareness she felt in his presence was beginning to drive her nuts, though in her defense, maybe she'd be able to ignore it if he didn't keep kissing her every five minutes.

Okay, fine. He'd only kissed her twice.

But those two kisses had packed a *hell* of a punch.

Her ears perked at the sound of pipes groaning, and then the water stopped.

Somehow, she found herself making her way to the corridor. She heard quiet noises from behind the bathroom door—footsteps, the squeak of the faucet, running water, a toilet flushing. When she saw the doorknob twist, she ordered herself to dash back to the living room, but her feet stayed rooted in place.

She was standing right outside the door when it opened.

Tate frowned the second he saw her. "What's going on?" he asked instantly.

Eva couldn't answer. Her vocal cords had stopped working the second she laid eyes on his bare chest. Hard pecs and washboard abs and sleek, golden skin assaulted her vision. He wore a towel that rode precariously low on his hips, a sight that made her entire mouth go drier than sawdust.

"What do you want, Eva?" he asked in a tight voice.

She met his green eyes and saw unmistakable arousal flashing back at her. The smart thing to do would be to walk away, but her feet refused to comply.

Tate waited a few seconds, then sighed when she still didn't answer. "Fine. We'll deal with this later. I'm getting dressed."

She blocked his path. Her gaze dropped to his towel, then moved back to his face. A wry note entered her voice. "Don't bother."

His eyes narrowed. "Don't bother what?"

"Getting dressed." She brought her hand to his chest and stroked the spot between his pecs. "We both know any clothes you put on will come right off, anyway."

Tate inhaled sharply and she felt his pectoral muscles quiver beneath her fingers. "You're playing with fire, sweetheart."

She tickled his flat, brown nipples with the pads of her

fingers. "We've both been playing with fire since the moment we met," she corrected.

Licking her lips, she reached for his hand. After a moment, he intertwined their fingers and studied her face one last time, his green eyes blazing with passion. "You sure about this?"

She stared at their joined hands, then met his gaze. "Who knows what tomorrow will bring, right?"

His voice came out gruff. "Meaning?"

"Meaning we may as well enjoy ourselves tonight."

Chapter 11

The bedroom was dark when they entered it. Eva paused at the foot of the twin bed and studied their darkened surroundings, baffled by the total lack of furnishings. Ben's room consisted of nothing but the bed, a table littered with books, and half a dozen duffel bags on the floor. No dresser, no desk, not even a closet.

Which was fine. Because all they really needed was that bed.

Her pulse sped up as Tate reached for the knot on his towel. Despite the surge of excitement, she also experienced a flicker of apprehension. Was she really going to do this? Sleep with a man she still barely knew?

Tate's towel hit the floor, officially making the answer to both those questions a big, resounding *yes*. He was the most incredible-looking man she'd ever seen. A warrior to the core, with long limbs, roped muscles and various scars marring his golden skin.

Her heart screeched to a stop, then took off full speed ahead as she watched his arousal grow before her eyes. Her mouth watered, and without any conscious thought, she found herself standing in front of him and wrapping her fingers around his erect shaft.

A low groan rumbled out of his chest. "Are you sure?" he asked again.

She nodded. "I'm tired of fighting this attraction." To prove it, she eased her hand along the hard length of him, then released him so she could reach for the hem of her T-shirt.

"We still don't trust each other," he reminded her, his dark green eyes locking with hers.

"Well, as someone once told me, sex and trust don't necessarily go hand in hand."

She took off her shirt and sports bra, and tossed them on the floor.

Tate's gaze instantly homed in on her bare breasts. Her nipples puckered in response, hard and tingly, and an answering flash of lust and appreciation lit his face.

But then he seemed to notice the bandage on her arm. "You're hurt," he mumbled. "You're not up to this."

She smiled faintly. "Says who?"

Without breaking eye contact, Eva unbuttoned her jeans and wiggled out of them, then peeled her panties down her legs. She straightened up and stood there fully naked, every inch of her skin burning as Tate devoured her with his eyes.

Three feet of distance stood between them, between their respectively naked bodies, between their mouths and their hands, but she refused to bridge that distance. She'd already made this first move, and now she wanted Tate to come to her. She wanted to watch *him* fall apart, to give in to the attraction that had been tormenting her hormones for days now.

It didn't take long before she got her wish. Tate raked his hot gaze over her one final time, then let out a growl that startled her, and the next thing she knew, she was flat on her back with his big warrior body crushing her on the bed.

He captured her mouth in a toe-curling kiss, stealing the breath right out of her lungs. As his tongue plundered and possessed, he rocked his hips, his heavy erection pulsing against her belly and making her moan with abandon.

"You taste so good," he muttered before kissing her again.

Long, deep and passionate. His drugging kisses had her head spinning, and when his hands began a slow exploration of her body, she nearly passed out from the incredible sensations. His callused palms scraped her hypersensitive skin. Teased, caressed, tickled. He cupped her breasts, feathering his fingertips over her rigid nipples and summoning another moan from her lips.

"You like this?" he murmured, and then he gently pinched her nipples.

"Yes." Her head flopped to the side, her arms coming around his broad shoulders, clinging to him, needing to steady herself. She was lying down, but she feared if she didn't have something to hold on to, she might actually be swept away by the unbelievable waves of pleasure coursing through her.

Planting a quick kiss on her lips, Tate dipped his head and inched his body lower, so that his mouth was level with her breasts. Without hesitation, he took possession of a nipple, flicking his hot, wet tongue over it before suckling. A bolt of heat sizzled from her nipple right down to the juncture of her thighs, and her hips shot off the bed, her aching core seeking relief.

Tate chuckled. He gripped her waist to steady her, then

shifted his attention to her other breast, getting the exact same reaction out of her.

"Please, I need more," she choked out. "I need you."

"Don't worry, sweetheart, you'll get me."

Amusement rang from his husky voice, but though his words were meant to reassure, his teasing didn't subside. While his mouth continued tending to her breasts, he glided one hand down her body and brought it between her legs, stroking her damp folds with barely there caresses that caused frustration to build in her body.

The tension between her legs was liable to kill her. And the heat. God, her skin was on fire, humming, crackling, threatening to burn her alive.

Sweat broke out on her forehead. *"More,"* she pleaded, her hand desperately moving between their bodies in search of his erection.

A strangled groan left Tate's lips, and when she focused her eyes, she realized that he was not as calm and blasé as she'd thought he was. His facial muscles were taut, green eyes glittering with dark hunger that would've scared her if she weren't feeling the same damn thing.

His voice was hoarse, strained, as if he were speaking through clenched teeth. "I'm trying to make this last, sweetheart." The tendons in his neck tightened as he forcibly moved her hand off his arousal. "It's been too long for me."

"For me, too," she mumbled. "Which is why I don't want to be teased right now. I want…" She moved her hand right back to his hard length and squeezed. "I want you. *Now,* Tate."

With a groan, he removed her hand again, and she nearly slugged him out of sheer frustration, but fortunately, he was simply donning a condom.

Anticipation gathered as she waited for him to sheathe himself. Her nipples tingled, her thighs clenched, her sex throbbed. She'd never felt this way before. Hot, needy, as if she'd actually die if she didn't have this man inside her.

And when he gave her what she craved and drove his cock deep, the anticipation transformed into an explosion of heat and ecstasy that made her cry out and convulse.

Waves of release shuddered through her from that very first stroke. She hadn't realized how badly her body had needed this, and as her climax skyrocketed into her and sent her soaring, Eva wrapped her legs around Tate's trim hips and rode out the release.

Her climax ebbed, leaving her feeling warm and sated and unbelievably contented. She watched Tate's face, floored by the passion she saw there, the naked need, the softness that she'd never seen before and probably wouldn't see again, at least not outside the bedroom. Watching this big, strong man come apart triggered another rush of pleasure, another tiny orgasm that skipped along her nerve endings and made her gasp with surprised delight.

"Eva." He said her name on a groan, and his thrusts quickened, shortened, then stopped altogether as he buried himself deep and jerked with release.

Running her hands along his muscular back, she smiled in the darkness and waited for him to catch his breath. She felt his heartbeat hammering against her breasts, and her smile widened at the knowledge that she'd put him in this state of frantic excitement.

When he rolled off her, she experienced a pang of disappointment, but to her surprise, he didn't get up and walk away. Rather, he slung his arm around her and pulled her close, and although his motions had a slightly awkward feel to them, Eva didn't complain.

"How's the arm?" he asked, his voice gruff.

"It's fine." She rested her cheek against his damp chest,

inhaling the clean, soapy smell of him, enjoying the way his light dusting of chest hair abraded her cheek.

After a moment, he idly began stroking the small of her back, the awkwardness in the gesture evident once more. Clearly he wasn't a cuddler, and a strange sense of joy tickled her chest over the fact that he was still here, snuggling in bed with her. She'd needed the sex, but she suspected she needed *this* more—nestling next to a warm male body that wasn't her son's, feeling sheltered in a pair of strong arms.

"What was your brother like?" she whispered.

His chest stiffened beneath her cheek. "Why do you ask?"

"I'm just curious. It's clear you loved him very much. I mean, you're willing to give up your own life just to avenge him." She paused, a faint smile tugging on her lips. "Was he a thorny, grumpy pain in the ass, too?"

She could practically feel Tate rolling his eyes. "No. He wasn't any of those things."

"Then what was he like?"

It took several seconds before he replied, and when he did, his voice was thick with grief. "An optimist. Will was the eternal optimist. He always looked for the best in people, gave you the benefit of the doubt even when you didn't deserve it. He was a damn good soldier, but he lacked that killer instinct. Don't get me wrong, he was tough as nails, and he could kill without batting an eye just like all the other men on the unit, but he didn't have that ruthlessness that a lot of us Special Forces guys have, and he definitely wasn't jaded, which is something that happens real fast in our line of work."

"So he was a glass-half-full kinda man."

"More like glass-is-overflowing-it's-so-full," Tate said, sounding wistful. "I never understood how he could be so damn happy all the damn time. I used to think it had to be an act, but Christ, it *wasn't*. My brother was actually one of those rare people who was completely happy with every aspect of his life."

Eva smiled in the darkness. "That's what I want for Rafe," she confessed. "I want him to grow up happy and positive. I don't ever want him to have that ruthlessness you just talked about."

Her heart began to weep as she realized it might already be too late. Rafe was only three, and his life was anything but normal. Moving around from place to place, no real family except for her, no friends, no house or picket fence or drooling golden retriever to toss a stick to. And being ambushed by Hector's men in Istanbul had scared him, enough to give him recurring nightmares. How could she ever hope for her son to be happy and positive when all she'd shown him so far was sad and negative?

"Hector needs to die." The lump in her throat was so enormous, she could barely keep talking. She gulped once, twice, blinking back tears. "Rafe won't be able to lead a normal life until that maniac is out of our lives."

Tate's touch was warm and surprisingly protective as he dragged his hand over her bare shoulder. "Cruz won't come after you or your kid again. I'll make sure of it, Eva."

Despite her rapid blinking, two tears slid out from the corners of her eyes and streamed down her cheeks. Before she could stop it, a rush of shame flooded her, and though she quickly tried to tamp it down, she wasn't fast enough. As a result, shivers racked her body and the tears fell a little bit faster.

Tate, of course, didn't miss either reaction. "What's wrong?" he demanded, tightening his grip on her.

"I'm the one who did this to my son." Her voice shook. "I'm the reason he doesn't have a normal life, Tate."

"Eva—"

"You know it's true," she cut in, unable to curb the bitterness that climbed up her throat. "If I hadn't been so caught up in saving the world I wouldn't have supported the ULF. I wouldn't have met Hector. Rafe would have a father who wasn't—" She halted abruptly, a vise of fear squeezing her gut at her slip-up.

"A father who wasn't what?"

"Dead," she finished. "A father who wasn't dead."

For the first time since she'd met Tate, the lie got stuck in her throat like a clump of hair in the drain. Maybe it was because they were naked in bed together. Lies seemed so out of place in such an intimate setting.

"You loved him? Rafe's old man?" Tate sounded oddly annoyed, as if he didn't want to ask but curiosity had gotten the best of him.

She wiped her eyes with the back of her hand, managing a quick nod. "I did. I loved him a lot."

For all of twenty minutes, she failed to add. It was true, though—she *had* loved Hector at the beginning. He'd been larger than life. A true rebel *with* a cause, and it was a cause she'd truly believed in: freeing the people of San Marquez from a government that was oppressing, starving and killing them. But when the ULF's methods had gone from peaceful to violent in the blink of an eye, Eva had realized that the "cause" had never been about saving anyone, only about fattening up Hector's wallet.

But she couldn't say any of this to Tate, not without the risk of revealing details she couldn't afford to reveal.

"Rafe will never know his father," she said sadly. "Hector made sure of that."

"Fathers are overrated," Tate quipped.

Biting her lip, she propped herself up on one elbow and studied his face. "Do you really never plan on having kids?"

"Nope."

"Is it a fear thing? You think you might end up like your dad?"

He chuckled. "You're reading far too much into it. I'm not afraid I'll end up beating my kids—trust me, that'll never frickin' happen. I just don't want to be responsible for another human being. Now that Will is gone, I don't owe anything to anyone. Only myself."

"Must be nice," she murmured, though she was only being half-serious. Truth was, she wouldn't trade Rafe for the world. She'd rather be overburdened with responsibility and have her son in her life than be worry free without him.

"You know what would be nicer?" He rolled her over without warning, his lips hovering over hers. "This."

He kissed her, softly at first, then with more urgency, until she was gasping for air and clinging to his sculpted shoulders. "Tate—"

"No more talking," he said hoarsely. "We already established that we might die tomorrow. Wouldn't we rather spend tonight doing more interesting things than talking?"

He had a point.

With a contented sigh, she closed her eyes and relinquished control, letting Tate bring her to new levels of passion, losing herself in the delicious sensation of him moving inside her, the release that sent her soaring to dazzling heights and reduced her to a hot, boneless mess when it finally receded.

Later, when they were once again sated, Tate pulled her into his arms and tucked her into his bare chest. With his big, warm body spooning her from behind, Eva fell asleep feeling safer than she'd felt in a long, long time.

Tate had just poured himself some coffee the next morning when Eva's voice wafted from the living room. "Tate, get in here. My friend just got back to me."

His shoulders went rigid. Gripping the tin cup, he stalked out of the kitchen. Rather than join Eva on the couch, he loomed over her, his tension levels at an all-time high.

"What did he find?" Tate demanded.

Ignoring him, Eva continued to peer at the computer screen with a look of extreme concentration. As she read, his impatience climbed higher and higher, until he finally put down his cup and crossed his arms over his chest before he gave in to the urge and snatched the laptop from her hands.

"Okay, this isn't much," she announced. "He couldn't find any record of that last mission, and all the files on you and the members of your unit have officially been locked. Only the highest security clearance can access them, and he didn't want to trigger any red flags by trying to infiltrate those restricted areas."

Tate fought a burst of disappointment. Granted, he hadn't expected some computer hacker to be able to solve this mystery in twenty-four hours when he himself hadn't learned diddly-squat in eight months, but he couldn't deny that Eva's confidence had gotten some of his hopes up.

"Oh, well. You tried," he said with a shrug, as he handed her back the laptop.

Her teeth dug into her bottom lip for a moment, while her gaze scanned the screen. "He found quite a lot of background information on that doctor, though. You said his name was Richard Harrison, right?"

Tate furrowed his brows. "Yeah."

"Is this him?" She angled the laptop so he could see the screen.

Squatting down, he studied the photograph and gave a brisk nod. The salt-and-pepper hair, ruddy cheeks and deep brackets around a thin mouth definitely belonged to Dr.

Harrison. The man looked the same as Tate remembered, minus the bullet between the eyes, of course.

Eva turned the laptop back, her sharp blue eyes narrowing the more she read. "Huh. That's weird."

Tate's instincts kicked into gear. "What's weird?"

"What do you know about Dr. Harrison?"

He searched his brain, trying to remember the details he'd been provided eight months ago. "Harrison worked for a medical research lab. I was told he was involved in developing vaccines and he came here to test the water in the towns and villages that were affected by that cholera outbreak a few years back."

Eva nodded absently. "Right, I remember that. Hurricane Isabella did a number on the water systems. More than a hundred thousand people died during that outbreak."

"Well, apparently Harrison was collecting samples—I guess he was trying to develop a more effective vaccination for cholera. He was working out of a small field hospital in Corazón to do his research. I think he brought a couple of assistants with him."

"Okay. But…" She drifted off, her tone distracted.

"But what?"

She wrinkled her forehead. "But Harrison didn't develop vaccinations. According to this, he was the department head for the lab's biological development unit."

Tate stiffened. "What?"

"It says so right in the file. Harrison worked for D&M Initiative, one of the biggest private research labs in the country. The world, actually. They work closely with the government, the WHO, CDC, pretty much all the big players in the health sphere. Like I said, Harrison's specialty was biological development."

Alarm bells went off in his head. "What the hell does that mean?"

"I'm guessing it's a euphemism for biological weapons," she said with a wry look. "The U.S. supposedly shut down its biological weapons program a long time ago, but the government still provides funding for medical defense. Private labs and government agencies are continually conducting research on how to defend against potential bio attacks." She shrugged. "Call me a cynic, but personally I think our government focuses on more than just defense. I think offensive programs are still going on, whether the White House admits it or not."

"Wouldn't surprise me," he agreed.

Eva turned back to the screen and bit her lip again, a gesture he was beginning to associate with puzzlement. "There's absolutely nothing here about Harrison being sent to San Marquez in relation to the cholera outbreak." Her breath hitched. "Wait a minute. It says he was there to coordinate with his lab's field researchers about something called Project Aries."

"Project Aries? What's that?"

"I have no idea. My friend couldn't gain access to the project file. He made a note saying it was *beyond classified.*" She scrolled down. "Yeah, apparently none of the databases would let him in. The firewalls were insane, which means someone really doesn't want unauthorized eyes seeing that file."

"So Harrison was in Corazón conducting some top secret project that had nothing to do with vaccination shots," Tate said slowly.

"That's what it looks like."

Frustration jammed in his throat. "That doesn't shed light on anything, Eva. In the end, Harrison was still taken hostage by Cruz and his men, who killed him before we could extract him. None of that explains why my unit was hunted down."

"I stand by my original suggestion—you must have seen something in the village."

Stifling a groan, Tate resisted the impulse to slam his fist into the nearest wall. He'd gone over the events of that op a thousand times already, and nothing, *nothing,* stood out as not ordinary. Dead doctor, dead villagers, rebels swarming the area, Will's throat slashed. That was all there was to it. Except evidently it wasn't that cut-and-dried.

So what the *hell* was he missing?

Eva must have picked up on his turbulent state of mind because she stood up and approached him. Her sweet, feminine scent floated toward him and his pulse immediately kicked up a notch.

At five-six, she wasn't a tiny thing, but she still had to tilt her head to look up at him, and when her blue eyes locked with his, he was reminded of the way those eyes had shone with passion last night.

The sex had been good. Really frickin' good. In fact, he'd been having trouble getting it off his mind all morning. And earlier, when he'd opened his eyes and found Eva's lush body curled into his, he'd nearly caved in and given her a wake-up call she would never have forgotten.

Instead, he'd quietly sneaked out of bed, knowing that what happened last night needed to remain a onetime occurrence. Sex had no place on this mission. Besides, with Ben accompanying them on this final leg of the journey, there wouldn't be many opportunities to get naked anyway.

And Tate was just fine with that, because as mind-blowing as it had been, he couldn't do it again. Sex was one thing, but cuddling the way they'd done last night? Totally uncool. He didn't want Eva getting any ideas about them—mainly, that they could have any sort of future, which was an absolute impossibility.

"Where did you find Harrison's body?" she asked, her

businesslike tone revealing she was oblivious to where his thoughts had drifted.

Tate forced himself to focus on the more pressing matters. "In the makeshift clinic in the village. The whole building was engulfed in flames, but the fire hadn't reached the office yet. Harrison was sitting behind the desk with a bullet in his head."

She grimaced. "Okay. Well, was there anything unusual about the office? Papers in disarray? Weird medical vials or something else that stood out to you?"

"There was a lot of smoke, so I can't be sure, but nothing stood out. The only thing that looked out of order to me was the dead man at the desk."

"And outside? What did you see outside?"

"Not much," he admitted. "The smoke was thick as hell. And the smell—" a cold shiver ran up his spine "—the smell made your eyes water as much as the smoke did. Have you ever smelled burned flesh, Eva?"

Her face paled. "No."

He swallowed. "It's not an odor you're likely to forget."

She faltered for a moment, as if trying to absorb that. "So Hector's men killed the villagers and burned the bodies and the buildings to the ground. Was there anything about the bodies that seemed suspicious?"

His frustration returned, eating a hole in his gut. "All I saw was charred corpses."

"Okay. What about…" She hesitated. "What about your brother's death? How did that happen?"

Pain jolted through him. "Cruz wasn't expecting to be ambushed by my unit. There was a lot of gunfire, rebels coming after us, flames everywhere. In the chaos, Cruz managed to escape into the brush. Will went after him."

"And you found Will's body later," she finished softly.

His heart constricted. "No. Will was alive when I found

him. Cruz took my brother hostage. He told me to lay down my weapon, and that if I let him go, he'd release Will."

"You believed him?"

"Pretty frickin' foolish of me, huh?" Sarcasm dripped from his tone.

"Tate—"

"Yes, Eva, foolish, moronic me put down my gun—and Cruz sliced Will's throat anyway."

She gasped.

Anger bubbled in his blood. "And instead of going after Cruz, I tried to help Will. I thought there might actually be a chance I could save him, but I couldn't, and so there you go. Another act of foolishness and Cruz got away."

"Trying to save your brother wasn't foolish," she said firmly. "You made the right choice."

"If you say so," he said dully.

Eva cupped his chin with her delicate hands, her grip surprisingly strong. "I do say so. You chose to help your brother rather than go after Hector. That *was* the right decision, and if you hadn't done it, and there was a chance that Will could've been saved? You would have never forgiven yourself."

"I don't forgive myself now." His voice came out harsher than he intended. The confession was unintended, too.

Christ, what was he doing, opening himself up to this woman?

Sure enough, his rough admission made those big blue eyes soften. She stroked the stubble coating his jaw, and though her touch was meant to be gentle and reassuring, it sent a bolt of heat right down to his groin and stirred his cock.

Gritting his teeth against the onslaught of desire, Tate stepped out of her touch, trying to steer his thoughts back to safe territory. But there was nothing safe about any of this, especially when the front door of the cabin suddenly flew open and Ben burst into the room as though his ass was on fire.

"They're on their way," Ben boomed at them. "You need to go. Now."

Chapter 12

Everything happened so fast Eva had no time to react. One minute she and Tate were talking in the living room, the next, Ben was flying through the door with a hard expression and tense demands.

"Get your pack," Tate barked at her when he noticed she was still rooted in place.

Snapping out of her bewilderment, she sprinted toward the bedroom where she'd left her backpack. She jammed yesterday's clothes into the bag and grabbed the handgun she'd left on the pile of books by the table beneath the window. She idled only long enough to pull her hair into a tight ponytail and shove the gun in her waistband, then hurried back to the main room, where she found Ben zipping up a duffel and Tate shoving a clip into his rifle.

"Who exactly is on their way here?" she demanded when neither man so much as glanced her way.

Tate checked his extra magazines before shoving them

in his pack. "Military. They were asking about us around town."

She swore. "How did they know we were here?"

Slinging his rifle over one shoulder, and the strap of his backpack over the other, Tate shot her a hard look. "Someone must have tipped them off."

The implication hit her hard. "You think it was *me?*"

"You were on the computer all morning..." He let the remark hang.

Indignation ripped through her. "Yeah, helping *you!* I didn't tell anyone where we were, Tate."

Even though they'd already determined that sex had nothing to do with trust, his lack of faith in her was still upsetting. And yet it wasn't surprising in the slightest.

What *did* surprise her were his next words.

"I believe you."

"You do?" she said warily.

He shrugged. "You've got nothing to gain by tipping off the military. Not when we're this close to getting Cruz."

It wasn't a declaration of trust, but she'd take it. "So then how did they find us?" she asked again.

"It's not improbable that they tracked us down. The unit in the jungle was tracking us for a while before they attacked—they must have reported our general movements to whoever they were checking in with, and you've got to assume reinforcements were dispatched after that unit went AWOL."

"So someone else picked up our trail?" she said, feeling queasy as she followed Tate to the door. "And tracked us here?"

"I wasn't making much of an effort to cover our tracks. Besides, it's common sense we'd end up here. Valero is the first town you hit once you reach the end of the river."

"And I'm the only American living in these parts," Ben

added in a grim voice. "If Tate was turning to anyone for help, it'd be me, and these men know that."

All talk ended, leaving Eva to panic in silence as she followed the men out the door. Outside, Tate shouldered the duffel bag Ben had brought back from town, the contents of which had yet to be divulged to her.

Ben tossed Tate a set of keys before stepping up to bestow his buddy with one of those macho-man side hugs. "ATV's stashed beyond those trees. You remember the coordinates I gave you?"

Tate nodded. "We'll see you there in two hours."

Eva swiveled her head to Ben. "You're not coming with us?"

"We'll rendezvous later. I've gotta deal with the soldiers."

She felt even queasier. "Deal with them how?"

The big African-American smiled, his white teeth gleaming in the morning sunlight. "I'm not gonna off them, if that's what you're afraid of. Don't worry, baby-cakes, I'll just send them on their merry way—and far away from you and Robert."

Relief trickled through her. "Okay." On impulse, she bounded over to Ben and threw her arms around him in a tight hug. "Be safe, okay?"

Surprise and unease flickered in his brown eyes, but after a moment of stiffness, he returned the embrace. "You, too, Eva."

Five minutes later, she and Tate were on an ATV, bouncing through the woods and putting miles behind them and Ben's cabin.

Though not as noisy and treacherous as the jungle, the mountainous terrain offered its fair share of obstacles. Thick brush, rotting logs and grand trees limited their path options, and the bugs were as plentiful and relentless as in the jungle, slapping Eva's face and hissing by her ears as Tate kept a solid foot on the gas and sped them to safety.

Each bump in the trail sent a throb of pain to her bandaged arm, and she readjusted her grip around Tate's waist, pressing her face between his shoulder blades and holding on tight. As they cut a path through the brush, the duffel bag he'd strapped to the back of the ATV kept jostling her knee. She wondered what was in it. Something important obviously, seeing as it had taken Ben all night to "procure" it.

At the thought of Ben, another tremor of panic skittered up her spine. "Do you think he'll be okay?" She shouted over the wind so Tate could hear her.

He didn't respond, but she felt his back stiffen against her breasts. He would probably never say it out loud, but she knew he hadn't liked leaving his friend behind to deal with the impending arrival of those soldiers.

She didn't doubt that Ben Hastings could handle himself—*look* at the guy, for Pete's sake—but she also couldn't help but remember the way that last military unit had pounced on them in the jungle. No hesitation, no attempt at civilized talk; those soldiers had been sent to kill Tate, and most likely her, too. What if the men who arrived to question Ben were of that same mentality?

She said a quick prayer for Ben's safety, knowing there was no point in worrying. At least not until they reached those coordinates. The two men must have arranged the meeting place when she'd been gathering her gear.

Nearly an hour later, Tate finally slowed the ATV, and Eva lifted her head to examine their surroundings. They were still amid the forested landscape, sheltered by a canopy of green, but the path was nearly impassable now. They'd been deeper inland before, but now they hugged the edge of the mountain, traveling alongside a steep, rocky slope where the foliage was sparser. Soon the ATV wouldn't be able to fit on any trail, and she wasn't surprised when Tate killed the ignition and told her to hop off.

"What'll we do with the ATV?" she asked as he unloaded their packs and Ben's duffel. "We can't just leave it on the side of the mountain."

"We won't." He swept his gaze around, squinting in the bright sun. After a moment, he cursed, dug his aviator sunglasses from his backpack and shoved them on the bridge of his nose. "Okay, check the GPS while I stash the ATV."

He rattled off the coordinates, which Eva had to memorize quickly because he only recited them once, and then he was gone, reversing the vehicle the way they'd come and disappearing into the brush.

She rummaged in Tate's pack until she found the portable GPS device she'd seen him use when they'd been in the jungle. She typed in the longitude and latitude he'd given her, and a moment later, the location appeared in the form of a red dot on the small digital screen. The green dot was their current location, and she gave a pleased nod at how close the two dots were to one another.

"We're two miles away," she told Tate when he reemerged from the brush ten minutes later.

He took the GPS, studied the display and offered a nod of his own. "Good. Let's book it, then. Won't take long to get there."

Eva fell in line behind him, not voicing a single protest about the two-mile walk. It was blistering hot out, but she wasn't going to complain about that, either, not when they were so close to Hector she could practically taste the freedom.

With the rugged terrain, it took them twenty-five minutes at a steady walk to reach the coordinates. At first sight, there was nothing special about the area, just a bunch of boulders and grass, hilly slopes marked by thorny shrubs and colorful wildflowers, but Tate seemed pleased with what he saw.

It wasn't until he pointed it out that Eva discerned the mouth of the cave hidden on a rocky incline ten yards away.

Taking out his pistol, Tate took a step toward the slope, glancing at her over his shoulder. "Wait here. Let me check it out."

She nodded, busying herself by sipping from her canteen while Tate ascended the hill to investigate. A few moments later, he let out a sharp whistle, which she took as her cue to join him.

Pebbles and twigs crunched beneath her hiking boots as she climbed up to the cave. Tate appeared at the top of the hill and extended his hand to help her up, and the moment their fingers touched, warmth seeped into her hand and spread in every direction.

Her heart skipped a beat when his mossy-green eyes landed on her mouth. She knew he was contemplating kissing her, and she nearly opened her mouth to blurt out the words *do it.* But at the last second, she bit back the demand. A good thing, too, because Tate's gaze abruptly shifted and his hand dropped from hers.

Message received.

Didn't mean she wasn't disappointed, though. In fact, disappointment had pretty much been her mood of the day, ever since she'd woken up to find Tate sneaking out of the room without so much as a good-morning kiss.

But what had she really expected? That one night of sex would lead to something long lasting? That they now shared a deep, meaningful connection? Of course it wouldn't, and of course they didn't. They'd given in to their carnal urges, enjoyed each other's bodies, and now it was business as usual: two people with a common goal, zero mutual trust and no future.

The cave's entrance was only four feet high or so, and Tate had to duck in order to walk inside. Eva trailed after him, cautious as she stepped into the shadows. Rays of sunlight sliced into the mouth of the cave, casting a weak glow over the rocky walls and dirt floor.

Fortunately, it didn't look as though they were sharing the space with any other living creatures, though the musky scent of dung in the air increased her wariness.

"Mountain lion," Tate supplied. "But the droppings are old. Ditto on the tracks, so you don't need to worry about any surprise visitors. We won't be here long, anyway."

The reminder made her glance at her watch, which showed that an hour and a half had passed since they'd left the cabin. Ben would be here soon, and then they'd need to be on the move again. And fast, depending on what happened with those soldiers back there.

"Are you hungry?" Tate asked, bending down to unzip his pack.

"Not really." They'd split a loaf of bread and a brick of soft Brie for breakfast, and though several hours had passed since, the excitement of the past couple hours had stolen any appetite she might have had.

Tate pulled out a package of beef jerky, tore off a strip and popped it in his mouth. He slid down the cave wall and sat on the ground, stretching his long muscular legs in front of him.

After a beat, she sat on the wall across from him and searched his face through the shadows. "Ben will be okay, right?" she said, trying to ignore the wave of anxiety that refused to subside.

His expression revealed nothing, but he sounded confident as he replied, "Ben can take care of himself."

"But what do you think the soldiers will do to him?"

"They'll ask a bunch of questions, maybe hurl out some threats." Tate shrugged. "They want me, not Ben, and once they confirm that I'm not at the cabin, they'll move on."

A cloud of annoyance and frustration swirled through her. "Doesn't it drive you crazy, not knowing why people are after you?"

"Yep."

"Can't you just…I don't know, call your former commander and demand an explanation?"

"You think I didn't already do that?" he answered dryly. "Once the third member of my unit was found dead—a mugging gone awry, of course—I put two and two together and started to see the pattern. I called my former CO with my concerns, which he brushed off."

"So you think he's in on it?"

"He's gotta be. I contacted him again after Berk died— Stephen Berkowski, a damn good soldier, the fifth and final one to die. My CO told me to quit asking questions and accused me of being paranoid. A few days later, someone nearly blew my head off on the street. So yeah, I think Commander Hahn is absolutely aware of what's happening and why."

Eva frowned, feeling angry on Tate's behalf. "Have you considered kidnapping this Hahn and torturing him until he tells you what the heck is going on?"

Tate laughed. "I'd considered it, yes, but Nick and Seb talked me out of it."

At the mention of Tate's men, a pang of longing tugged at her heart, and the image of her little boy's blue eyes and mischievous grin flashed across her brain.

"When can we call Nick again?" she asked. "I haven't spoken to my son in two days."

"Nick would've contacted us if anything was wrong."

"I know that, but I still want to hear Rafe's voice and tell him that his mother loves him." Her lips tightened. "Is that too much to ask?"

Tate arched his brows. "I didn't force you to leave your son behind, Eva. Going after Cruz was your idea, remember?"

Her shoulder sagged. "I know. I'm sorry. I just miss my son, that's all." Before she could stop them, tears pricked her eyes. "He's all I have, Tate. For the past three years, he's been the only constant in my life. I can't see my parents, my family, my friends." A laugh popped out. "I'm twenty-five years old, and my only friend and confidant is a three-year-old boy. How sad is that?"

"You're still young," he said roughly. "You've got a lot of time, Eva. Once you get Cruz off your back, you can start over. You'll have your family and friends back in your life, and you'll make new friends, fall in love, you know, all that stuff normal people do."

His last comment brought a smile to her lips. "Let me guess, you don't consider yourself one of those normal people, do you?"

"Me? Normal?" He shot her a self-deprecating grin. "Baby, I'm thirty-four years old, on the run from my own government, living in a fortress in Mexico and trekking across this godforsaken country to murder a man. Tell me, is that normal?"

Despite the dismal facts he'd recited, she had to giggle. "Definitely not."

They both fell silent after that and Eva used the time to mull over everything Tate had said, coming to the conclusion that it probably *was* for the best if they didn't sleep together again. His life was even more complicated than hers, and he was right—*nothing* was normal about his situation.

But for her, normalcy was almost within her grasp. Once

Hector was gone, Rafe would be safe. She would be safe. And the two of them could start over, just like Tate said.

The longer the silence dragged on, the sleepier Eva became. The darkness of the cave made her eyelids droop and her limbs loosen, and she must have fallen asleep, because the next thing she knew, someone was shaking her shoulders.

Blinking in disorientation, her eyes focused to find Tate bending over her, a grave look on his handsome face.

"Did I fall asleep?" she mumbled, sitting up straighter and rubbing her eyes. "Is something wrong?"

"Yes, and I don't know." His voice sounded grim. "I'm heading back to the cabin."

His announcement snapped her into a state of full alertness. "What? Why?"

"Because Ben still hasn't shown up. It's an hour past the time we were supposed to meet."

"Maybe he's just late," she said feebly.

"Maybe." Tate rose to his full height, and his head was inches from bumping the ceiling. "I want you to stay here while I find out what the holdup is."

She hopped to her feet, panicked. "You're leaving me?"

"Only for an hour or two. I'm going to do some recon on the cabin and see what's up."

"Then I'm coming with you."

"No." His tone brooked no argument. "You're staying here. You'll only slow me down."

Indignation hardened her jaw. "Have I slowed you down so far?"

He ignored the question. "You're not coming." He abruptly turned away from her and grabbed his rifle. "I'm leaving the packs and duffel here. If you get hungry, there's a ton of MREs in my pack. Beef teriyaki or veggie bean-and-rice burritos—take your pick. But don't start a fire."

Eva knew there was no protesting or changing his mind. He was a man on a mission—his broad shoulders set high, his jaw tight, green eyes gleaming with fortitude. Yet beneath the commanding demeanor, she sensed something else. Desperation? Fear? She couldn't put her finger on it, but she knew without a doubt that Tate was not as calm and composed as he was acting.

He was worried about his friend, and frankly, as she glanced at her watch and noted the time, she was getting pretty worried, too. She hadn't known Ben for very long, but she liked the man, and he wouldn't even be involved in any of this in the first place if it weren't for her.

As she watched Tate go, she bit her lip and prayed that Ben was all right.

Because if he wasn't, she knew Tate would hold her responsible for it.

Hell, she'd hold *herself* responsible.

Death was in the air.

Tate couldn't explain it, but the moment he neared the woods behind the cabin, his heart sank to the pit of his stomach like a cement block and he knew he was too late.

Maybe it was the silence—the forest was too damn quiet for his liking—or it could be the coppery scent in the breeze, though he suspected he wasn't actually smelling blood.

Just anticipating it.

Keeping a solid grip on his rifle, he positioned himself at the edge of the rocky slope that would provide him with a better view of the cabin. The rear of the structure looked innocuous. No soldiers, no Ben, no sign of foul play, yet Tate's instincts continued to buzz, persistent and ominous.

Moving soundlessly, he crept through the trees and headed for the front of the cabin. His breathing was steady, his pulse regular—neither of those vitals changed, not even when the gruesome sight assaulted his vision.

But a part of him died. Right there, on the spot.

"Goddamn it, Ben," he mumbled, as hot agony streaked up his throat to choke him.

Ben's body was sprawled on the bottom steps of the porch, one lifeless arm flung out, stiff fingers still wrapped around a 9 mm that he probably hadn't even had a chance to use. Blood from the bullet hole in Ben's forehead continued to drip onto the dirt, forming a crimson puddle that made Tate see red. Literally and figuratively.

But he wasn't surprised. Oh, no. There had only been one possible explanation for Ben being a no-show at the rendezvous point. But hell, those soldiers hadn't even given him a chance. They must have stalked up to the cabin and shot him point-blank. Had they even asked him about Tate's whereabouts before they blew his brains out?

A fire of rage scorched a path through his veins. His gaze stayed glued to his friend's dead body. Damn it. God-frickin-*damn* it. He'd known Ben since they were eighteen years old, for Chrissake. Other than Will, Ben was the only person Tate had trusted implicitly and without question, and now he was gone. All because Tate had involved him in this foolish quest to kill Hector Cruz.

He wanted to go to his friend. Give him a proper burial, touch his hand, try to express how much Ben had meant to him all these years. But he couldn't. His gut told him the soldiers who'd killed Ben were long gone, but from his vantage point, he couldn't get a good look at the cabin's windows. For all he knew, those bastards were lying in wait inside, hoping Tate would walk right into an ambush like some kind of novice.

Ben will understand.

Right. Ben would understand that his only friend had

no choice but to leave his dead body lying there to rot in the sun.

Fury skyrocketed through him.

"No," he said through clenched teeth. "No frickin' way."

He couldn't just leave his buddy there, couldn't let him become food for scavengers. If an ambush awaited him, then so be it. He refused to disrespect Ben, not after everything the man had done for him.

Raising his rifle, Tate emerged from the brush, hyperaware that he was out in the open and that any amateur with a sniper rifle could pick him off. To his relief, no bullets plowed him down as he made his way toward his friend's body.

He was ten yards away when he noticed another pool of blood on the dirt, and a wave of satisfaction swelled in his gut. Ben *had* managed to fire a shot before he'd died. The size of the puddle hinted that the recipient of Ben's bullet had lost a decent amount of blood. Good.

Tire tracks also streaked the dirt, which told him that the soldiers had come and gone in a military-issued jeep. It was a reassuring sign—perhaps nobody was waiting for him in the cabin after all.

When he neared his fallen comrade, he found himself unable to keep it together. His pulse suddenly went off-kilter, his throat tightened to the point of suffocation, and it felt as if someone was pinching his chest with rusty pliers.

Ben's dark brown eyes were open. Expressionless, and yet Tate could swear his friend was glaring at him in accusation.

The only way to get through the next ten minutes was to shut down. Mentally. Emotionally. Moving on autopilot, he carefully dragged Ben's massive body around the side of the cabin, toward the edge of the woods where the dirt wasn't as compact.

He didn't breathe, barely blinked, just located the shovel from the tin shed behind the house and dug a grave for his friend as if it were something he did every day. The whole process took an hour. One hour for four feet of earth to dislodge from the ground, for Ben's body to slide into that hole, for that dirt to cover it, for Tate to construct a cross from two branches.

One last thing before he could walk away. He dug a hand in his pocket and fished out the silver chain he'd removed from Ben's beefy neck. Dog tags, remnants of Ben's army days.

Looping the tags around the makeshift cross, Tate stared at the grave for several long moments before finally wrenching his gaze away.

His friend was dead. Another casualty of the war he'd found himself fighting. A war he didn't even know *why* he was fighting.

But he knew one thing, and that was that Ben Hastings was not going to die in vain.

The San Marquez military was clearly in cahoots with the United States in tracking Tate and his men down, but a bunch of soldier grunts weren't calling the shots. Someone with more clout, someone of importance, was giving the orders. That someone had ordered the unit in the jungle to shoot first and ask questions later, and now they'd done the same thing again with Ben.

Well, Tate was going to track that someone down, and when he did, maybe he'd take a page out of these bastards' book and do the exact same thing.

Don't ask questions.

Just shoot to kill.

Chapter 13

Eva was waiting outside for him when Tate strode back to the cave hours later. He'd taken his time walking back because he'd wanted to avoid the questions Eva would surely have, and he'd needed to say goodbye to his friend in private.

Ironically, the weather had decided to match his mood. It was only four in the afternoon, but the sky had turned gray sometime during the walk from the cabin to the cave. Black thunderclouds loomed overhead. The temperature had grown cooler, and the wind picked up, rustling the tails of his olive-green long-sleeved shirt.

"Hey," Eva called tentatively when he ascended the slope.

"Hey," he said, keeping his tone neutral.

After almost a week with Eva, he'd learned that she was too damn caring for her own good, and he had no doubt that she would shed tears for Ben, despite the fact that she'd hardly known him at all. A part of him was tempted to withhold Ben's death from her just to avoid an emotional situation, but not telling her wasn't even an option, because she took one look at his face and seemed to know exactly what happened.

And sure enough, tears filled her eyes.

"Oh. Oh, God, Tate. Is he dead?"

He swallowed.

"Is he?" she said, her voice wobbling.

After a second, he finally nodded. "Shot to death. I…I buried him."

His voice wobbled, too, and the evidence of his shaken composure annoyed the hell out of him. He didn't want this woman to know how much Ben's death had torn him apart. Keeping his emotions hidden was a skill he'd mastered at a young age; it had been the only way to gain the upper hand with his old man. His father could smell weakness and vulnerability from miles away, and if Tate revealed either shortcoming, the beatings would be substantially worse. Needless to say, he'd quickly learned to bury his emotions.

He didn't like giving Eva a glimpse of what lay beyond the composed, indifferent mask he usually wore, and when she did precisely what he'd expected and stared at him with those big, sympathetic eyes, tears clinging to her sooty lashes, anger replaced his irritation.

"Why are you crying?" he muttered. "You didn't even know him, for Chrissake."

Two strands of tears slid down her cheeks, and she reached up to wipe them away with her sleeve, shooting him a scowl as she responded with, "Are you seriously telling me I'm not allowed to cry for him? Because too bad. I *liked* Ben, and his death saddens me, so if I want to cry about it, I damn well will. And FYI, he's not the only one I'm crying for."

Tate frowned.

"That's right, I'm crying for *you,* too. You lost your friend, Tate. It must be tearing you apart, but we both know you're not going to admit it. You'll just pretend it's no big deal. You know, because you're a big, tough military man who doesn't let his emotions get the best of him."

"Save your tears," he snapped. "I don't need you or anyone else crying on my behalf, sweetheart."

No sooner than the words left his mouth than the sky cracked with thunder and the clouds released sheets of rain that fell so hard they nearly knocked him over. The downpour was so violent he and Eva were drenched in a matter of seconds.

Cursing, he grabbed her arm and herded her into the cave, where total darkness enveloped them. He couldn't see a thing, but he sure as hell felt it when Eva pressed her lips to his.

Although he'd promised himself he wouldn't sleep with Eva again, Tate couldn't resist parting his lips to grant her tongue access to his mouth. Here in the dark, he didn't have to see the compassion in her eyes, or risk her seeing the absolute agony in his, and he knew the kiss was Eva's way of offering comfort.

"Make love to me again." Her voice came out throaty, her breath warm against his lips.

Groaning, Tate ran his hands down the sleeves of her wet shirt before peeling the garment off her slender shoulders and tossing it aside. He couldn't have stopped this even if he'd tried. He was too pissed off right now, too wrecked and too broken to care about anything other than getting Eva naked and losing himself in the pleasure she had to offer.

After their damp clothing was tossed aside, he yanked her against him, and naked flesh met naked flesh. He was mindful of her injured arm, but it didn't seem to be bothering her because she raised both arms and tightly twined them around his neck, forcing his head down for another kiss.

There was something desperate about the entire encounter. He found that his hands were shaking as he roamed her endless supply of curves, squeezing her perfect breasts, skimming his fingers over her hips, cupping her firm bottom.

Each breath came out ragged, each beat of his heart sending a jolt of pain through his body. He couldn't stop thinking about Ben's empty eyes. Ben's lifeless body.

Damn it. He'd gotten Ben killed by involving him in this mess. How many more people had to die because of him before he learned his damn lesson?

"Don't think about it."

Eva's soft voice cut into his dark thoughts. Her hands gripped his jaw, forcing him to look at her. Her face was cloaked in shadows, but he saw the intensity in those blue eyes, the firm set of her sexy lips.

"Put the pain away," she whispered, dragging her thumb along the line of his jaw. "Let me help you forget, at least for a little bit."

As his shoulders sagged in defeat, Tate allowed her to guide him into the cave wall. Cold stone chilled his bare back, but the rest of his body was on fire, the flames growing stronger as Eva sank to her knees in front of him and took his erection in her hands.

Somehow he managed to do what she'd asked. He put the pain away. Cleared his mind of the unwanted images and incensed thoughts. Closed his eyes. Tangled one hand in Eva's silky hair.

At the first brush of her lips over his cock, a moan slipped out of his mouth. His hips thrust of their own volition, seeking Eva, seeking relief. She didn't hesitate. She took him in the warm, wet recess of her mouth and sucked him so delicately that shivers skated up his spine.

A part of him felt unworthy of the worship she bestowed him with. She teased him with her fingers and lips and tongue, until the pressure in his groin was too much to bear.

"I'm too close," he murmured, stilling her loving movements by cradling her head. "Come up here."

She rose without a word, her arms coming up to loop around his neck, her head tilting and lips parting in anticipation of his kiss. Taking possession of her mouth, he kissed her roughly, that thread of desperation once again coiling inside him, threatening to snap at any moment.

He left her only to grab a condom from the kit in his pack, and then he was sheathed and ready and lifting her up. She wrapped her legs around him as he took her right there, standing up against the wall. They both groaned at that first upward thrust.

Pressure built in his groin, in his throat, his heart, and he couldn't have controlled his rough, hurried thrusts even if he'd tried. He wanted her too badly, needed this too greatly, and so he closed his eyes and lost himself in Eva. Each stroke sent him careening closer to the edge, and he slammed into her, over and over again, latching his mouth to her neck and sucking on her hot flesh as his body drove them straight to paradise.

When he felt her inner muscles clamp over him and heard her cry out in release, he let himself go. The climax shook through his body with the force of a hurricane. His heart thundered and his knees almost buckled, and as he struggled to catch his breath, he was vaguely aware of something wet tickling his shoulder.

Breathing hard, he glanced down to see Eva's eyes sparkling with tears. She was crying again, but before he could question her, she let out a shaky breath and said, "Don't tell me I can't cry for you. Because I can."

He didn't argue. Instead, he just stood there, still lodged deep inside her warmth, holding her tightly against him as she cried the tears that he couldn't.

Three hours later, the rain hadn't let up. If anything, it only got worse, the wind increasing in velocity and gusting into the opening of the cave, bringing a chill into the dank, shadowy space. Eva snuggled closer to Tate, who was lying on his back with one arm wrapped around her. They'd gotten dressed after the intense encounter against the wall, but rather than putting distance between them once their clothes were back on, Tate had surprised her by creating a makeshift bed for them on the cold ground and pulling her down beside him.

They lay under a thermal blanket, but even without it, she would have been toasty warm. Tate's body was like a furnace, radiating heat even while a torrential storm raged outside the cave.

"I didn't think tropical storms reached this far inland," she mused in the darkness, listening to the shriek of the wind.

"Me, either." He jostled her by giving his trademark shrug. "But hopefully it'll stop raining soon so we can get moving."

Uneasiness crawled up her throat like a colony of ants. "Tonight? You want to leave tonight?"

"I want this over as soon as possible," he replied in a flat tone. "The faster I slit that bastard's throat, the faster I get back to my men, and you get back to your son."

His brutal words painted a grisly picture, but Eva didn't begrudge him his bloodlust. Hector had brutally murdered Tate's brother, after all. And the more she got to know Tate, the more she realized he wasn't the indifferent, ruthless warrior he made himself out to be. He cared about people a whole lot more than he let on. The ravaged look in his eyes when he'd come back from burying Ben had said more than Tate's gruff words ever could.

He'd lost a friend tonight. He'd lost a brother. He'd lost his team.

And all that loss ate him up inside, no matter how much he pretended it didn't.

"You really just want to be alone?" she heard herself asking. "You want to live your life without letting a single person in?"

He stayed quiet, and she could feel the discomfort rolling off him in waves. "Why does it bother you so much?" he finally muttered. "There are worse things than solitude, Eva."

"I know. It's just…don't you ever get tired of your own company? Don't you feel the need to get close to someone else?"

"Getting close always ends in one thing—misery." A tiny note of bitterness hung on his words. "One day you'll learn that the only person you can trust is yourself, sweetheart."

"So you didn't trust your brother?" she challenged.

"I trusted Will as much as I could. But one hundred percent pure, blind trust? Nobody will ever get that from me."

"That's sad."

His harsh laughter echoed in the darkness. "You want sad? I trusted the woman who gave birth to me to take care of me, and she chose to take care of herself instead, by pumping poison into her veins. I trusted the man who sired me to step in and fix things, and he decided to use me as a punching bag instead. I trusted my government to protect me, and now I'm being hunted like a dog." His ragged breathing heated her forehead. "How's that for sad, baby?"

Her heart wept for him. "Tate—"

"No pity, Eva. No sympathy, no reassurances. I've accepted the cold hard reality of it—you get close, you get betrayed. That's the running motif of my life, and that's why I'm not just okay with being alone, I *embrace* it."

"I guess I understand that," she conceded. "But me? I don't think I'd want to be alone."

He chuckled. "One thing I've discovered over the years is that not a lot of people can stand their own company. In fact, they're so uncomfortable with themselves and out of touch with who they are that they surround themselves with other people in order to define themselves."

"Oh, I know who I am, and trust me, I'm fine with it. I can be alone if I need to be, but like I said, I wouldn't *want* to. I like having someone else to talk to, someone to share my thoughts and feelings with." Her throat closed up. "I've been lonely the past three years. Do you ever get lonely, Tate?"

To her surprise, he caressed her shoulder, his rough-skinned fingers tickling her skin. "Yeah," he admitted. "I do."

"What's your coping strategy? How do you cheer up when you feel lonely?"

"I remind myself of all the crap that's happened in my life. I remind myself why I chose to be alone."

"That's…depressing."

He hesitated. "What do *you* do?"

"I think of my son. Everything I've done these past three years, all the new houses and new names and new places— they were all to protect Rafe. So it doesn't matter if I feel happy and fulfilled, all that matters is that Rafe is, and it doesn't matter if I'm sad or lonely, as long as he *isn't*. That little boy is my entire life. He's the only thing that matters."

Tate fell silent again. She felt his heart beating beneath

her ear, a steady, comforting rhythm that brought a sense of peace she hadn't felt in years. Tate might be rough around the edges, cold at times, arrogant at others, but she couldn't deny that he made her feel protected. She'd actually managed to get some real, satisfying sleep since she'd teamed up with him. She could close her eyes and let her guard down because she knew that Tate would keep her safe, and the realization brought prickles of discomfort to her skin.

She trusted him. Somehow, during this past week, she'd come to trust Tate.

"Let's get some shut-eye." His raspy voice broke through her disconcerting thoughts. "I want to head out the moment the rain stops."

"Okay," she murmured, snuggling closer.

But she was still thinking about what it all meant—trusting Tate—as she drifted off to sleep.

When two days passed and the storm showed no indications of abating, Tate was beginning to think he and Eva would never be on the move again. Outside, the slope had turned into an ocean of mud, making it difficult to leave the cave without the risk of being carried away by a mudslide. He and Eva only ventured out to use nature's bathroom, and each time they did, the rain and wind nearly knocked them off their feet.

Fortunately, they had plenty of food in the form of the MREs, beef jerky, crackers and bottled water Tate had shoved into Ben's duffel before they'd left the cabin. They couldn't start a fire because the cave didn't offer much in terms of a chimney, but they had a blanket, and they could share body heat—which they did. A lot. With nothing to do but sit and wait out the storm, getting naked had become the best way to pass the time.

And though he'd never say it out loud, he'd enjoyed

being with Eva these past two days. He'd enjoyed it immensely.

"Why don't you believe me?" she demanded.

Her annoyed tone made him chuckle. So did the way she scowled at him, as if he'd accused her of committing a major crime when all he'd done was express a teeny bit of doubt about her response to his question. Out of sheer boredom, they'd started talking about what they envisioned to be the perfect life, and Eva's description had definitely triggered his skepticism.

"Because it doesn't seem like something you'd be into," he replied, rolling his eyes. "You want to live out in the boonies, have a bunch of dogs, let your kid run wild and pretty much isolate yourself from society."

Her scowl deepened. "What's wrong with that?"

"Nothing's wrong with it. In fact, it's exactly…"

Exactly what he wanted for himself. Minus the kid part, of course.

But he didn't finish that thought. Instead, he trailed off, and searched her gorgeous blue eyes for a sign that she was joking around.

Her expression remained dead serious. "I hate cities," she said frankly. "I grew up in Manhattan and hated every second of it. The crowds, the traffic, the pollution, the noise. I told you how every summer my parents would rent a cabin in Vermont, right? Well, it was all I looked forward to all year. That's when I knew I belonged in the boonies."

"Yeah, and what about your trusty computer?" he countered. "Seems like your love for technology doesn't mesh with the country life."

She shrugged, causing several strands of black hair to fall over one of her bare shoulders. The only light came from the flashlight resting on a ledge above Eva's head, and the yellow glow created a halo effect and made her blue eyes sparkle.

She was sitting cross-legged beside him, while he was sprawled on his back, and he reached out to tuck her silky hair behind her ear. For some reason, he'd been touching her far too frequently during this forced confinement, and not just during the sex. Stroking her hair, rubbing her back, brushing his fingers over her slender arm. He couldn't seem to stop himself, and damn, but it felt nice touching Eva. She was so soft and warm and womanly that he simply couldn't resist.

"All I need is an internet connection," she said. "I already told you, I want to design software, maybe contract myself out to companies who are worried about the security of their websites and databases. I can do that from anywhere."

"True," he agreed. "But I still can't picture you living in the middle of nowhere."

"I'm a simple girl, Tate. I like the outdoors, I love big, open spaces, and I hate all the superficial stuff that so many people are obsessed with." Her perfect lips quirked in a smile. "I don't want my son to be superficial, either. I want him to run around outside and have fun adventures and discover new things, not sit inside playing video games all day. It's important for him to learn how to use technology, but I don't want that to define him, you know?"

Tate had already lost count of how many times he'd had to hide his deep approval for this woman. Eva continued to surprise him—she was far more intelligent than he ever would have guessed, had a sensible head on her shoulders, fiercely spoke her mind, was quick to laugh, easy to talk to.

He couldn't remember ever liking or respecting a woman this much, and it troubled the hell out of him that his guard was slowly lowering in her company. He wasn't supposed to trust or care about her, yet the longer this storm raged on, the more his defenses began to crumble. He couldn't even believe half the stuff he'd told her—about his family, his brother, his need for solitude. He always tried to keep a distance from other people, but with Eva…damn it, with Eva, he only seemed to pull her closer and closer.

"Oh, no." She suddenly grimaced. "I have to pee."

Tate had to grin. "I already told you, it's fine if you want to go in the corner. I'll close my eyes."

She looked horrified. "I refuse to do my business in this cave. I'd rather get wet and muddy."

He laughed as he watched her stumble to her feet. She wore nothing but a white button-down shirt and black bikini panties, and her legs were long and smooth, her delicate feet bare. With her hair loose and her cheeks flushed, she made a truly spectacular picture. His body, of course, immediately responded to her, which wasn't a surprise seeing as getting hard for this woman had become a habit he couldn't kick.

"I'll be right back," she said, reaching for the second flashlight sitting on top of her pack.

She switched it on and pointed the shaft of light at the entrance of the cave. The rain was still pouring, a constant stream of water that didn't seem at all interested in easing up. The only upside was that the air itself remained hot and humid, so when you stepped into the rain, it was like entering a warm bath.

After Eva left the cave, Tate sat up and rummaged around for his T-shirt, which he pulled over his head before searching for his pants. Once he was dressed, he did a quick inventory of his pack, made sure their food and water supply wasn't dwindling, checked his ammo situation and examined the contents of the first-aid kit. That final task had his eyebrows shooting up. He'd lost track of the number of times he and Eva had wound up naked over the past forty-eight hours, but judging by the solitary condom left in the plastic pouch, they'd clearly reached nymphomaniac status.

Zipping up the bag, he stood up and headed to the cave's entrance, swallowing his rising frustration as he gazed out at the relentless rain. They'd already been delayed two days, and he didn't like it one damn bit. The only saving grace was that the soldiers who'd ambushed Ben at the cabin were probably grounded, too. This area was notorious for mud- and landslides—nobody would be stupid enough to be on the mountain in this weather. Nevertheless, he'd feel better once they were no longer sitting ducks, and on the move.

"Eeeek!"

The shrill female cry interrupted the steady pounding of the rain and made Tate's stomach go rigid.

"Eva?" he shouted.

When there was no answer, he sprang to action, a rush of adrenaline whipping through his veins and making his pulse speed up.

He didn't bother putting on his boots, just tore out of the cave barefoot, cringing when his feet sank into a thick layer of slimy brown mud. It was late morning, but the sky was so overcast it looked more like twilight. Running wasn't an option, not unless he wanted to slide down the slope and break both his legs, and panic hammered a reckless beat in his chest as he moved as fast as he could in the direction Eva usually went to take care of business.

"Eva!" he yelled again.

No answer.

His panic intensified. Christ, why wasn't she answering?

He followed the muddy terrain toward a set of huge jagged boulders in the distance, unable to control the frantic thumping of his heart. What if the soldiers had grabbed her, or an animal attacked her, or—

He staggered to a stop when he rounded the boulders and spotted her.

"Thank God," he blurted out.

Then he noticed her predicament and burst out laughing.

"Don't you dare laugh at me," she ordered, her jaw so tight he knew she was grinding her teeth.

"You okay?" he asked between chuckles.

Looking pissed off and mortified, Eva lay on her back, covered from head to toe in mud. Her shirt was no longer white but brown, and the mud and rain had caked her hair to her head and was dripping down her face, making her look like a creature out of a horror movie.

"I tripped," she grumbled. "Got the wind knocked out of me. Tried to get up and tripped again."

Tate stifled another laugh and managed a supportive nod. "I can see that." He tilted his head. "You need a hand, or are you just going to lie there in the mud for the rest of the day?"

Her bottom lip stuck out in defeat. "I need a hand."

Lips twitching with amusement, he carefully walked over to her and extended his hand. The second their fingers touched, he realized her evil intentions, but by then it was too damn late.

Eva tugged on his hand and he came crashing down on top of her, sending wet muck sailing in all directions.

"You little…" He spat mud from his mouth, then tried to wipe his face only to make it worse.

"That's what you get for laughing at me," she said, wiggling beneath him. "A true gentleman politely keeps his mouth shut in the face of a lady's humiliation."

"I'm no gentleman, sweetheart." And then he proceeded

to prove it by sliding his wet, dirty hands beneath her wet, dirty shirt.

She squeaked in surprise, then moaned and arched her spine, pushing her breasts into his palms. Her enthusiasm made him groan. She was always so eager for him, so ready and willing and welcoming, no matter when he reached for her, no matter how rough he was.

He hated to admit it, but he didn't have the upper hand anymore. He'd lost that sometime over the past two days, when his desire for Eva had reached a new level of desperation that both shamed and thrilled him.

"I love it when you touch me like this." She sighed happily as he gently squeezed her breasts.

"I love touching you like this," he answered gruffly.

He swept his thumbs over her distended nipples, and she moaned again. The husky sound teased his senses and stirred his cock, which grew hard, heavy, pulsing with need.

Neither of them seemed to care that they were lying on the wet, muddy ground. In fact, Tate was completely oblivious to his surroundings as he captured her mouth with his and kissed her, long, deep and thorough. The rain continued to fall, soaking them both as they lay there kissing, drowning out all sound and reason.

"I didn't bring a condom out," he murmured.

"That's probably a good thing, because I don't think I want mud getting all over my delicate parts," she said wryly. She slid her hand between their bodies and rubbed her palm over the bulge in his pants. "But I think we can arrange something for you."

"You don't have—"

But she wasn't listening. She'd already unbuttoned his pants and reached inside.

Tate's head lolled to the side as she tormented him with

her hand. When he could barely support his own weight, he rolled onto his back. The raindrops felt like little needles as they fell into his face, but he barely noticed the downpour. With Eva curled up at his side, her hand wrapped around his shaft as she pumped him in fast, sensual strokes, the rain was the last thing on his mind.

"Oh, sweetheart, I'm close," he rasped.

She increased her speed, tightened her suction, and within seconds, he lost himself in a mind-shattering release that made him gasp for air. When he regained his faculties, he found Eva watching him with a satisfied gleam in her blue eyes.

"Do you forgive me for pushing you down in the mud?" she teased.

It took him a moment to find his voice. "I forgive you."

"Good." She bent her head to plant a kiss on his lips, then carefully got to her feet.

Tate watched as she tipped her head up to the sky and let the rain wash the brown streaks from her face. In fact, within seconds, her face and bare legs were totally clean, but her white shirt was beyond saving.

His heart rate had just steadied after that explosive climax, but it quickly sped right back up when Eva began unbuttoning her shirt. She peeled it off her slender shoulders, and then she was gloriously naked save for her bikini panties. Her gorgeous, golden limbs assaulted his vision and made his mouth go dry. Everything about her reignited his arousal—her bare breasts, round and full, the raindrops clinging to her pebbled nipples and sluicing over her flat belly, the sexy curve of her buttocks.

His gaze landed on the dirty bandage covering her upper arm, and he stumbled to his feet with a frown. "We need to change your dressing," he said firmly. "And you should take another antibiotics shot."

"Later," she answered, and then she continued to wash up, running her hands over her breasts and belly.

Trying to ignore the sexy sight, he followed her lead and let the rain wash him clean. The faster he got this mud off him, the faster he could be back in the cave with Eva, making use of that last condom in his pack.

She must have read his mind, because she shot him a broad smile. "You're totally going to have your way with me, aren't you?"

He responded with a rogue smirk. "You complaining?"

"No." She donned a thoughtful pose. "But you've got to do one thing for me before I give you free rein of my body."

"Yeah, and what's that?"

"Admit you like me."

His jaw tensed, just for a second, but he quickly forced it to relax. The playful look in Eva's eyes told him she wasn't making demands of him, but he knew there was a lot more to that lighthearted request.

He was perfectly aware that he hadn't given her any indication of what he felt for her. She must know he was wildly attracted to her—fat chance of him hiding *that*—but in terms of where his head was at? His heart? He understood her need to figure that out, and he didn't blame her; he'd learned a long time ago that the women in your bed sometimes needed a little reassurance.

So he opened his mouth and told her what she wanted to hear.

"I like you." He shrugged awkwardly. "I like you a helluva lot, Eva."

Except then something strange happened, something that almost made him topple right back into the mud.

He realized that he'd meant every damn word.

Chapter 14

"Okay, so what's the plan?" Eva asked the next morning.

Tate's green-eyed gaze swept over the piece of paper he'd spread out on the boulder near the cave. The rain had ceased right after dawn, almost as quickly as it had started, and Eva was still having trouble adjusting to the blinding sunlight beating down on her head. Although some parts of the area were still wet and muddy, most of the earth had dried up, leaving streaks of brown clay on the soles of their boots.

She and Tate had eaten breakfast outside, both of them needing the fresh air after being cooped up in the cave for forty-eight hours, and now Tate was all business as he examined the drawing she'd made of Hector's bunker. She'd included every detail she could remember, which Tate seemed to appreciate, but she still had no idea how the two of them would manage to sneak in and out without being shot on sight.

"Ben and I came up with something before, but…" Tate drifted off, his expression strained.

Knowing how difficult it was for him to talk about his friend, she reached out and took his hand, squeezing it gently. "What did you come up with?"

"He would provide a distraction while I went in from the tunnel over here." He pointed to the exit she'd labeled on her map, the one located in the foothills that the bunker's tunnel led out to.

"Okay. What kind of distraction?"

"A full-on assault. Rig the area over here—" he pointed again "—with explosives, and take out the entrance with an RPG."

Her eyebrows flew north. "A rocket launcher? You've got one of those?"

Tate's mouth quirked. "That was one of the supplies Ben went to get."

"Oh. Okay. So what was supposed to happen after he took out the entrance?"

"The camp would be in chaos. All the guards would be drawn to the explosion. They'd try to make sense of the commotion, Cruz would most likely send a team out to investigate. Ben would've strategically detonated explosives and lured any rebels away from the camp, while I went in from the foothills, took out Hector and snuck back out."

"Wow. All right. Well." She pursed her lips. "Why can't I be the one in charge of the distraction? I'm sure I could handle a rocket launcher without screwing it up too badly. It's just point and shoot, right?"

His expression hardened. "No way."

"I can do it," she insisted. "I'll hide out in the trees over here—" she jammed a finger at the map "—and when you give me the go-ahead, I'll take out the entrance. And I can work a remote detonator. When the rebels come out to investigate, I'll make them all go boom."

He didn't look the slightest bit amused by her attempt at humor. "No. Way."

His tone invited absolutely no argument, and it elicited a burst of irritation.

"I won't screw it up," she muttered. "And I take direction really well. All you have to do is tell me how to—" She stopped abruptly as it dawned on her. "It's not that you think I can't handle it, is it? You don't *trust* me to do it. You think I'll screw you over or something."

Pain squeezed her throat, but really, why did that surprise her? Tate had made it clear from day one that he didn't trust her, and their sleeping together didn't change that. Heck, that was *another* thing he'd made clear—sex and trust were one hundred percent mutually exclusive.

Yet his lack of faith brought a dull ache to her heart. She might have lied to him about her relationship with Hector, but she hadn't lied about anything else. Her life story, her love for her son, her thoughts and fears and hopes. There had been nothing false about any of that, and it troubled her how willingly she'd confided in Tate about those things.

She wasn't supposed to let another man in. After her disastrous and reckless involvement with Hector, she'd promised herself to be warier around men. Not to give her trust so easily, and yet here she was, putting all her faith in another soldier. Another ruthless alpha male who didn't care about her at all.

"Forget it," she mumbled when he didn't respond. She averted her eyes, pretending to study the map. "If you don't trust me to be part of this mission, then fine. We'll do it your way."

Her peripheral vision caught a flash of movement, and she jumped when Tate's rough hand gripped her jaw. His touch was surprisingly tender, his gaze even more so as he forced eye contact.

"That's not it," he said gruffly.

She swallowed. "What are you talking about?"

"I won't let you play Rambo and blow things up, and that's not because I think you're going to screw me over." A strangled breath flew out of his mouth. "It's because it's too damn dangerous and I refuse to let you get hurt."

Astonishment rippled through her. "What?"

"Once things go to hell, all those rebels will be running out to find the source of the chaos. They'll be pissed off and trigger-happy and gunning for the person who had the nerve to blow up their lair."

His hand dropped from her chin and curled into a fist that he slammed on the dirt. "You're not dying on my watch, Eva. I refuse to let you die. You understand?"

Her shock only deepened. "Why?"

"Why what?" He sounded—and looked—embarrassed.

"Why don't you want me to die, Tate?" She softened her tone. "Yesterday you told me you liked me, but I think you were saying that more for my sake than anything. You've made it clear from the beginning that you don't particularly care about my wellbeing, so what's changed? Why do you suddenly care whether I live or die?"

His silence dragged on and on, and she'd just given up on ever receiving an answer when he cleared his throat and offered an awkward shrug. "Your kid. I want you to live so your kid can grow up with his mother."

Before she could question—or challenge—that statement, Tate stood up. "I'm gonna grab some water and then we can talk this through some more. Want anything from the cave?"

She shook her head, then watched him stride off, feeling incredibly perturbed.

I want you to live so your kid can grow up with his mother.

She had to wonder, was that really it?

Or was it possible that maybe, just maybe, Tate was actually starting to care about her?

It took twelve hours to reach their destination, but Tate didn't feel the slightest bit winded. If anything, he was riddled with adrenaline, fraught with tension and champing at the bit. Hector Cruz was less than a mile away. One measly mile. For the first time in eight months, the man who'd murdered his brother was within his grasp.

Although he preferred to travel at night, impatience and eagerness had overruled his need for caution, and so he and Eva had navigated the mountainous terrain while the sun beat down on their heads, leaving them hot and sweaty. They'd discussed their options during the trek, but Tate hadn't come up with a workable plan of action yet.

Eva insisted that she should be in charge of causing a distraction, but he was loath to put her in the line of fire like that. Ben would've easily been able to disappear in the woods and evade the men who would no doubt be dispatched to comb the mountainside. But Eva? She was no soldier, and he'd be damned if someone else died under his watch.

Right, that's why you're so concerned.

The nagging voice brought a frown to his lips. He'd been battling those same doubts all frickin' morning, and he'd yet to make a single lick of sense about the strange emotions swirling through his chest. He didn't want Eva to die. That much he knew, but...but why the hell should he care if she did?

Because they were sleeping together?

Because her kid would be orphaned?

Because he'd be losing something...*worthwhile* if she wasn't in his life?

Ridiculous. All those options were utterly ridiculous, and only increased his annoyance. He'd be just fine if Eva was no longer warming his bed. He didn't care about her kid. And he certainly didn't need or want her in his life.

"The sun will set soon," she remarked, coming up beside him. "What's our plan, Tate?"

Other women would probably look exhausted and disheveled after a twelve-hour hike, yet Eva seemed downright cheery. Her eyes flickered with determination, and she held her shoulders high, despite the fact that a backpack had been weighing those shoulders down all day long.

"When it gets dark, I'll go on ahead and do some recon," he replied.

Her eyes narrowed. "Alone?"

"Yes, alone." He arched a brow. "Will I get an argument from you?"

"No, but..." Her teeth nibbled on her bottom lip. "But what if something happens? What if the guards spot you?"

"They won't." Confidence lined his tone. "I'm black ops, sweetheart. I'm invisible."

"Somehow that doesn't reassure me."

Sighing, he moved closer and rested a hand on her shoulder. "It'll be fine. I was trained for this kind of thing, Eva. And I work better alone, so you're going to stay here like I ordered and let me do my thing, okay?"

"Okay," she said in a grudging tone.

He dipped his head, brushed his lips over hers and forced himself not to question this need to reassure her. The two days in the cave had created an intimacy between them that made him unbelievably uncomfortable, yet at the same time, he found himself almost soothed by it.

Oh, brother. He was in deep trouble.

Stepping backward, he headed over to their gear and unzipped Ben's duffel. Along with the aluminum case containing the RPG-7, there were also a handful of grenades, trip wires and enough C4 to blow up a small country. He was pleased to discover that Ben had even done most of the prep work—the explosives just needed to be rigged and armed, and then Tate could detonate them remotely if need be. As far as strategies went, this one was flimsy at best, but without Ben, there weren't many other options.

Tate gathered up the supplies he needed and stowed them in his pack, then grabbed his rifle and glanced over at Eva. Overhead, the sky had darkened, the sun steadily dipping toward the horizon line.

"Stay out of sight," he told her, gesturing to the crude blind he'd constructed for her in a cluster of dense shrubbery.

Her expression was resigned. "I will." Then she bent down, picked up her backpack and dutifully ducked into the hiding spot he'd fashioned.

Fighting the stupid urge to yank her out of the tree and kiss her goodbye, Tate dragged the heavy duffel into the brush and covered it with fallen branches and dead leaves. A moment later, he slung his rifle over his shoulder and took off walking.

It was the first time he'd been alone in days, and he welcomed the respite, the silence. He moved through the wilderness without making a sound, and this time, he made an effort to cover his tracks. He hadn't bothered in the jungle or on the way here, because, frankly, he didn't give a damn if anyone knew where he was going. Let the hunters follow him—as long as he killed Will's murderer before they caught up to him, he'd die happy.

Yet he couldn't seem to maintain that careless indifference any longer. He might not care whether he lived or died, but he sure as hell cared if Eva did. For some reason, protecting her had become a priority for him, and if that meant covering his tracks so that his enemies didn't stumble across her, then so be it.

Tate's instincts began to hum as he maneuvered the foothills that made up the base of the small mountain range spanning San Marquez's western coast. The sun had set completely by then, shrouding the entire area in darkness. Since he couldn't afford to make a single wrong move, he stopped only to remove his night-vision goggles from his pack. He slipped them on, and his surroundings immediately came alive again.

He kept walking. The trees thinned as rocky slopes and craggy hills appeared, making it all the more important to stay invisible. The enemy was close. He felt it with a bone-deep certainty, and the conviction was validated when he finally laid eyes on the prize he'd been seeking for months.

Hello, Cruz.

Eva hadn't lied. At first glance, one would think they were looking at a wall of solid rock surrounded by heavy shrubbery. In the distance, the jagged peaks of the mountains seemed to glow thanks to his goggles, but they weren't the only things glowing. In the daylight, the copper-colored door built right into the rock formation up ahead would probably be mistaken for dirt and rock, but the night-vision goggles picked up on the inconsistency, making that particular feature glint like the metal it was.

Like Eva had said, the entrance was guarded, but there weren't as many men as Tate had expected. He counted ten. Two at the door, four stationed higher in the hills, armed with rifles and binoculars. Four more walking the perimeter.

All were rebels, which was clear thanks to the unkempt brown uniforms and the potluck collection of weaponry—

AKs, M-16s, handguns, a shotgun or two. The ULF rebels were organized for the most part, but when it came to supplies, they took what they could get. Rumor had it Cruz had deals in place with several major arms dealers, but it also wasn't uncommon for the rebels to raid military camps or villages to steal weapons.

Since he needed to get a sense of the perimeter guards' movements before he did anything, he hunkered down behind a couple of boulders and spent the next two hours watching and learning.

It turned out the guards didn't travel far. They simply circled the compound every ten minutes in teams of two, following the same path each time. Every now and then, they'd light up a cigarette and stop to chat near the half-dozen Jeeps and pickup trucks littering the base of the slope.

Cruz's hideout was no maximum-security prison. More like the place you sent perpetrators of tax fraud or petty crime, but then again, that made total sense. Cruz wouldn't want to advertise his presence, and making this particular camp seem unimportant was a nice touch. Anyone who caught wind of this place would never dream to think that the leader of the ULF was hiding here, out in the open with barely any protection.

It took Tate no time at all to set up a few strategically placed explosives, and then he was heading back the way he came, putting distance between himself and the rebels who'd been oblivious to his presence.

He was halfway back to Eva when his body started humming again. His back stiffened and the hairs on his nape stood on end. His rifle snapped up instinctively as he slid behind a gnarled tree trunk, where he stayed out of sight. Waiting. Listening.

Nothing sounded out of place. Just the night noises of the creatures that inhabited these woodlands.

So why couldn't he shake the feeling that he was being watched?

One minute passed. Two. Five. Ten. By the time the fifteen-minute mark crept up, Tate was wondering if his intuition was on the fritz or something. Whatever danger he'd sensed was gone. If the threat had even existed in the first place.

Reluctant, he stepped out and continued making his way back to camp, but the hairs on the back of his neck tingled the entire damn time.

"That is a *terrible* idea!" Eva hissed a few hours later, after Tate divulged the details of his plan.

The moonlight cast a glow over his handsome face, emphasizing the determined line of his mouth. "It's the best one I've got," he said in a low voice.

She shook her head, unable to fathom how he could sit there so calmly after outlining the flimsiest, most suicidal plan she'd ever heard in her life.

To make matters worse, he'd completely misled her. The two of them were ducked behind a cluster of thick shrubs about twenty yards from the rusted metal hatch that was barely visible through the brush. That hatch led to the tunnel, which in turn led to Hector's bunker, and by bringing her here, Tate had made her believe he needed her help with this mission.

Apparently that wasn't at all the case.

"I'm going in alone." His tone was firm, his expression inflexible. "I already told you that a dozen times before."

"But that was when Ben had your back. Now you're on your own." She frowned. "What happened to the rocket launcher plan? The big distraction?"

"That was when Ben had my back," he mimicked. "With Ben watching the front and me here in the rear, there would have been no chance of Cruz getting away, but now, Cruz could flee the bunker while I'm blowing the main entrance to smithereens, and I won't be here to stop him."

"I could watch this exit while you blow things up," she offered.

"No."

"Fine, then let *me* blow things up."

"No."

Frustration spiraled through her. "Stop saying no to everything. This plan of yours sucks. You're just going to waltz through that hatch without trying to distract any of the guards standing right on the other side of that hill? And then you're going to shoot your way to Hector, kill him and shoot your way back out?" An amazed laugh popped out of her mouth. "You're nuts, you know that?"

He merely shrugged.

"And let's not forget about *my* part in all this. What's my part again?" She faked an epiphany. "Oh, right, *nothing.*"

Tate ignored the sarcasm. "Same deal as before, Eva. Get yourself to the coordinates I gave you. Take the sat phone, and if I'm not there at the arranged time, call Gomez and he'll come pick you up."

She scowled. "Just like that, huh? What happened to what you said about the government shooting unauthorized aircraft out of the sky?"

"Gomez won't be flying you off the island, just taking you to the coast. You can make your way to Tumaco from there, and then Gomez will rendezvous with you in Cali and bring you back to Mexico. Back to your kid."

The thought of seeing Rafe brought a rush of longing to her chest, but the fear and concern already swimming there overpowered the new addition. No matter how much she wanted to be reunited with her son, she couldn't let Tate undertake this crusade alone. Walking into Hector's hideout like he owned the place? With no contingency plans in place? No backup? No guaranteed way out?

The stubborn fool was going to get himself killed, damn it.

Her gaze drifted toward the unguarded hatch in the distance. Tate had said there were nearly a dozen rebels on the other side of the rocks, but back here, the hills were dark and deserted at four in the morning.

She understood his point about not wanting to risk Hector escaping, which was a real possibility if Tate was forced to take out the front entrance and then rush all the way over here. By then, Hector could already be halfway down the mountain in one of those off-road vehicles Tate had seen.

"I'm coming with you," she announced.

"No."

She lifted her brows in defiance. "Say no all you want. It won't change a damn thing."

Reaching around, she pulled her gun from the waistband of her jeans, ignoring the way Tate's green eyes smoldered with menace. In the darkness, with his angry expression and thick beard, he looked deadlier than usual, but Eva wasn't about to let him push her around.

Somehow during the past week, she'd come to care about this man, and she refused to let him die, especially not when she was the one who'd dragged him to San Marquez in the first place.

"Eva…" His voice thickened with annoyance.

"Tate," she replied, her voice calm.

"You're not coming."

"Like hell I'm not."

"Eva."

Now she rolled her eyes. "Quit saying my name. And

quit arguing with me. I'm going into that tunnel with you, whether you like it or not."

He let out an exasperated breath. "I won't let you."

"You don't have a choice." She removed the magazine of her gun and checked to make sure she had a full clip, then shoved it back in and cocked the weapon. "I'm coming."

"Why, damn it?"

Because I'm in love with you and I don't want you to die!

The thoughts whizzed to the forefront of her mind so fast that her brain nearly shorted out. Shock slammed into her, but she scrambled to maintain her composure, to remain expressionless.

God. It couldn't be true. She couldn't have fallen in love with Tate.

Right?

As her throat became dry and tight, she gulped a few times, searching for an excuse, an excuse Tate would believe. Because no way could she tell him the truth. He wouldn't be comfortable with the idea that she wanted to help him because she cared, and as that notion settled in, she realized the best answer she could give him was the one that catered to his natural cynicism.

"Because I want to see Hector's dead body with my own eyes," she said with a shrug.

A deep crease dug in his forehead. "I see."

"I thought you would. Trust, remember? You don't trust me, and I don't trust you. How am I supposed to know you'll actually kill Hector?"

"Oh, I'll kill him," Tate declared, a fierce look entering his eyes.

"Well, forgive me if I can't take you at your word. I'm coming with you, Tate."

His head tilted pensively as he appraised her. "To make sure that I actually kill Cruz."

"Yes."

For a moment, she thought he'd continue to argue, but apparently her appeal to his cynical side had worked.

It was pretty damn sad that he couldn't accept worry or affection as a reason for her to offer backup on a mission, but fear of betrayal? He had no problem buying that.

Even sadder? That she might actually be in love with a man who, given the choice, would probably prefer her distrust to her love.

Tate was acutely aware of Eva as the two of them moved through the shadows toward the unmanned hatch. He wanted to throw her over his shoulder in a fireman's carry and cart her back to safety, but after days of traveling with the woman, he knew she wouldn't take too kindly to being pushed around. She'd made up her mind about coming along, and nothing he said or did would change that.

I want to see Hector's dead body with my own eyes.

Her words continued to float through his head, bringing a multitude of emotions he couldn't quite get a handle on. On one hand, he absolutely understood her need to ensure that Cruz truly met his demise. He wouldn't be satisfied with secondhand confirmation, either—oh, no, he'd need to see that bastard's head on a spike before he believed Cruz was dead.

On the other hand...well, he supposed it shouldn't bother him that Eva had so little faith in his ability—and his promise—to follow through and kill Hector.

But it did bother him. It bothered him a helluva lot.

It shouldn't, though, seeing as he didn't trust her, either.

Yes, you do.

He nearly froze in his tracks. Had to force himself to keep moving, even as that alarming revelation continued to flash through his head like a strobe light. Was it true? Did he trust Eva?

Christ, did he *care* for Eva?

Stricken, he forcibly banished each and every disturbing thought from his mind. Now was *not* the time to ponder any of it. Maybe after he killed Cruz. Or after he managed to get him and Eva out of this alive. Maybe *then* he'd let himself think about the answers to those terrifying questions.

"Stay behind me." His voice was barely a whisper as they came upon the entrance of the tunnel.

Raising his rifle, he reached for one of the rusted handles on the two halves that made up the metal hatch. The opening was low to the ground and on an angle, which meant Tate would be looking down at whoever happened to be behind those doors.

"Ready?" he murmured.

As Eva offered a soft assent, he said a quick prayer, then yanked open the door. Despite the thick layer of rust on it, the hatch didn't make a single sound as it opened. No creak or groan or croak. Someone must have been oiling the hinges regularly, a fact that Tate was incredibly grateful for at the moment.

When they didn't encounter a single guard behind that door, however, his gratitude transformed into suspicion. He stared at the three concrete steps leading to the gaping opening, then glanced at Eva. "You said there should be a guard here."

She looked confused. "There was the last time I was here."

Frowning, he carefully descended the steps and entered the tunnel. The overhead lights flickered incessantly, humming like insects in the musty-smelling space and bringing a throb to his temples.

He turned at the sound of Eva's quiet footsteps and

raised his finger to his lips to signal her silence. She nodded slightly, falling behind him once more as they made their way down the narrow tunnel. It was only fifty yards or so before the tunnel ended in front of a metal ladder built into the wall.

Tate glanced up and spotted yet another hatch at the top of the ladder. Eva had mentioned there'd be guards up there, too, but considering they hadn't encountered a single man in the tunnel, he was beginning to question everything she'd told him.

Sure enough, they didn't run into any trouble once they slid through the second hatch. This one led to a small room with cinder-block walls and no furniture, and as he crept to the door, rifle in hand, Tate's uneasiness continued to grow, until his gut was damn near overflowing with it.

Nothing about this seemed right.

Battling his rising apprehension, he slowly pushed on the door handle and peered out into the corridor. Empty. Why wasn't he surprised?

He replaced his rifle with his pistol, which was affixed with a silencer, then gestured for Eva to follow him. He'd memorized her drawing, and knew exactly where to go, provided her intel was solid.

The bunker was deceptively larger than it seemed from the outside, and Tate felt far too exposed as he and Eva moved deeper into the enemy's domain. The lack of security continued to unnerve him—not only the absence of guards, but he didn't see a single camera mounted on any of the walls, either. Maybe Cruz didn't deem it necessary. Maybe Cruz was so arrogant that he believed himself to be untouchable.

Wouldn't surprise him. He'd witnessed that same arrogance eight months ago when Cruz had nonchalantly murdered Will. The rebel had considered himself untouchable then, too.

On the other hand, maybe the lack of precaution had nothing to do with arrogance, Tate decided as he noted the bad lighting and poor ventilation, the cracked cinderblock walls and dirty cement floor. The ULF wasn't as well funded as other "freedom" groups, and he doubted Cruz had specifically built this bunker for the purpose of having a secret hideout. The rebel leader had probably just stumbled upon this lair and knew a good thing when he saw one.

"Hector's quarters are this way." Eva's voice was barely over a whisper.

Tate still wished she'd agreed to stay behind, but it was too late to second-guess his decision to let her come. He just hoped this all didn't blow up in his face.

After rounding another corner, they descended a set of low stairs and crept down another hallway, this one narrower than the others. They took a left, then a right—and suddenly found themselves face-to-face with the startled eyes of a dark-skinned guard.

Odd as it was, the notion that they weren't alone brought a blast of relief to Tate's gut. He'd been starting to think this damn bunker was abandoned, and he was happy for some proof that it wasn't.

Still, that didn't mean he enjoyed the killing the man.

He had no other choice, though. He pulled the trigger and shot the guard between the eyes, then darted forward to catch the limp body before it toppled to the floor. The suppressor screwed to the barrel of his pistol ensured that the kill had been soundless, and nobody came running to the guard's rescue.

As he lowered the dead man's weight to the floor, his peripheral vision caught Eva flinching.

Without remorse, he offered a dry look and murmured, "You have something to say?"

She slowly shook her head, but her cheeks were pale.

Tate got to his feet and stared at the wooden door the dead man had been guarding, then glanced at Eva in an unspoken question.

When she nodded, he gestured for her to move behind him. She did, all the while holding her gun in a two-handed pose, her breathing soft and steady.

Taking a steadying breath of his own, he tucked his pistol in his belt and raised his rifle instead.

You ready for me, Cruz?

The notion that his brother's murderer was right behind that door flooded his mouth with saliva. As bloodlust ripped into him, he aimed at the doorknob, pulled the trigger and let the bullets spray. The deafening sound of gunfire reverberated in the corridor, making his ears ring and Eva yelp.

Adrenaline burned a path through his veins, giving him a boost of energy as he kicked open the bullet-ridden door and bounded into the room that lay behind it.

A yellow glow filled a room that turned out to be half a bedroom, half a library. But it wasn't the abundance of books stacked on every available inch of the small space that triggered Tate's bewilderment. Nor was it the futon across the room, or the laptop blinking on a round metal table, or the wine bottles sitting on the floor.

No, what had him gaping in disbelief was the man on the ratty beige couch that spanned one cinder-block wall. Hector Cruz. Sitting there with a semiautomatic Ruger resting on his knee as if he had no care in the world. In fact, he looked downright bored as his gaze collided with Tate's.

"Hello again," Cruz said with a pleasant smile.

White-hot rage funneled through his body and lodged

in his throat like a piece of spoiled food. The son of a bitch looked the same as he remembered: curly black hair, mocking eyes, unkempt goatee. Only his attire was different— he didn't wear a brown uniform, but a pair of black cargo pants and a threadbare gray tank top that revealed the tattoos covering both his biceps.

Bad call.

Tate couldn't get the taunt out of his head. It repeated in his mind like a continuous loop, until all he could hear were those two teasing words and all he could see was the blood gushing from Will's throat as—

Sucking in a breath, Tate blinked once. Twice. And then he pointed his rifle at Cruz and finally found his voice. "Anything you want to say before I kill you?"

Cruz's smile widened. "I suppose a thank-you would be in order."

He faltered. "What?"

"Thank you." The rebel leader shrugged. "For bringing my woman back." He craned his neck, peering past Tate's shoulders. "Where is she, by the way? Eva, are you out there in the corridor?"

His jaw stiffened. He opened his mouth to tell Cruz to shut up, but the rebel kept talking—and his next words made Tate's blood run cold.

"Eva, *mi amor,* did you bring our son?"

Chapter 15

Our son.

Those two words left Tate momentarily frozen. Just for a second, but it took only one second of hesitation to send everything to hell, and that was exactly what happened.

Before he could blink, something hit him from behind with the force of a Mack track. His rifle clattered out of his hands as he went sailing forward. A female scream registered, but he couldn't move, couldn't look in Eva's direction, because now there was a five-hundred-pound weight crushing his back.

Pain jolted through him as his arms were yanked violently behind him. He felt himself being disarmed—guns, knives, all gone—and then his wrists were twisted and tied together, and his equilibrium abandoned him once again as he was hauled to his feet.

It happened so damn fast Tate didn't know what hit him,

and he bit back a string of expletives for allowing himself to be caught off guard like that.

A quick assessment of the situation he'd found himself in, and Tate realized he was out of luck. Four more rebels with assault rifles had entered the room, joining the one who'd tackled him, a beefy man with the shoulders of a linebacker. With all those AKs pointed at him, he had no chance in hell of fighting his way out.

And where was Eva? He shifted his gaze, then stiffened when he saw her standing in the doorway. Her blue eyes were glued to Cruz, her cheeks paler than snow and her slender shoulders trembling like leaves in the wind.

There were no guns pointed at Eva. *That* he didn't miss. *Our son.*

"Don't worry, *mi amor,*" Cruz spoke up, his voice strangely somber. "I understand why you didn't bring our *hijo.* There are probably some matters to straighten out before we involve our boy."

Tate's jaw tightened further, a response that Cruz noticed, because those black eyes focused on him. "Judging from the look on your face, I gather she didn't fill you in on our history, did she, amigo?"

A shaky breath sounded from the doorway. "Tate—" Eva stammered.

Cruz interrupted her. "Quiet, Eva. I can handle this." With a jovial smile, the rebel rose from the sofa and strode toward Tate.

It took all his willpower not to launch himself at the other man, but he knew he'd be shot down like a dog if he did. He couldn't afford to be stupid about this. He'd already made a grave error by letting Cruz's revelation distract him, and if he wanted to get out of this mess alive, he had to play it cool from this point on.

"I don't know what she told you," Cruz began, "but I

suppose she said whatever was necessary to get you here."
Those black eyes moved to Eva. "It's all right. I don't hold
it against you. I treated you very badly, didn't I?"

Eva said nothing.

From the corner of his eye, Tate saw her mouth set in
an angry line. *Ha.* He doubted she was as angry as he was.

He still wasn't a hundred percent on what the hell was
going on, but one thing remained clear: Eva had lied to him.

Cruz was the *father* of her kid.

The resulting rush of rage, combined with an unwelcome burst of jealousy, set his insides on fire. Just pictur-
ing Eva in Hector Cruz's bed brought bile to his mouth.
And the memory of her kid…Christ, he'd left his men behind to protect *Cruz's son.*

Goddamn it.

"I'm afraid I wasn't very good to our Eva," Cruz told
Tate, his tone rueful. "But you know how it is, right, Captain? Love drives people to behave in crazy, irrational ways.
So does stress. And I'll admit, times were stressful then,
more so than they are now."

The rebel's eyes softened as he looked at Eva. "I don't
blame you for running away. I behaved very, very badly,
mi amor, and I truly regret that."

Tate couldn't stop himself for turning his head to study
Eva's expression. Her face was a mask of disbelief. "You
behaved badly?" she blurted out. "You turned me into a
prisoner in my own life!"

Cruz recoiled. His strained gaze darted to the five rifle-
wielding rebels in the room, as if it pained him to have
this dirty laundry aired in front of them, and then his eyes
flashed and he shot Eva a hard look. "Let's not trouble everyone with the boring details. We'll continue this discus-
sion in private."

Cruz cocked his head at one of his men. "Take my

woman to the room we prepared." He spared Eva a pithy glance. "I'll be there shortly."

A yelp of protest flew out of her mouth as a rebel grabbed her arm and began leading her to the doorway.

"Tate!" Her voice was thick with anguish. "Don't believe anything he says, Tate. Don't trust—"

He didn't hear the rest of that sentence. Didn't really care to, either. The word *trust* hung in the air, making him want to laugh uncontrollably.

She was actually talking to him about trust? The woman had been lying to him from day one. Which didn't surprise him in the slightest, did it? He'd known all along that she hadn't told him the entire truth, but this? Covering up the fact that Hector Cruz was the father of her child? That she'd had a relationship with the man?

Anger and disgust burned a path down to his gut and seized his insides. He'd slept with the woman who'd once shared Cruz's bed.

The man who'd murdered his brother.

Jesus.

As he choked down his revulsion, he was tempted to throw smarts into the wind and do something foolish, like rush at the rebels holding guns on him. That'd probably earn him a tidy little bullet in the head, but at this point, did he really care? He wasn't getting out of this alive anyway. Might as well take out a few sons of bitches before he met his maker.

"Don't." Cruz's voice was deceptively soft, his gaze knowing as he glanced at Tate. "They'll shoot. And that would be a shame, wouldn't it?"

"Right," Tate said sardonically. "Because you're really going to let me walk out of this alive."

"I am. I have no intention of killing you, Captain Tate."

Cruz's tone or expression didn't reveal any mistruth, but Tate didn't buy it. Not one damn bit.

He feigned a bored look. "Oh, really?"

"Really. You don't know how impressed I am that you made it here alive. I heard about the ambush in the jungle, and it seems you evaded another attack a couple of days ago, too." The rebel chuckled. "The Americans are desperate, no?"

Tate narrowed his eyes. "Why do you say that?"

"Because they've teamed up with my military to hunt you down, and we both know your government likes to clean up its messes on its own. They'd probably be better off, too. I'm afraid the military in my country is nothing but a joke. But you already know this, since you made it here in one piece."

"And I'm supposed to believe you want me to stay in one piece, huh?"

"I do," Cruz confirmed.

"Yeah, and why is that?"

"Because I'm going to put you to use instead."

The laugh he'd been holding earlier slipped out, a harsh, bitter sound that resonated in the air. "Sorry to disappoint, but that's not going to happen. I'd rather let your men shoot me."

Cruz gave a chuckle of his own before nodding at his men. "Leave us," he told them. "But stay close."

After the rebels shuffled out of the room, Cruz gestured to the sofa. "Sit."

Tate didn't move. He stared down the ULF leader, feeling the odds return once more in his favor. Even with his wrists tied behind his back, he could disarm Cruz and snap the bastard's neck with his legs if he got him on the ground and in a good lock.

"Oh, Captain, you are so very predictable," Cruz said

with a sigh. "You could at least try to hide your desire to kill me."

"Why should I?" He offered another callous laugh. "You slit my brother's throat, you son of a bitch."

Surprise flickered across the other man's face. "Your fellow soldier, you mean?"

"My brother." Fury constricted his throat. "So you might as well kill me now, Cruz, because the two of us? We won't be reaching any goddamn agreements, not unless they involve me slitting *your* throat, amigo."

The rebel's answering sigh was heavy with annoyance. "My condolences about your brother, Captain, but it wasn't personal. I did what I had to do to save myself, so I could live another day to fight."

"Fight? All you do is rob and cheat and kill, under the guise of freeing your people from oppression. But all that money you squirrel away, where does it go, Cruz? To buy food and medicine and clothes for the people you're pretending to care about? Or does it go directly into your wallet?" He laughed again. "Don't bother responding—we both know the answer to that."

"Your arrogance astounds me, Captain, and I'd prefer if you didn't speak of things you know absolutely nothing about. I *protect* my people—"

"Protect them? Is that what you did in Corazón when you murdered hundreds of innocent people? You *protected* them?"

"My men and I did not harm those villagers."

"No, you just burned them to death."

Sarcasm dripped from Tate's voice, and he nearly launched himself at Cruz out of sheer anger and frustration. He couldn't believe they were standing around talking about that day as if it were a normal topic of conversation.

Burning villagers. Slitting throats. Just another day in the life of Hector frickin' Cruz, huh?

As his bound hands curled into fists and bloodlust flooded his mouth, Tate's gaze flicked to the Ruger dangling idly from Cruz's hand. Five steps and he could tackle the son of a bitch to the ground before the man even raised that gun.

"I'm sorry to burst your bubble, but those people were dead before my men and I even got there," Cruz informed him.

Tate raised his eyebrows. "And the doctor? I suppose he was dead, too?"

A dark smile graced the man's mouth. "Oh, no, he was very much alive, at least before I had the pleasure of putting a bullet in his brain."

"And why would you do that?" Tate said sarcastically.

Just like that, for the second time in less than thirty minutes, Cruz threw him for another loop.

"Because the bastard is the one who killed all those innocent villagers you're so concerned about."

Eva was numb. She couldn't move a muscle, couldn't form a coherent thought, couldn't even breathe properly. Her reaction back in that room shamed her. She was the *worst* backup on the planet. A cataclysmic failure. She hadn't even managed to get a shot off before one of Hector's men had ripped her gun from her hand. And she hadn't even *tried* to give Tate an explanation after Hector dropped that bomb on him.

In her defense, she'd been too damn shaken. She hadn't heard Hector's voice in three years, hadn't seen his face since the day he showed up at her parents' Manhattan co-op and demanded that she and Rafe return to San Marquez with him. Seeing him again had knocked her off balance.

She'd frozen in place like a deer in the headlights, seeing that car careening in her direction and unable to do a thing but let it slam into her.

And by the time she'd regained her composure, Tate had already been restrained by Hector's men and was looking at her as though she'd committed the ultimate betrayal.

You did. You had a child with his brother's murderer.

The mature, rational part of her pointed out that she'd had that child long before Tate's brother had died, but she knew that wouldn't make a difference to him. In his eyes, she'd become the woman who'd warmed a murderer's bed, and she knew nothing she did or said would change that.

Damn it. Why had she insisted on coming with him? She should've known that a confrontation with Hector would lead to the truth coming out. If she'd let Tate go alone, her name probably wouldn't have even come up, Tate would've killed Hector, and her secret would've been safe. But she hadn't been able to stomach the thought of Tate doing this alone. Of Tate getting hurt.

Except now he *would* get hurt. Who knew what Hector would do to him, and it was all thanks to her.

As agony ripped her heart to shreds, Eva rose from the four-poster bed that didn't belong in a room made up of cement walls.

Hector hadn't been kidding when he'd said he'd "prepared" a room for her. It wasn't the same one she'd occupied the last time she'd been here. No, that room had been more like a nursery, with a crib and rocking chair and changing table, items that were gruesomely out of place in this dark bunker. But Hector had insisted she spend her pregnancy in a safe place. He'd allowed her to go outside— under a watchful guard, of course—but every night, he'd make sure she was back in her room, locked up nice and safe for the night.

Her lips curled in a frown as she looked around. Along with the elaborate bed, which featured a mountain of pillows and a soft burgundy comforter, there was a small bookshelf crammed with all her favorite novels and an antique armoire filled with clothes that were her exact size. The one thing that was conspicuously absent? A computer, which told her Hector was as smart as she remembered. No way would he leave her alone with a computer; even if this bunker didn't have an internet connection, she'd still find a way to contact the outside world.

She started to pace, wondering what the hell Hector was expecting to happen. His reaction to seeing her had not been what she'd expected. He'd seemed happy. And *regretful*.

"He's playing you," she muttered to herself.

Yeah, he had to be. His apologetic admission about treating her badly was nothing but a ploy. She might be locked up in this room, but she still had the upper hand thanks to Rafe. Hector would never dream of hurting her as long as their son was still out there somewhere and she was the only person who knew where.

A sharp knock sounded on the door, putting a stop to her pacing. "Are you decent, *mi amor?*" came Hector's voice.

She experienced another burst of surprise. Since when would her state of undress deter him from marching into a room?

When she didn't respond, the lock creaked and then the door opened. Stepping into the room, Hector swept his dark eyes over her and frowned. "You're still wearing those filthy clothes. I had thought you'd want to be more comfortable. Didn't you see all the things I bought for you?"

"I saw them," she said stiffly. "They just didn't interest me."

When his eyes blazed, she instinctively moved backward, anticipating an outburst. Hector wasn't known for his restraint. If you angered him, you were punished, and nobody was immune to his wrath.

Or at least that was how he'd behaved in the past. Now, the rage in his eyes burned hot for only a few seconds before dimming into resignation. "I won't hurt you," he said in a quiet voice. "I already did enough of that three years ago."

Eva clenched her teeth. "Stop it. Just stop it already. I don't buy this remorseful act of yours. I don't know what game you're playing, but—"

"No games."

He didn't make a single move toward her. Just stood there with his hands dangling at his sides. He wasn't even holding a weapon, she realized.

"I mean it, Eva," Hector went on, his voice heavy with regret. "I was out of control back then. I was reckless and desperate for change, and nothing was happening. The cause was stalled, those bastards in our 'government' were refusing to hear our demands. Our people were dying at the hands of our military, dying from disease and starvation."

She stifled an irritated groan. She'd heard this all before, many, many times. Four years ago, his "dedication" to the cause had been inspiring, but he no longer fooled her. Hector was a tyrant who used violence to advance his cause, who used children to fight his wars, and she refused to believe he had anything good inside him.

"I took my frustration out on you," he said, gazing at her with earnest eyes. "And when you got pregnant, I was angry. Angry that yet another child would have to be born in this miserable country, a dictatorship operating under the guise of democracy. I kept asking myself, how could we bring a child into the world when every day children in San Marquez are dying?"

"Spare me the idealistic crap," she retorted. "I don't care

how angry or frustrated or scared you were. You had no right to *hit* me. No right to become my warden and control every aspect of my life." She shook her head angrily. "For God's sake, I had to *beg* you for *permission* to take our newborn son to New York so he could meet his *grandparents*."

His black eyes blazed with belligerence. "And I was right to deny you, was I not? You used that trip as a ruse to run away from me!"

"You made my life a living hell for eighteen months," she said coolly. "Nine of which I spent pregnant, right here in this dark, horrible bunker."

"I brought you here to keep you safe," he insisted.

"You brought me here to keep me under your thumb."

A frustrated growl left his mouth, and then he marched toward her, not stopping until his hands were gripping her waist like a vise. "I'm sorry. Is that what you want to hear, Eva?"

"I don't want to hear anything from you," she said bitterly. "All I want to know is what you did with Tate."

Something dark and sinister flickered in his eyes. "You're sleeping with him."

Her lips tightened. "What did you do with Tate?"

"Answer the question."

"You didn't ask one. But I did. So tell me what you did with him."

They stared at each other for several long moments, and then Hector's expression relaxed once more. She had no idea how to handle this new side to him. She was used to the volatile Hector, the one who exploded at the slightest provocation, who solved problems with his fists and cared for nobody but himself. This new Hector was calmer, more analytical, more restrained.

"The good captain is in a quiet place, where he can think about everything we talked about," Hector finally revealed.

"What the hell does that mean?"

"It means Captain Tate and I share a common goal. I made him an offer and now he must ponder it."

Both confusion and relief swept through her. She had no clue why Hector was keeping Tate alive, but she wasn't one to look a gift horse in the mouth. Tate was safe. For now, anyway.

And now she had to figure out a way to get them both out of this mess.

She shot Hector a wary look. "Why didn't you kill him?"

"Because he's of more use to me alive than dead." Hector waved a dismissive hand. "Why do you think it was so easy for the two of you to get in here, Eva? I've been expecting you both, and the guards were ordered to stay out of your way."

Surprise jolted through her. "Why were you expecting us?"

"Well, more you than the captain," Hector conceded. "I figured your uncle would take care of Captain Tate. That was our compromise, after all."

"My uncle? What are you talking about—" Her surprise transformed into a rush of hot outrage. "Miguel told you I was coming after you?"

"Of course he did. Miguel has been aiding the ULF agenda for years, *mi amor.*"

She blinked in horror. "You're lying."

But all she had to do was look into his eyes to know that he was telling the truth. Her uncle, a military *general,* was on the ULF's payroll.

She'd gone to him for *help,* damn it. Miguel had been the one to tell her about Tate, the one to voice his agreement that her son couldn't live a normal life as long as Hector was still alive. God, her uncle had all but encouraged her to hire Tate to kill Hector.

"Miguel called me the moment he knew you were on your way here. He's the one who told me you'd be bringing Captain Tate along."

"What was the compromise?" she demanded.

"I'm afraid the Americans really want Captain Tate dead, so Miguel had no choice but to send a unit to eliminate the man. He has a pretense to put up, after all, as a loyal member of the military. As much as I wanted to use the captain, I agreed to let him be killed, as long as you were brought to me, safe and sound."

Eva gaped at him. "So my uncle agreed to *bring* me to you?"

"Yes, but it was unnecessary. The captain managed to stay alive. He's good, I'll give him that." Hector offered a self-deprecating smile. "Miguel didn't warn me that you were sleeping with the man, though." He held up his hand before she could speak. "It's all right, Eva. I forgive you. I drove you away and I accept responsibility for anything you've done during our separation."

Disbelief sent her eyebrows soaring.

"But although I've developed a new appreciation for patience and restraint, I won't tolerate my woman screwing around on me. Like I said, I need Captain Tate's assistance, but you're to stay away from him, Eva. I don't want my son near that man, either, once we bring him here. Now that you're back, I expect you to—"

"Back?" she cut in, her jaw falling open. "God, Hector! You're completely delusional. I'm not *back*. I don't love you anymore, I don't want to be with you, and I'm not letting you anywhere near my son!"

A short silence ensued.

For the first time since this sick reunion, Eva caught a glimpse of the Hector she remembered. The cold, cruel Hector who killed anyone who got in his way, who trained children to murder and steal, who orchestrated a prison break rather than pay for his crimes.

As his rugged features twisted in rage and his black eyes glittered like burning coal, Eva saw the man she'd run away from, and fear trickled down her spine like water from a leaky tap.

"My son belongs with me," he said, his voice so soft it sent a chill through her body.

"*My* son will never get anywhere near you."

A second silence hung over the room. Hector took a step back, crossing his arms over his chest. His biceps flexed, causing the tattoos on his skin to ripple ominously. His left arm boasted a tattoo of a red snake coiled around a machete—the ULF's symbol—while the right arm was completely covered with text. The cause's mission statement.

However, when Eva peered closer, she noticed a new line of text near his wrist.

RAFAEL.

Lord, he'd inked Rafe's name and birth date on his skin.

"My son belongs with me." Hector repeated himself in a lower, deadlier tone. "He needs to be groomed to lead the people once I'm no longer able to."

Terror erupted in her belly.

"Hopefully by then, there will be no need for rebellion— the country will be what we desire it to be," Hector went on, oblivious to her stunned expression, "but if not, my son will possess the skills necessary to lead. Now, I'd prefer if the three of us could be a family, the way it was intended, but if you choose to opt out of that arrangement, that's your decision. But Rafael—"

"Don't you dare say his name!"

"—will grow up with his father. Where is my son, Eva?"

A hysterical laugh lodged in her throat. "Somewhere you'll never find him."

Hector merely shrugged. "I'm afraid you're wrong about that. I have no doubt that our son is safely hidden at the moment, but it's not difficult to figure out where he'll be after I kill you."

Her heart lurched with horror.

"You would've named your parents as his guardian in the event of your death, isn't that right?" Hector smiled. "So really, all I have to do is put a bullet in your head and then send someone to New York to fetch my boy. I met your parents, Eva. They're not equipped to protect Rafael from the likes of me."

Anger swirled through her like a tornado. "I won't let you near him, Hector. I won't let you corrupt him."

"Corrupt him?" He sounded irritated. "That's rather melodramatic, don't you think?"

"What I think is that you're poison," she shot back. "You kill and destroy anything and anyone that stands in your way. Rafe is an innocent little boy—I refuse to let you—"

Pain stung her cheek as Hector backhanded her, stunning her into silence.

"You refuse?" he echoed. "You *refuse?* You have no say in this, Eva! That boy is mine! Not yours, but *mine.* Mine to do whatever I damn well please with."

She tasted the coppery flavor of blood in her mouth and realized that he'd split her lip. Wiping the corner of her mouth with her sleeve, she stared at the father of her child with undisguised bitterness.

"You're a different man, huh?" she mocked. "Because you seem like the same volatile, spoiled, angry man that I remember, a man who strikes out first and thinks about it later."

Ragged breaths flew out of Hector's chest, and she could

see him struggling to maintain control. Both his hands were curled into fists, and she instinctively moved back, anticipating an attack.

To her surprise, it didn't come.

"I think we both need some time to calm down," he said wearily. He took a step to the door, then stopped, turning to face her with a glint of humor in his eyes. "I've missed you, Eva. Your fire, your strength and determination. I don't want to have to kill you."

She barked out a laugh. "Gee, thanks."

"I want you to consider my offer. You, me, our son. A real family."

Another laugh, this time loaded with incredulity. "You escaped from prison and you're living in a bunker. What kind of life is that for a little boy?"

Annoyance crossed his expression but it faded quickly. "I mean it, Eva. I want to make this work." He paused. "In fact, as a show of good faith, I'll even do you a small kindness."

Her eyes narrowed. "What are you talking about?"

He extended his hand. "Come here."

She stayed rooted in place.

Hector's mouth tightened. "Come. Here."

With the taste of blood lingering on her tongue, she reluctantly approached him, but she didn't take his hand, much to his obvious displeasure. Yet again, he displayed that newfound sense of restraint, because he didn't react to the rejection.

She followed him out of the room, flinching when he rested his hand on her upper arm, and this time he *did* react.

"It would behoove you to be a little nicer to me, Eva. Keep being rude and maybe I'll change my mind and take you back to your room."

She ignored the threat. "Where are we going?"

"You'll find out soon enough."

They turned the corner and followed the hallway until its end, pausing in front of a solid steel door.

"See if you can persuade him to my way of thinking," Hector said as he stuck a metal key into the lock.

"What? Who are—"

Her words died as Hector pushed open the door and she found herself staring at Tate.

Chapter 16

Tate lifted his head as the door creaked open. Hector Cruz's mocking face entered his line of vision, but it wasn't the sight of the rebel leader that quickened his pulse. It was Eva, who apprehensively appeared at Cruz's side.

He didn't want to look at her, but his gaze refused to comply despite his brain's command to look away. When he spotted the blood dripping down her chin, he had to forcibly stop himself from jumping to his feet and pulling her into his arms.

That he could still feel concern for her sent anger shooting up his chest, and he quickly armored himself with that rage, refusing to let Eva see that he still gave a damn about her.

Sitting on the floor, with his legs stretched in front of him and his wrists tied behind his back, Tate watched as Cruz stepped into the room, a semiautomatic dangling loosely from his grip.

"I thought you two might like to chat," Cruz said, sounding both amused and annoyed. Those black eyes pierced Tate's face. "Have you given any more thought to my proposition?"

Tate didn't reply.

Cruz sighed. "I see you need more time to consider it. Fine. Maybe Eva will have more luck." Now he gave her a pointed stare. "Knock on the door when you're ready to return to your room. Javier is right outside."

Cruz took a step to the door, then stopped and tossed a casual glance at the security camera mounted in the corner of the ceiling. "Feel free to untie him, but don't do anything foolish, *mi amor*. I'll be watching you." He smirked, then marched out of the room and closed the door behind him.

Once the lock clicked into place, Eva dashed across the room, her expression awash with concern. "Are you okay?" she asked in an urgent tone.

Tate shrugged.

She dropped to her knees, leaning behind him to tug at the restraints binding his wrists. Her hair got in his face, tickling his nose and making him want to throw his fist into something. Why did she have to smell so good? And why the hell was he reacting to her nearness? Didn't his traitorous body know that this woman was nothing but a liar?

Her breathing was shaky and irregular as she untied the knots, her fingers cold as they brushed his skin. When the ropes finally came free, Tate brought his arms back to his front and rubbed his chafed wrists.

Noticing that Eva was still half-draped over him, he shot her a hard look and said, "Thanks. You can move now."

She didn't say a word as she crawled away from him. She ended up stumbling to the other side of the small space and settling in a sitting position on the cold cement floor.

Although Tate didn't make eye contact, he felt her gaze on him, felt the desperation radiating from her slender body.

"Tate. Look at me."

He spared her a terse look.

"I'm sorry I lied. I should have told you that Hector was Rafe's father, but I knew that if I did, you wouldn't agree to help me."

A groan lodged in his throat. He wanted to block out the sound of her voice, but clearly he was a masochist, because he found himself hanging on to her every word. He gave her no sign of it, though, maintaining a cool, indifferent mask even while fighting the insane urge to go to her and wrap his arms around her.

What the hell was the matter with him?

This woman had *lied*. She'd *slept* with Cruz, had a child with that monster. She didn't deserve Tate's sympathy or concern, and certainly not his forgiveness.

"Everything I told you about my past was true," she said softly. "My reasons for coming to San Marquez, my support of the ULF. The only thing I lied about was Rafe's true father. I…" Her voice cracked. "I was in love with Hector. Stupidly in love with him."

The streak of jealousy that soared up his spine irked the hell out of him. He wisely kept his mouth shut, knowing that if he said something, Eva might see through his uninterested façade. But hell, why *was* he interested? He shouldn't want to know the unholy details of that unholy union, and yet the need for details, the need to make sense of it all, gnawed at his gut like a hungry scavenger.

"It only took six months before he showed his true colors," Eva went on, sounding ashamed. "He was cold, violent, had a hair-trigger temper. Things weren't going well for the cause at that point, a lot of arrests and strife, no money coming in. Hector was furious about everything, and he took it out on me."

"And yet you stayed with him," Tate couldn't help but snipe. He immediately regretted that show of emotion, but added, "What, was the violence a turn-on?"

Her blue eyes flooded with sadness. "No, it wasn't a turn-on. I decided to leave him after the first time he hit me, but then I found out I was pregnant. I made the mistake of telling him, and he refused to let me go. I wasn't kidding about being a prisoner—I had guards on me at all times. I couldn't go anywhere alone, couldn't talk to my parents without Hector being in the room. He hovered over me during the entire pregnancy, and eventually I played along. I made him think that I'd calmed down, that I wasn't planning on leaving him once the baby was born."

Tate raised his eyebrows. "And he believed it?"

"I'm very convincing," she said dully.

Oh, he didn't doubt that. Not one bit. Another rush of jealousy filled his gut at the notion that Eva might have used her sexuality to convince Cruz of her sincerity.

"I made him believe I was still in love with him and that I wanted us to be a family. He bought it, and eventually he stopped keeping such close tabs on me. After Rafe was born—" her smile was dry and bitter "—he was born here, actually, in this bunker. And after his birth, I convinced Hector to let me fly to New York so my parents could meet their grandson. He agreed, as long as I took a couple of guards with me."

She uncrossed her legs, stretching them out in front of her, and Tate couldn't help but remember how amazing those shapely legs felt wrapped around his waist as he moved inside her.

The memory brought a silent curse to his lips. Christ. What was *wrong* with him?

"The moment the plane touched down on American soil, I knew I was free. Hector tried to bring me back, but my parents helped me leave town, and, well, you know the rest of the story," she finished. "Three years of running, and then I found my way to you."

"And conned me into helping the mother of Hector's child," he muttered.

Her tone grew chilly. "Rafe is *my* child. It's not my son's fault that his father is a monster. I've spent three years trying to keep Rafe away from that man. Everything I've done has been to protect my little boy."

Tate frowned. "You should have told me the truth."

"Would you have teamed up with me if you knew?"

"No."

"Then I'm glad I didn't tell you," she said bluntly. "Because the only way to keep Rafe safe is to remove Hector from his life, and I needed you in order for that to happen."

Tate snorted, gesturing around the cramped, windowless room. "How'd that turn out for you, Eva?" Now he chuckled. "You know, you would have had a better shot of me killing Hector if you'd stayed behind like I wanted you to. I would've killed the SOB in a heartbeat, instead of hesitating because I was too damn shocked to hear that he's your *lover*."

"Was," she corrected, her voice stiff. "The only thing I feel for that man now is loathing and disgust."

"Oh, I know all about disgust, sweetheart. I'm feeling quite a bit of it right now."

She flinched as if he'd struck her. "That's not fair."

"You really wanna talk about fair when we're locked up in a room by the father of your kid?"

Even from six feet away, he could see her pulse vibrating in her delicate throat. Panic moved over her face as she studied their surroundings, and he saw exactly what she was seeing—no furniture, no windows, no weapons. A locked door with a guard behind it, and a slim-to-none chance of escape, leaning closer to *none.*

You had your shot and you didn't take it.

The reminder only deepened his foul mood. Yeah, he'd had his chance to kill Cruz, hadn't he, but he'd let the bastard blindside him with that baby-daddy bullcrap. Now he had to pay the price for that asinine move.

The silence dragged as each of them sat in their respective corners. Tate kept his gaze on his feet, but he felt Eva watching him intently. Sure enough, when he tipped his head up, he noticed her astute blue eyes focused on him.

"What?" he muttered.

"Before he brought me in here…" She visibly swallowed. "He told me he doesn't plan on killing you. He said the two of you share a common goal. What did he mean by that?"

As much as he wanted to be juvenile about this and give her the silent treatment, Tate couldn't fight the need to talk this entire baffling development through. He still couldn't believe everything Cruz had told him, and now that he was reminded of it, the perplexing details began flashing through his head again.

Torn between making sense of it and shutting out a woman he clearly couldn't trust, he drummed his fingertips on the cement floor, feeling Eva's curious eyes on him.

"Tate?" she said quietly.

He released a long breath. "Cruz claims the villagers in Corazón were dead before the rebels even got there."

She looked dubious. "That sounds suspect. And how did they supposedly die?"

"From the virus that Richard Harrison tested on them."

Her breath hitched. "What?"

"Project Aries," Tate said. "Cruz says Harrison's lab

manufactured a biological weapon that was being tested in remote villages throughout the country."

"And how on earth does Hector know this?" she demanded, sounding skeptical.

"That's what Harrison supposedly told him before Cruz killed the guy. It was all the information Cruz managed to get—he claims to have no idea who gave the green light for Harrison's project, or if either of our governments is even aware of it. All he knows is that when he and his men showed up at the village, everyone was already dead."

"So why did they burn the bodies?"

"To control the infection," he said grimly. "They weren't sure if the virus was contagious."

"Hector isn't a doctor," Eva muttered. "How does he know those people were even infected with something?"

"He says the only visible symptoms were nosebleeds, and that it looked like some of the villagers had foamed at the mouth. But he was pretty much convinced of foul play when he discovered Harrison and his staff examining the bodies and taking notes."

Eva's blue eyes blazed. "Harrison was still in the village, *cataloging* the dead bodies?"

"According to Cruz, yes. Supposedly the village was a test site for this disease."

Eva went quiet for a moment. "Then it must have been approved by the American government," she said steadfastly. "And now they're trying to cover up what happened in the village. That's why they're trying to kill you, Tate."

"Then why send my team to begin with?" he pointed out. "Why put us in the position to discover what Harrison was up to?"

She shrugged. "They needed Harrison. Hector took him hostage, right?"

"He denies that. Says that he and his men interrogated

Harrison for six hours, seven hours tops, before my unit showed up. Which makes no sense," Tate said in frustration, "because we were told that Harrison had already been a captive for twenty-four hours at that point."

"I think it's safe to assume that everything you were told was a lie," she replied. "And it doesn't matter what the details are. Maybe Hector is lying and he *was* holding the doctor hostage and trying to negotiate with the U.S., or maybe Harrison managed to get an SOS out before the rebels swarmed the village. Maybe he contacted someone in the government and asked to be extracted. Like I said, doesn't matter."

"And why not?"

"Because either way, Harrison was still the head of that project, and our government couldn't afford to lose him. They probably thought, hey, we'll send in a team to see what's going on and try to bring the doc home if he's alive. Tell them it's an extraction and then deal with shutting their mouths once they come home." Her mouth set in a grim line. "The second your team was exposed to that village, someone was already planning on making sure you couldn't talk, regardless of whether you figured out the truth while you were there."

It made sense. It also grated, how levelheaded Eva was about this all, and how quickly he'd confided in her when he shouldn't be saying a damn word to her.

"What exactly does Hector expect you to do for him?" she suddenly asked, sounding uneasy.

"Help him take down his government."

Her jaw fell open. "Are you serious?"

"Yep. He wants me to go back to the States and expose what happened in Corazón. He'll offer me money and protection, and give me a fleet of guards if necessary, as long as I take this all the way to White House."

Now she laughed. "And do what?"

"He wants the American alliance with his country severed. He wants our troops and our relief workers and our doctors out of San Marquez."

"That's...ambitious."

Tate rolled his eyes. "Apparently I'm the man to make that happen. His reasoning is that if we threaten to expose that the U.S. government is actively developing biological weapons while telling the world it isn't, they'd happily cut ties with San Marquez in order to cover that up."

"Does he not know our policy of not negotiating with terrorists?"

"I didn't say his reasoning made sense."

Sense? It suddenly occurred to him that maybe what didn't make *sense* was the way he was sitting here and chatting with Eva as if nothing had changed between them.

The absurdity of his actions settled over him like a black cloud, but what infuriated him even more was the awareness that picking Eva's brain had become so natural he didn't even question it anymore. He hadn't realized how much he'd come to enjoy having her around, talking to her, bouncing ideas off her, sharing his frustration about that mission gone awry that he still didn't understand. Somehow, this woman had sneaked through his defenses, and that pissed him off beyond belief.

"Don't shut down on me."

Her strained voice jerked him back to the present. "What are you talking about?"

"You're about to shut down. I can see it in your eyes." She sighed. "For a moment you forgot that I lied, and you were talking to me like everything was normal, but now you're going to shut down again and pretend I don't matter to you."

"News flash, sweetheart—you don't." He didn't regret

the callous words, not even when he saw the flash of pain in her eyes.

Pain that quickly transformed into steely fortitude. "You're lying," she retorted. "You care about me. If you didn't, you wouldn't have freaked out at the thought of putting me in harm's way, or tried so hard to make me stay behind outside the tunnel."

"Maybe I didn't want you in my way—did you ever think of that?"

"You care about me," she repeated. "You like me and you respect me and you wouldn't be so angry with me right now if I didn't matter to you. I'm sure people lie to you all the time, Tate—do you react this way every time it happens? I doubt it."

"Eva—"

"Tell me I matter," she interrupted. "Stop patronizing me and tell me I matter to you, damn it."

You matter.

"You don't" was what he said, and as a result, her beautiful face collapsed. "Don't fool yourself, Eva. The only thing between us was sex. No relationship, no hope for a future. It was just sex."

"Just sex," she echoed, her voice laced with sadness.

"That's right. All I ever wanted from you was your body. I never made any promises or led you on. I never made you think it would be all rainbows and sunshine and happily-ever-after for us."

But a part of him *had* secretly wondered if it was possible, hadn't it?

That cold, embarrassing truth burned a hole in his gut. Christ, he *had* considered it. A lot, in fact, during those two days they'd been stuck in the cave. Holding Eva, talking to her, laughing with her—for a few brief moments, he'd gotten caught up in the foolish notion that he and Eva might be able to keep this going after Cruz was dead.

But who the hell was he kidding? He knew better than that. Getting close to people only resulted in heartache. And Eva in particular? The woman was no good for him. She was nine years younger, and she had a *kid.* Make that *Cruz's* kid, for Chrissake.

"You never made me any promises," she agreed. "I didn't make any, either. But I'm promising you something right now—I didn't lie because of some secret plot to lure you out of hiding or to bring you to Hector, or whatever other suspicions are running through your head. I lied because I was scared. I needed you, and I was scared you wouldn't help me if you knew the truth about my relationship with Hector."

She slid up to her feet and crossed the room, kneeling before him once more. When her hands came out to cup his chin, Tate stiffened, but he didn't have the strength to push her away.

"Maybe I don't matter to you, but *you* matter to *me,*" she said fiercely. "You know why I fought to confront Hector with you? It wasn't because I didn't trust that you'd kill him, it was because I didn't want you to get *hurt.* I wanted to have your back just in case you ran into trouble—because I care about you and because the thought of losing you was too much to bear."

He swallowed, hoping she couldn't see the rapid hammering of his pulse in his throat.

"I trust you, Tate, and I care about you. All this time we've spent together has taught me that not all men are like Hector. You've treated me like an equal on this entire journey. And yeah, you're ruthless and grumpy and cold at times, but you're also sweet and tender and funny—" her breath caught "—and I'm falling for you."

As her confession hung in the musty air, it took several moments for it to register in Tate's brain. When he absorbed what she'd said, his initial reaction was unexpected—his heart did a pathetic flip, his breath hitched the slightest bit, and he experienced a hot, unfamiliar emotion that was akin to...*joy?*

Just as quickly, that feeling faded, replaced by something equally hot but this time familiar: anger. Directed at Eva. Directed at himself.

Especially at himself, because what the hell was the matter with him? He shouldn't feel joy over the fact that this woman might love him. He didn't want or need her love.

Suddenly he couldn't even look at her. His body was overcome by a heap of volatile emotions he couldn't define, and his anger intensified, so powerful he could swear he felt the walls move from the force of it.

It wasn't until he saw the look of shock and fear on Eva's face that he realized his fury wasn't manifesting itself in this room.

The bunker was under attack.

As a deafening boom reverberated in the air, the walls literally shuddered, pieces of cement breaking off from the ceiling and fluttering down to the floor like confetti.

Tate shot to his feet just as he heard a second blast. Muffled, as if it had happened far above them. Without questioning his actions, he launched himself on Eva and shielded her with his body, keeping his head down as he anticipated another explosion.

It didn't come. Other than a slight ringing in his ears and Eva's shallow breathing, everything had gone silent.

He awkwardly shifted his weight, annoyed that his first instinct in the face of danger had been to protect Eva, but before he could question the impulse, gunfire erupted beyond the door. There was a startled cry, another gunshot, and then footsteps approached the room.

Just as the door swung open, Tate stood up and pushed Eva behind him.

And came face-to-face with a pair of familiar gray eyes.

"Are you frickin' kidding me?" he demanded.

Sebastian Stone flashed a rogue grin. "Mornin', Captain. Fancy meeting you here."

Eva blinked a few times to make sure that was actually Sebastian standing there in the doorway. Short blond hair, mocking gray eyes, rugged features. Yep, that was him. He was the last person she'd expected to walk in, but boy, was she happy to see his face.

She had no clue what was going on beyond this room, but it didn't sound pretty. Gunshots, explosions, tremors. Was someone waging a small war out there?

"What the hell are you doing here?" Tate barked, scowling at the sandy-haired man who'd waltzed in as if he owned the place.

In his dirt-streaked T-shirt, army fatigues and military-issued boots, with an assault rifle in his hands, Sebastian looked every bit the warrior he was. Only the smirk on his face seemed out of place.

"Saving your ass," he replied. "So come on, let's not waste time. Cruz's sorry excuses for soldiers are up there scrambling to figure out why they're under attack, but they won't stay confused for long."

"What exactly did you do?" Tate asked, as Sebastian tossed him the rifle.

The other man pulled a handgun from his waistband and cocked the weapon. "I blew up the entrance, and most of their vehicles."

Eva didn't miss the amusement on Tate's face. "How'd you swing that?" he asked.

"Note to Tate—don't leave a rocket launcher lying around in the shrubs," Sebastian replied with the roll of his eyes. "Someone else might come across it and blow up a rebel leader's secret lair."

Tate snorted.

"Those explosives you set all over the perimeter didn't hurt, either," Sebastian added. He grinned and held up a small silver device that Eva guessed to be a detonator. "I figured you wouldn't mind if I hijacked your bombs."

"Not at all," Tate said solemnly. He adjusted his grip on the rifle. "Come on. Let's beat it."

Sebastian's gray eyes flicked in Eva's direction. "She coming with us?"

Tate hesitated.

Eva's heart dropped to the pit of her stomach.

He'd hesitated.

He'd actually *hesitated.*

But before she could fully absorb the implications behind that one little beat of silence, Tate was already nodding. "Yeah," he said gruffly. "She's coming with us."

Without checking to see if she was following, the two men bounded out the door, leaving Eva to tail after them while continuing to battle that frigid burst of clarity.

Her heart felt as if someone had pummeled it with a baseball bat, and the hot tears stinging her eyes made her vision go cloudy. She was vaguely aware of two dead rebels sprawled on the corridor floor. Sebastian's doing, most likely.

They moved at a breakneck speed, navigating hallways that were surprisingly quiet and threat free. Why weren't rebels popping out and trying to shoot them? Where was Hector? He'd had a camera in that room, for Pete's sake.

He had to know that she and Tate had escaped, so where the hell was he?

"There's just one more thing I need to do before we blow this joint."

Tate's low voice jerked her from her troubled thoughts.

"Already way ahead of you," Sebastian said, as they turned another corner.

"Obviously not, or you'd know we have to go *this* way," Tate replied, his green eyes flashing with irritation as he took a step back toward the opposite end of the hall.

Sebastian grinned. "Just trust me. We're going this way."

Reluctance creased Tate's features, just for a moment, but then he nodded and allowed the other man to take the lead.

Eva tried not to feel upset in the face of Tate's easy acceptance of Sebastian's "trust me." It shouldn't have bothered her, or hurt her, that he trusted the other man. After all, they'd known each for years.

Yet it *did* hurt, how readily he trusted Sebastian when he'd viewed her with nothing but distrust since the day they'd met—even after spending hours naked in each other's arms.

And he'd *hesitated* when Sebastian asked whether to take her with them.

Ignoring the pain squeezing her heart like a boa constrictor, she forced herself to match the men's swift pace. The cinder-block walls whizzed past; overhead lights hummed and flickered as they raced through the bunker toward the room that led to the tunnel entrance.

Five minutes later, they'd ducked down the hatch and were hurrying toward the end of the tunnel, and when they finally emerged from the second hatch, Eva blinked wildly as bright light assaulted her. They'd entered the bunker when it was still dark out, but now the sun sat high in the morning sky, shining down and marring her vision with sunspots.

When the scent of smoke wafted toward them, she turned her head and saw thick black plumes rising from the other side of the rock face. Muffled shouts could be heard in the distance. Then Sebastian clicked the silver device in his hand, and suddenly the ground beneath their feet shook. Another column of smoke swiftly rose from beyond one of the craggy hills.

"This way," Sebastian said, leading them in the direction of a rock-strewn slope a couple of yards away.

Eva noticed Tate frowning as they trailed after the other man. Her own brows knit together, then soared when she spotted the dead man lying at the top of the slope. The man was sprawled on his back, and the front of his brown ULF uniform boasted a dark stain. Blood.

She'd barely absorbed the sight when she noticed the Jeep parked ten feet away. And the other two bodies. The pools of blood spreading beneath the rebels' heads made her blanch.

"You've been busy," Tate murmured.

Sebastian shrugged. "Like I said, saving your ass. Come on. Got a surprise for you."

Eva felt unbelievably uneasy as Sebastian gestured to the Jeep. She hung back, unsure she wanted to see this "surprise." Instead, she watched as the two men stalked off, with Sebastian in the lead. The Jeep's top was down, so she could still see both men as they rounded the vehicle.

Tate's green eyes dropped to the ground, focusing on something out of her line of vision, and when she heard him mutter a savage curse laced with satisfaction, Eva knew exactly what was back there.

Swallowing hard, she staggered toward the Jeep and peered around it.

Lying on the dirt, tied up and gagged, was the father of her child.

Chapter 17

The bittersweet taste of satisfaction filled Eva's mouth as she stared at Hector's immobilized figure. He wasn't blindfolded, and his eyes snapped open when she walked up, oozing with betrayal as they locked with hers. But he didn't make a single sound. He just stared at her with those burning eyes, his face an angry accusation.

"Caught him trying to flee after I blew up the entrance," Sebastian explained with a smirk. "Figured you'd want the honor of ridding the earth of this bastard."

For a second, Eva thought he was talking to *her,* but when Tate let out a growl of approval, she realized the comment had been directed elsewhere.

"We don't have a lot of time," Sebastian added, taking a step back. "I'll give you some privacy."

Eva scarcely noticed the man walk away. She was too focused on Hector's outraged black eyes and Tate's strained profile.

Her hands started to shake, her heart beating irregularly as she waited for Tate to do something. Anything. And yet when he finally made a move, slowly lifting his rifle, she nearly yelled, "Stop!"

Could she really stand here and let him kill a man in cold blood?

This is the man who terrorized you!

The internal reminder didn't ease the sudden tightness of her throat.

"I would have preferred to end it with a knife," Tate said in a calm voice, his green eyes fixed on Hector, "but you disarmed me back there, so I'm afraid I'll have to make do with this." He waved the barrel from side to side, just in case Hector hadn't noticed the rifle pointed at him.

Eva's entire body went cold with fear and indecision. "Tate, maybe—"

"Maybe what?" he cut in. "Maybe I should spare this bastard's life?"

She gulped down the lump wedged in her throat. "I…I don't know."

"I should have known you didn't have the stomach for this. Go wait with Sebastian, Eva. You shouldn't be here."

He was right. She shouldn't be. She also shouldn't stand by and watch him murder an unarmed man, yet she couldn't move a muscle. She was frozen. Numb. Unable to think clearly.

"I want to ask him something first," she blurted out.

Irritation flickered in Tate's gaze. He lowered the rifle. "Is that really necessary? Everything he'll tell you will be a lie."

"I don't care." She stubbornly lifted her chin. "I want to ask him anyway."

She failed to add that whatever she did next depended on the answer Hector gave her. Wholly depended on it, in fact.

Because she could fight Tate. She could demand he spare Hector. She could throw herself in front of that rifle if need be, as long as it meant living the rest of her life with a clean conscience, one that didn't harbor the burden of knowing she was a murderer.

The irony didn't escape her. She'd *asked* Tate to kill Hector for her. She'd brought him here for that exact purpose, and now that the opportunity was here, now that the only thing standing between herself and her freedom was Hector, she couldn't in good conscience let it happen.

"Take off his gag," she said softly.

With a sigh, Tate bent down and grabbed Hector by the armpits, yanking the man up into a sitting position, with his back against the rear wheel of the Jeep and his bound wrists resting in his lap.

Tate pulled the rag out of Hector's mouth, and immediately, the rebel spat at him. Unperturbed, Tate wiped the spittle off his chin, stood up and glanced at Eva.

She stepped forward and peered down at Hector, whose eyes took on a calculating gleam. "You know you don't have it in you, Eva," the man she'd once loved accused. "If you let him kill me, you'll live with it for the rest of your life."

She drew in a slow breath. "I want to ask you something. And I want an honest answer."

Hector's lips set in a wary line, but the suspicious expression faded fast, replaced by a soft look that reminded her of the day they'd met. The day they'd spent hours passionately talking about what they wanted for their country.

"Ask me anything, *mi amor*," he said, his voice gentle yet seductive. "I'll answer honestly."

She exhaled in a rush. "What does Rafe mean to you?"

His proud forehead furrowed in puzzlement. "I don't understand."

With a burst of frustration, she sank to her knees in front of him. "What does he mean to you?" she repeated. "Why do you want him in your life? What do you want for his future? Why do you love him, Hector?"

Now he seemed incredibly frazzled. "Because he's my son! He's my blood, and he belongs with me."

"Why?" she pressed.

"Because I need him to lead when I can't! Because I want him to be a symbol for hope, a symbol for this revolution! His future is here in San Marquez and I'm going to raise him to appreciate his roots, to fight for them, to—"

She was done listening.

My son. My blood.

Hector didn't love his son. No, Rafe was just a pawn in his power play, a *symbol,* and Hector would eventually destroy that little boy. Raise him to fight and revolt and do his bidding.

That was the difference between her and Hector. He didn't care about Rafe's future, only his own, while she... well, she'd gladly give up her life if that ensured Rafe would have a safe and happy future.

And she'd also sacrifice her conscience.

She glanced over her shoulder, her gaze locking with Tate's. "You're right," she whispered. "This needs to happ—"

Before she could finish her sentence, she was yanked backward as Hector looped his arms around her neck and jammed his forearm into her throat.

She gasped for air, her windpipe burning, her heart pounding.

Hector's wrists were restrained, but that didn't take away from his strength. "Put the rifle down," he hissed, "or I break her neck."

Eva looked up at Tate, whose green eyes had gone cold

with fury. Rather than lower his weapon, he continued to aim it at Hector.

"Lay down your weapon," Hector demanded. "We'll go our separate ways, amigo, and Eva lives." His spittle splashed the side of Eva's cheek, the scent of sweat, anger and desperation filling her nostrils.

Tate still didn't make a single move.

Her pulse raced with panic. Oh, God. What if he stood by and let Hector snap her neck?

But the fear was unwarranted. With a harsh chuckle, Tate took a small step forward. "You honestly think I'm going to fall for that line of bullcrap again?"

And then he pulled the trigger.

The gunshot was deafening. It exploded in her ear, making her head ring like a carnival game. The pressure on her windpipe eased, and Eva stumbled forward, sucking in deep gulps of oxygen. Something warm and sticky stained her cheek.

Hector's blood. Hector's brains.

The nausea hit her hard and fast. Crawling away from Hector's lifeless body, she threw up, unable to control the horror that continued to spiral through her. When she had nothing left in her stomach, she crouched in the dirt dry-heaving, until she finally felt a hand on her shoulder.

She looked up and saw Sebastian looming over her, his gray eyes gleaming with impatience. In her peripheral vision, she caught sight of Tate dragging Hector's body away from the Jeep. The blood oozing from the bullet hole in Hector's forehead brought a fresh wave of queasiness.

Numb. She felt numb. And so very cold, but she got the feeling the chill wouldn't go away for a long, long time.

She might not have pulled the trigger, but she was as guilty of killing Hector as Tate was.

He would've killed you. He would've destroyed your son.

She clung to that reminder, knowing with bone-deep certainty that Hector's death was the only guarantee of her son's safety.

"Let's get outta here."

She turned at the sound of Tate's gruff voice. Their gazes collided and held. He'd saved her life. She knew without a doubt that Hector would have snapped her neck if Tate hadn't pulled that trigger.

"Thank you," she whispered.

He remained expressionless. "I didn't do it for you. I did it for Will."

Her throat tightened. Of course. This had always been about avenging his brother, the only person he'd ever cared about. She was an idiot to think that Tate might actually care about her wellbeing, that he'd been protecting *her* when he'd shot Hector. He would've killed Hector regardless.

Lord, maybe Tate really *was* the heartless bastard she'd thought he was when they'd first met. Maybe she'd been fooling herself by believing they could have something real.

Collecting her composure, she staggered to her feet and headed for the Jeep. Without a word, she slid into the backseat, while Sebastian took the wheel and Tate got in the passenger seat.

Before Sebastian could step on the gas, she leaned forward and gripped Tate's shoulder.

He turned around, his face expectant. "What?"

"You were considering it," she said dully.

His eyebrows lifted.

"Leaving me in the bunker," she clarified. "You hesitated. Like you were actually considering leaving me."

He was quiet for a moment, and then he offered that careless shrug she was beginning to loathe. "That's because I was," he said coolly, and then he turned around and banged on the dashboard, a signal for Sebastian to go.

Agony punched her in the gut. Her hand dropped from his shoulder, and she sagged backward into her seat, working valiantly to control the tears threatening to break free.

Heartless bastard, indeed.

Paraíso, Mexico

Tate had never glimpsed a more beautiful sight than the crumbling exterior of the stone fortress. It still astounded him that only six hours ago they were running out of a bunker in the Marqueza Mountains. Even more astounding was that the three of them had made it back here in one piece. They hadn't encountered a single hiccup, not during the chopper ride to the harbor, the boat to Ecuador, the private plane to Tijuana. Somehow, not a single thing had gone wrong, and Tate was starting to believe a higher power was looking out for them.

During the entire trip home, Eva hadn't said a solitary word to him. Sebastian hadn't spoken much, either, despite the fact that the man clearly had *a lot* on his mind.

Tate would never say it out loud, but he was damn proud of the sergeant. Aside from that one moment in the woods, when Tate's instincts had screamed that he was being watched, he hadn't picked up on Sebastian's presence in the slightest, despite the fact that Sebastian had tailed them all the way to Hector's hideout.

He'd trained the other man well, that was for sure. Maybe a little *too* well.

Didn't mean he was happy about the way Sebastian had blatantly disregarded his orders, though. He'd already verbally assaulted him for it, which was probably why the man was acting so moody.

"Mommy!"

The high-pitched voice drew their gazes to the door beneath the watchtower, which burst open as Eva's son dashed out of the fort, with Nick hot on his heels. For a toddler, the kid could sure move, but Prescott scooped the boy up before he got close to the Jeep. The little boy proceeded to wiggle like an eel in Nick's arms, crying out for his mom, who didn't even wait for the Jeep to come to a complete stop before she dove out.

As Eva made a beeline for her kid, Tate couldn't help but watch the reunion. An odd lump of emotion rose in his throat. He choked it down, disgusted with himself. So what if she was hugging that kid as if she never wanted to let him go? So what if her eyes sparkled with tears and her voice overflowed with pure love as she spoke to her child?

Cruz's child.

Then again, did that even matter anymore now that Cruz was dead?

The reminder brought a rush of saliva to Tate's mouth, a sense of deep satisfaction. He'd fantasized about this for eight months, and now it had finally become reality. The man who'd murdered his brother was dead.

"Good to have you back, Captain."

Tate tore his gaze from Eva and Rafe, and leaned in to give Nick a quick side hug and back slap. "Good to be back." He arched a brow. "Not happy that you kept me in the dark, though. You could've given me the heads up that Stone went AWOL."

Nick looked sheepish. "I figured you'd make the tail within two minutes."

He let out a breath. "I was a bit distracted."

Fortunately, Prescott had the good sense not to hazard a guess about the source of that distraction. The guy already knew, anyway, judging by the way his amber-colored eyes gleamed knowingly when Eva made her way over to them.

The kid was clinging to her like a monkey, but he lifted his head when Eva came to a stop, and peered at Tate with big curious eyes.

"Thank you for taking care of my son," Eva said quietly, her eyes shining with gratitude as she looked at Nick.

"It was my pleasure. He's a great kid." Nick reached out and ruffled the little boy's hair, eliciting a peal of laughter from the boy.

Tate experienced a burst of discomfort. He wasn't great with children, and he didn't like the way the kid kept staring at him. As though he was an alien from another planet or something.

"What?" he grumbled when the kid refused to quit it.

Rafe's bottom lip dropped out for a moment, a shy expression playing over his face, and then he grinned, pointed at Tate's face and said, "You're hairy!"

Despite himself, Tate cracked a smile, which earned him surprised looks from both Nick and Eva.

"Yeah, kid, I guess I am," he answered, dragging one hand over the thick beard covering his jaw. The thing was starting to itch, too. He definitely needed to shave.

Eva turned to Nick. "Do you mind giving us a moment?"

The other man nodded. "No problem."

As Nick drifted off toward Sebastian, who was loitering near the Jeep, Eva shifted Rafe to her other hip. "What now?" she asked softly.

"Mommy, I want down," her son whined. "Wanna go to Nick!"

She gave the boy an indulgent smile before setting him on the ground. He barreled off toward Nick, giggling in an easy, carefree way that brought another wave of discomfort to Tate's gut and had him wincing.

Eva didn't miss his reaction. "You don't like him."

Her blunt tone made him scowl. "I don't even know him."

"And you don't want to, right?"

His jaw tensed. "What the hell are you really asking me, Eva?"

Sadness washed over her beautiful face. "Do you want me to stay, Tate?"

He had no idea what to say to that.

"Because if you say the word, I'll stay." Her voice grew husky, thick with emotion. "I wasn't lying in the bunker. I'm in love with you."

Something hot and painful pinched his heart. "Eva—"

She didn't let him finish. "I don't know what kind of future we can have, but I'm willing to find out. I could stay. *We* can stay, me and Rafe." Hope burned in her blue eyes. "I know you're still angry I didn't tell you that Hector was Rafe's father, but I didn't keep the truth from you out of malice. And now Hector is no longer a threat. He's gone. My son is safe. And I'd like for Rafe and me to stay here. With you." She searched his face intently. "Ask us to stay, Tate."

Indecision burned a path up to his throat, nearly choking him. Was it that easy? Just ask her to stay?

But what was even the point? What kind of relationship could they have with him living in hiding? And would she expect him to be a father to that kid?

How could he be? He wasn't fatherhood material, wasn't interested in love or commitment or any of that emotional garbage.

So then why did his heart constrict at the thought of letting Eva go? And why did his gaze keep drifting toward that little boy happily playing with Nick ten feet away?

His silence stretched on and on. He couldn't seem to

get a solitary word out, and the longer he stayed quiet, the sadder Eva looked.

"Okay." She cleared her throat. "Okay, I get it. I'll…ah, I'll just go inside and pack up our stuff and, um, I'll ask Nick to drive us into town. Rafe and I can stay in the motel there until I book a flight back to the States."

His chest ached so badly it felt like a thousand-pound Sumo wrestler was sitting on the damn thing, but he still couldn't seem to utter a word.

"Um, well, then, I guess I'll just say goodbye now." Her throat worked as she swallowed. "So…goodbye, Tate."

Chapter 18

"I love you, too, Mom, and I can't wait to see you guys," Eva murmured into the phone. "You still there, Dad?"

"I'm here, sweetheart." Her dad's warm baritone voice emerged from the speaker, and he sounded as choked up as she felt. "I'm dying to see that grandson of mine! The pictures you've been emailing aren't nearly enough."

Eva smiled through her tears, her gaze drifting toward the bed in the center of the motel room, where Rafe was sleeping soundly. "You'll see him soon enough, Daddy."

In fact, she would've preferred to be on her way to the airport already, but all the evening flights had been canceled thanks to a hurricane bearing down on them from the Gulf, so there was no point in hanging around the Tijuana airport waiting for the storm to pass. Might as well stay warm and cozy in this motel, and hope that the planes were back in the air tomorrow morning.

"Will Miguel be taking you to the airport?" Her mother

didn't sound thrilled by the idea, which wasn't surprising. Miguel LaGuerta was a nationalist to the core, and he made no secret of the fact that he disapproved of his younger sister's marriage to an Italian, and subsequent move to America. They'd been estranged for as long as Eva could remember.

But at the mention of her uncle, Eva's shoulders stiffened. Hector's accusation flashed in her mind, reminding her that she'd eventually need to confront Miguel about his part in all this. Someone had warned Hector that she and Tate were coming to him, and the only person who'd known about her plan was Miguel.

At this point, though, she didn't give a damn if Miguel was on the ULF take or if Hector had been lying. She was done with San Marquez. She didn't care what her uncle did or who he may or may not have betrayed. Now that Hector was gone, she had no reason to ever return to that godforsaken country.

"Miguel didn't come with us to Mexico," she told her mother.

Because I couldn't risk telling him where we were, she almost added, but stopped herself at the last second.

"So we'll take a cab to the airport," she finished.

"Okay, well, get some sleep, honey," her mother replied.

"That way you'll feel fresh and energetic tomorrow when you come home to us," her dad piped up.

She blinked back another rush of tears. It was so nice to hear her parents' voices. Even nicer to know that she'd be coming home to them so very soon.

"I will," she promised. "I'll call you guys tomorrow with my flight details, okay?"

After she hung up, she stared at the prepaid cell phone for a few seconds, tempted to dial another number. The number Nick had slipped in her hand earlier, the one for the men's satellite phone.

But she resisted the urge, knowing there was no point.

Tate hadn't asked her to stay.

He hadn't *wanted* her to stay.

She shouldn't be surprised, shouldn't allow it to hurt her, but she was, and it did. Despite the callous way he'd treated her back at the bunker, she understood where his anger had stemmed from—she'd kept something important from him, after all—but she also knew it was about more than one little lie. Tate had opened up to her during their time together, and that had scared him to death.

His bleak childhood had hardened him. He'd shut down, convinced himself that he preferred a life of solitude to a life filled with love. By letting her in and letting himself care for her, he'd probably broken the number-one rule in his emotionless warrior code.

You're better off.

Was she? In one sense, she supposed she was. Tate was a difficult man. Ruthless, dominating, prickly. And if they got together, she'd have to sacrifice her and Rafe's freedom once again, at least until Tate came out of hiding, and who knew when that would happen?

On the other hand, was anyone *really* better off without love in their life?

She hadn't planned it, hadn't wanted it even, but somehow, she'd fallen for the man. She'd glimpsed past his gruff exterior and discovered a man who could be sweet and tender, a man who'd protect her with his dying breath, who treated her like an equal and made her body burn with the simplest touch.

So no, she didn't feel better off.

Not by a long shot.

* * *

"A virus," Nick muttered, shaking his head for the hundredth time. "That's all Cruz said?"

"That's all he said," Tate confirmed.

The trio was up on the watchtower again, safe from the downpour thanks to the stone overhang above their heads. Tate had already filled them in earlier about everything Cruz had told him, but Nick and Sebastian were still visibly bewildered by it all.

"So the doctor we were ordered to rescue released some killer virus in Corazón," Sebastian said, shaking *his* head for the hundredth time.

"According to Cruz," Tate emphasized. "But I'm inclined to believe it might be true, especially since Eva came across that mysterious project Harrison was working on. Project Aries."

He was rather proud of himself—his voice didn't crack at all when he said Eva's name. And his heart had ached only a little, as opposed to the excruciating sense of being sledgehammered in the chest, which he'd felt earlier as he'd watched Nick drive away in that Jeep with Eva and Rafe.

"They're trying to shut us up then," Sebastian said, sounding confident. "Our government is experimenting with biological weapons and testing them on *human beings*. When they sent us to the village, they probably knew all along that we'd have to die, just in case."

"That's what Eva suspects," Tate admitted.

Sebastian got a funny look on his face, but it disappeared fast. "They can't be sure what we saw in the village, or whether we had contact with the doctor before he died. Either way, they need to silence us."

"So what's our next move?" Nick asked. "Find out who authorized Harrison's project? Maybe take this to the White House? Alert the media?"

He rubbed his hand over his freshly shaved chin. "I don't know yet. Let's sit on this for a while, let it settle, before we figure out a plan."

Nick nodded. "Sounds good."

Sebastian offered a nod of his own. "Agreed."

A flash of lightning lit the sky, drawing his gaze back to the steadily falling rain. The wind continued to pick up speed, and the sky was so black and cloudy you couldn't even see the moon.

No flights will be leaving here tonight.

Tate swallowed. He had no idea why that thought had crept into head.

Okay, fine. He knew exactly why he'd thought it.

"Hey, Prescott, give us a minute, will ya?" Sebastian said lightly.

Although his brows furrowed, Nick didn't object. "Yeah. Sure. I'll head inside and see if the wireless is working. I wouldn't mind doing a little online digging about that lab Harrison worked for."

After Nick disappeared, Sebastian didn't pull any punches. He simply crossed his arms over his broad chest and said, "Why the hell did you let her go?"

Tate blinked. "Pardon me?"

"Don't play dumb, Captain. Why did you let Eva go?"

"Because there was no reason for her to stay," he muttered. "We both got what we wanted. Cruz is dead. She and her kid can go back to New York now."

Sebastian's gray eyes flickered with irritation. "She doesn't want to go back to New York. She wants to stay here with you."

"Yeah, what makes you say that?"

"The woman is in love with you. Any idiot can see that."

Tate stared out at the rain sliding down the crumbling stone walls of the fort. Ignoring Sebastian's frank words, he shrugged and said, "We were right, by the way. She was lying right from the start. Cruz was her kid's father."

"I kind of gathered that. I heard what she said to him." Sebastian cocked his head. "Is that why you told her to get lost? You can't stomach the idea of raising Cruz's kid? Because if that's the case, shame on you, Captain."

He gaped at his fellow soldier.

"I'm serious," Sebastian said angrily. "I'm not much of a kid person myself—they're bratty and annoying and grubby—but even I know better than to blame an innocent child for his father's sins."

"I'm not blaming anyone for anything," Tate grumbled.

"So it's not that you can't raise Cruz's kid?"

"I can't raise *any* kid, Seb. I'm not father material."

"Bull." Sebastian actually had the nerve to laugh. "You'd make a good father. You wanna know why? Because you're a good man. Any kid would be lucky to have you as their old man, Captain."

He arched a brow. "What's with all the compliments? This is unlike you."

The other man shifted in embarrassment. "Look, I was following you and Eva for days. I couldn't risk getting too close, but sometimes, well, sometimes it couldn't be helped. And sound carries in the jungle and in the woods, so I'd hear things, whether I wanted to or not. But there was one thing in particular that I kept hearing, something I couldn't wrap my head around."

"What?" Tate said gruffly.

"Laughter." Sebastian grinned, and his white teeth gleamed in the darkness. "She made you laugh. A lot."

Gnawing on the inside of his cheek, Tate stepped toward the edge of the tower. Instantly, a gust of wind blew rain into his face, but he didn't bother wiping it off. He welcomed the cool drops, wishing the rain would wash away all the confusion plaguing him at the moment.

"That's when I knew that she was good for you," Sebastian went on. "The woman challenges you. She makes you come alive."

Tate gritted his teeth. "Where are you going with all this?"

"Will's dead, Tate."

A jolt of pain smacked him square in the chest. "I know that."

"He was the only person in your life that you opened yourself up to. I'd like to think that me and Nicky are important to you, too—"

"You are," he said roughly.

"But we both know you've always held a part of yourself back." Sebastian shrugged. "I get it, and I know why you do, but face it, it's not healthy. You can't close yourself off to people, otherwise you're in for a damn lonely life."

"Maybe it's the life I want."

"No, you don't. Nobody does." Sebastian blew out a frustrated breath. "Let's say you let her in, man. What's the worst that could happen?"

Uncomfortable, Tate shifted his gaze back to the rain, but Sebastian didn't take the hint and drop the subject.

"If you feel something for Eva, don't ignore it. Don't shove it aside and pretend she doesn't matter."

Tate sighed. "What's your point, Seb?"

"All I'm saying is…if you wanna go after Eva, and bring her and the kid back here, I wouldn't stand in your way. And if you want my opinion? I think that's exactly what you should do."

With that, the other man drifted toward the door, disappearing through the threshold and leaving Tate alone with his thoughts.

What's the worst that could happen?

Sebastian's question continued to float through his head, and the answers came in the form of images.

His mother's bluish skin as she lay OD'd on the floor.

His father's meaty knuckles coming toward his face.

When you let people in, they either betrayed you or abandoned you. People were selfish. They pretended to care, pretended to love you, but in reality, they only loved themselves. Selfish.

Not Will, a little voice pointed out. *Not Ben.*

And not Eva.

His breath caught as he glimpsed the truth in that. Eva wasn't selfish. She'd lied to him, yes. Convinced him to help her kill Cruz, yes. But not for her own self-interests. She'd done it for her kid. Ever since her son was born, she'd put that little boy first, which was something neither of his no-good parents had ever done.

Eva wasn't selfish. She was smart. Sassy. Determined. Courageous.

Not only that, but she was in love with him. For some asinine reason, that woman actually *loved* him.

And he was just going to let her walk out of his life? *Idiot.*

Eva smoothed a lock of hair off Rafe's forehead and smiled at her sleeping son, who'd conked out the second she'd put him down and hadn't stirred since. Apparently he'd had the "bestest time ever" with Nick this past week, though he'd admitted to having a few nightmares and wetting the bed twice. Hearing that absolutely killed her—it broke her heart that she hadn't been there to comfort her son.

Because she'd been too busy *killing his father.*

God, what would she do when Rafe asked her about his

father? Surely he would, at least when he got older. What on earth was she going to tell him?

Her heart pounded as she imagined that inevitable conversation. She definitely needed to decide how much to tell Rafe, but she knew one thing for sure, she would never, ever tell him that she'd played a part in killing his father.

Swallowing, she stroked Rafe's cheek one last time, then stood up and headed for the kitchenette. She doubted she'd get any sleep tonight, not with the windows rattling and the walls shaking from the wind and rain, but maybe a cup of decaf tea would make her drowsy.

The motel had an electric kettle in the cabinet beneath the sink. She filled it with water and plugged it in, clicking the button just as a sharp knock sounded on the door.

Her pulse immediately sped up, her first instinct to grab the gun sitting on the table, but she quickly berated herself for it. Hector was dead, damn it. His men weren't behind that door. Neither was his ghost.

Only one person could be out there, and Eva's heart raced even faster as she hurried to the door. She undid the chain and threw open the door, and sure enough, there he was. Soaking wet, his black Windbreaker plastered to his chest, droplets clinging to his clean-shaven face. He was ruggedly handsome, undeniably sexy, blatantly masculine.

"What are you doing here?" she said, having to raise her voice over the din of the wind.

"Asking you to stay," Tate answered sheepishly.

She stared at him in surprise. "What?"

"You heard me." His voice came out gruff. "Now, are you going to invite me in or should I grovel out here in the rain?"

Overcome with both shock and amusement, she opened the door wider so he could step inside. As he entered, he unzipped his jacket and carefully draped it on one of the kitchen chairs, then turned to shoot her an apologetic look. "Sorry, I'm dripping all over the place."

"It's okay." She smiled. "So, what was it you were saying about groveling?"

Remorse flickered in his green eyes. "I shouldn't have let you go like that. Without telling you that…uh…" He exhaled shakily. "You matter, okay? You matter to me, Eva."

Her heart somersaulted. "Really?"

Tate nodded in earnest. "My whole life, I've tried to keep my distance from people. It was the only way to guarantee I wouldn't get hurt, but over the years, I've let a few people in. My brother. Ben. Sebastian and Nick. And you. I let you in, Eva, and now that you're under my skin, I can't get you out."

When she narrowed her eyes, he held up his hand. "I don't *want* to get you out. My entire life has been one bleak, miserable mess. I'm surrounded by violence and death and darkness, and I was okay with that, at least before I met you."

He offered his trademark shrug, which brought a smile to her lips and tears to her eyes.

"You brightened everything up for a short while, and then you left and the darkness was back, and I realized I didn't want to live like that anymore." He shifted awkwardly. "I'm in love with you, and I don't want you to go."

Tate's sandpaper-rough voice made her heart skip a beat. She wanted so badly to throw her arms around him and tell him she wasn't going anywhere, but one thing held her back. Her gaze shifted to the little boy sleeping on the bed. *Her* little boy. The only person who mattered more than Tate, more than life itself.

Tate followed her gaze, and his green eyes softened. "I know it's a package deal, sweetheart. If you'll let me, I want to be a father to your son."

Astonishment slammed into her. "Are you serious?"

He offered another nod. "I don't know if I could ever be a good role model for a kid, but I'll try to be the best man I can be, for you, and for your son."

Before she could answer, Rafe chose that exact moment to wake up. With a loud, childlike yawn, her son sat up like a light, rubbed his eyes and said, "Mommy, I'm thirsty." Then he noticed Tate and wariness widened his eyes. "Mommy?"

"It's okay, little man. This is Tate. You remember him, right? Tate's the one who took me on that trip."

Wrong thing to say, she realized, as Rafe's expression turned cloudier than the sky outside.

As Rafe glared at the man responsible for taking his mother away from him for so long, Eva suppressed a sigh and took a step toward the bed, but Tate swiftly moved in her path.

"Let me?" he murmured.

Intrigued, she hung back and let him approach her son, watching in bewilderment as he lowered his big body on the edge of the mattress. Rafe stared at the intruder with suspicious blue eyes, but Tate wasn't perturbed.

"You're mad at me because I took your mom away, aren't you?" he said gruffly.

After a second of reluctance, Rafe nodded.

"Yeah, I kinda figured. I'm sorry I did that. I guess I was a little greedy, huh? I just wanted your mom all to myself, but that wasn't cool at all, was it?"

Tate flashed that crooked grin of his, and Eva hid a smile when she noticed her son fighting hard not to grin back.

"Well, I promise you right here and now that next time your mom and I want to go on a trip, we'll bring you with us. Your mom said you like adventures, so what kind of adventure should we pick? River rafting? Rock climbing?"

And just like that, Tate won her son over.

"I wanna see giraffes," Rafe blurted out. "And a big castle. And a dragon. And snow."

As her smile reached the surface, Eva drifted toward the kitchenette to get Rafe a cup of water. He was still babbling a mile a minute, reciting everything he'd ever wanted to see or do, but he stopped talking to gulp down the water.

"All right, we'll continue thinking of adventure ideas tomorrow," she said firmly as Rafe handed her the empty cup. "Right now, you're going to bed, little man. Say good-night to Tate."

"G'night, Tate."

Rafe didn't give her any arguments as she tucked him back in and read him a quick story. As usual, he passed out the second his head hit the pillow, which earned her a mystified look from Tate. He'd been sitting at the table while she'd put Rafe to bed, but now he stood up and quietly approached her.

"Your kid doesn't put up a fight at bedtime?"

She grinned. "Never. I must be the only mother in the world whose kid *loves* bedtime. I'm lucky."

Tate's sensual mouth curved in a smile. "I think I'm the lucky one."

Their eyes held for a moment, and then his expression turned serious again. "Do you forgive me for the way I acted at the bunker?" He swallowed. "When I hesitated about leaving you behind, it was my anger talking. I felt—"

"Betrayed. I know. And I forgive you." She searched his face. "Do you forgive me for not telling you the truth about Hector?"

"Yes."

Their gazes locked again.

"So what now?" she asked softly. "How will this work?"

Unhappiness creased his features. "I want to make you

so many promises, Eva, but I can't. Not while I've still got a target painted on my back. I need to find a way out of this mess, figure out who ordered the hits on me and my men."

"I can help," she said immediately.

"I'd appreciate that. But I'd also understand if you want to go. You've been running for three years, sweetheart, and now you don't have to anymore. You can go to New York, reunite with your family, build a life for yourself and Rafe." His voice grew hoarse. "It's not fair of me to ask you to hide out with me, because that's what I'm going to keep doing, at least until I can be sure my life is no longer in danger."

She gave him a gentle smile. "I'm not going anywhere, Tate."

Frustration crossed his face. "I have no right to ask you to stay. I'm a total ass for doing it."

"Like you said, I've been running and hiding for three years. What's a few more months?"

He stepped closer and stroked his knuckles over her cheek. "Are you sure?"

"I'm not going anywhere," she repeated. "You helped me get rid of my demon—it's only fair that I help you get rid of yours."

His hand continued to caress her face, and she covered it with hers, running her fingers over his rough-skinned knuckles. She lifted her other hand to his chest and placed it directly over his heart, feeling it beating beneath her palm. Strong and steady, just like Tate.

They stared at each other for a moment, and then he lowered his head ever so slowly and kissed her. Their mouths fused, lips parted, tongues explored. Tate drove the kiss deeper, fueling the fire building in her core, and she was gasping by the time they broke apart.

"Are you sure?" he asked again.

"I'm sure. I love you, and I want to be with you, even if

it means hiding out for a while longer." She leaned on her tiptoes and brushed her lips over his smooth jaw. "I just have one requirement."

"What's that?"

"We relocate to a better hideout. I love the outdoors, but I also love indoor plumbing. And real beds." She flashed an impish grin. "With that said, I've still got a lot of money."

"Stolen money," he said dryly.

She shrugged. "I like to think that I earned it, after everything Hector put me through. And I can think of nothing better than using Hector's money to find the five of us a secure place to lie low until we get you out of this mess."

"The five of us?"

She shot him a "duh" look. "Rafe and I are a package deal. Nick and Sebastian are *your* package. We're not leaving them behind."

The emotion shining in his green eyes took her breath away. "You're an amazing woman, Eva Dolce." His voice roughened. "And I promise you, I'll protect you and Rafe with my life."

"I don't need your protection," she murmured. "Just your love."

His mouth curved in a smile. "Well, that you've got. Anything else?"

"Yes, actually. One more thing."

Tate arched one dark brow. "Which is?"

"Your trust."

He reached for her hand. "Remember when I said that trust and sex don't have to go hand in hand?"

She nodded.

"Well, trust and *love?* Now, that's a whole different story, sweetheart." He slowly brought her hand back to his heart and held it there, flattening his palm over her knuckles. "You've got my heart, Eva. You've got my love. And you've got my trust."

Emotion clogged her throat, making it difficult to say a single word. But she managed four. "Right back at you."

Epilogue

Two Months Later

"Seb, get in here."

Halfway to the kitchen, Sebastian detoured and ducked into the living room of the beach house, where Nick was peering at one of the laptop screens.

"What's up?" he asked.

"Come read this."

Furrowing his brow, he came up beside Nick and studied the medical report on the monitor. Key phrases stood out: *Malaria. Possible outbreak. Six dead. Containment. Valero, San Marquez.*

Sebastian hissed out a breath. Thanks to Eva's not-so-legal software, they'd been keeping tabs on any unusual medical emergencies in San Marquez, monitoring every hospital and clinic on the island. They'd yet to determine whether Hector Cruz had been telling the truth about a virus killing the people of Corazón, but they couldn't afford to ignore the potential lead, even if it had come from a dead rebel leader.

"Should we check it out?" Nick asked, his expression conveying his lack of enthusiasm.

"I don't think we have a choice, but let me go ask Tate what he thinks."

His gaze drifted to the window, which provided a view of the turquoise ocean and endless stretch of white sand. At the water's edge, Tate was crouched next to Rafe, pointing at the waves as he explained something to the little boy. Eva stood a few feet away, her black hair loose and ruffling in the warm breeze as she watched the two males with a smile.

Sebastian moved his gaze from the happy family and squared his shoulders. Forget *asking* Tate. No, he'd *tell* the captain that someone needed to check out this San Marquez outbreak situation. And that someone was not going to be Tate. The captain had a lot more to lose these days. A woman he loved. A kid he adored.

Sebastian, on the other hand, had absolutely nothing to lose.

"Call the airfield," he barked at Nick. "I want to leave for San Marquez. Tonight."

* * * * *

COMING NEXT MONTH FROM

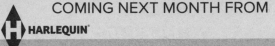

H HARLEQUIN®

ROMANTIC suspense

Available February 19, 2013

#1743 WHAT SHE SAW
Conard County: The Next Generation
by Rachel Lee

When Haley Martin poses as Buck Devlin's girlfriend to help solve a murder, she never imagines that he's putting her life, her dreams and her heart at risk.

#1744 A BILLIONAIRE'S REDEMPTION
Vengeance in Texas • by Cindy Dees

Willa Merris may be off-limits, but Gabe Dawson is a billionaire and can break all the rules to keep her safe... if she'll let him.

#1745 OPERATION REUNION
Cutter's Code • by Justine Davis

Will family loyalty ruin Kayla Tucker's chance at a true, lifetime love, and will past secrets destroy everything she holds dear?

#1746 COWBOY'S TEXAS RESCUE
Black Ops Rescues • by Beth Cornelison

Black ops pilot Jake Connelly battles an escaped convict and a Texas-size blizzard to rescue Chelsea Harris, but will he also lose his heart to the intrepid small-town girl?

YOU CAN FIND MORE INFORMATION ON UPCOMING HARLEQUIN® TITLES, FREE EXCERPTS AND MORE AT WWW.HARLEQUIN.COM.

HRSCNM0213

REQUEST YOUR FREE BOOKS!
2 FREE NOVELS PLUS 2 FREE GIFTS!

H HARLEQUIN®

ROMANTIC suspense

Sparked by danger, fueled by passion

YES! Please send me 2 FREE Harlequin® Romantic Suspense novels and my 2 FREE gifts (gifts are worth about $10). After receiving them, if I don't wish to receive any more books, I can return the shipping statement marked "cancel." If I don't cancel, I will receive 4 brand-new novels every month and be billed just $4.49 per book in the U.S. or $5.24 per book in Canada. That's a savings of at least 14% off the cover price! It's quite a bargain! Shipping and handling is just 50¢ per book in the U.S. and 75¢ per book in Canada.* I understand that accepting the 2 free books and gifts places me under no obligation to buy anything. I can always return a shipment and cancel at any time. Even if I never buy another book, the two free books and gifts are mine to keep forever.

240/340 HDN FVS7

Name	(PLEASE PRINT)

Address	Apt. #

City	State/Prov.	Zip/Postal Code

Signature (if under 18, a parent or guardian must sign)

Mail to the **Harlequin® Reader Service:**
IN U.S.A.: P.O. Box 1867, Buffalo, NY 14240-1867
IN CANADA: P.O. Box 609, Fort Erie, Ontario L2A 5X3

Want to try two free books from another line?
Call 1-800-873-8635 or visit www.ReaderService.com.

SPECIAL EXCERPT FROM
HARLEQUIN® ROMANTIC SUSPENSE

RS

Harlequin Romantic Suspense presents the third book in the thrilling Black Ops Rescues miniseries from best-loved author Beth Cornelison

Black Ops pilot Jake Connelly battles an escaped convict and a Texas-size blizzard to rescue Chelsea Harris, but will he lose his heart to the intrepid small-town girl?

Read on for an excerpt from

COWBOY'S TEXAS RESCUE

Available March 2013 from
Harlequin Romantic Suspense

A rattle came from the trunk lock, and she tensed. *Oh, please, God, let it be someone to rescue me and not that maniac killer!*

The lid rose, and daylight poured into the pitch-dark of the trunk. She shuddered as a stiff, icy wind swept into the well of the trunk, blasting her bare skin.

"Ah, hell," a deep voice muttered.

Her pulse scampered, and she squinted to make out the face of the man standing over her.

The gun in his hand registered first, then his size—tall, broad shouldered, and his fleece-lined ranch coat made him appear impressively muscle-bound. Plenty big enough to overpower her if he was working with the convict.

A black cowboy hat and backlighting from the sky obscured his face in shadow, adding to her apprehension.

"Are you hurt?" he asked, stashing the gun out of sight and undoing the buttons of his coat.

"N-no." When he reached for her, she shrank back warily.

Where was the convict? She cast an anxious glance around them, down the side of the car, searching.

She jolted when her rescuer grasped her elbow.

"Hey, I'm not gonna hurt you." The cowboy leaned farther into the trunk. "Let me help you out of there, and you can have my coat."

His coat... She almost whimpered in gratitude, anticipating the warmth. When she caught her first good glimpse of his square jaw and stubble-dusted cheeks, her stomach swooped. *Oh, Texas!* He was a freaking *Adonis*. Greek-god gorgeous with golden-blond hair, cowboy boots and ranch-honed muscles. He lifted her out of the trunk, and when he set her down and her knees buckled with muscle cramps, cold and fatigue, she knew she couldn't dismiss old-fashioned swooning for at least some of her legs' weakness. He draped the coat around her shoulders, and the sexy combined scents of pine, leather and man surrounded her. She had to be dreaming....

Will Chelsea find more than safety in her sexy rescuer's arms? Or will the convict come back to finish them both off? Find out what happens next in COWBOY'S TEXAS RESCUE

Available March 2013 from Harlequin Romantic Suspense wherever books are sold.

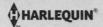